Wynne-Jones has won numerous
⋯r his work, including an Edgar Award, the
⋯ General's Literary Award, and a *Boston
Goose-Horn Book* Award. He is a faculty member
at Vermont College, teaching courses in the MFA
Program in Writing for Children and Young
Adults, as well as the author of more than twenty
books for children and young adults, including the
novel *The Uninvited* and the popular Rex Zero
books. T⋯ ⋯la
with his f⋯

BLINK&

CAUTION

Tim Wynne-Jones

WALKER
BOOKS

Also by Tim Wynne-Jones

The Uninvited

First published in Great Britain 2012 by Walker Books Ltd
87 Vauxhall Walk, London SE11 5HJ

2 4 6 8 10 9 7 5 3 1

Text © 2011 Tim Wynne-Jones
Cover Illustrations © Dimitri Vervitsiotis/
Digital Collection and Photographer's Choice/Getty Images

The right of Tim Wynne-Jones to be identified as author of this work has been asserted by him in accordance with the Copyright, Designs and Patents Act 1988

This book has been typeset in ITC Galliard

Printed and bound in Great Britain by Clays Ltd, St Ives plc

British Library Cataloguing in Publication Data:
a catalogue record for this book is
available from the British Library

ISBN 978-1-4063-3741-9

www.walker.co.uk
www.undercoverreads.co.uk

For all the lost boys and girls

Part 1

Chapter 1

Look up at the Plaza Regent, Blink, in the shivery morning light. Count the floors—take your pick.

You're wearing the Blessed Breakfast Uniform: the Adidas, sparkly white; the tan Gap cargos; the yellow Banana Republic polo; the red cotton hooded full-zip. Lifted, all of it, from a gym locker at Jarvis Collegiate, where the posh children drift down from Rosedale on shining bikes or are disgorged from BMWs. You picked a boy about your size. You followed him to school one day, which was against the rules. It's never hard to find a locker room; your nose shows you the way. These fine clothes of young master Rosedale were doused with Eternity when first you put them on, though that fragrance has been lost with repeated wear.

The BBU lifts you up. You are no street punk now. Just look at your fine self: your hair plastered down, your hands clean. Curl your fingers up, boy, so they don't see the nails, ragged from scratching out an existence in this anxious city on the edge of winter. You're uptown and hungry. Farther uptown than you have ever ventured before, driven to this new hunting ground. The edge of winter, the edge of the world. The brink of something. Because that's what edges are.

Wear the uniform like you own it, Blink. Walk like you mean it. No gazing at the ground as though there's a dime there with your name on it. Nothing in this whole wide world has your name on it.

Shoulders back now, so that the lobby guys say, *Good morning, sir,* like you just stepped out for a morning walk to get your appetite up to speed. He's opening the door for you, the tall fella in the long black coat with the red stripes on the shoulders and the little red monkey hat. Smile nice now, Blink, but not so much that you look like the monkey holding the door.

There's another one inside, with cheeks so shiny pink you'd swear his mama just scrubbed them with a toothbrush. He tips his hat like you're a king, and you acknowledge him with your chin, as if you'd say, *Good morning,* right back at him if you weren't so busy being rich.

You're on your way, Blink, you clever monkey, you.

You've played this breakfast game for a month or so, but it only ever lasts a few days. The smiles soon dim; the *good morning*s wither; then some suit strides your way wearing his good-bye face, and out you fly through the revolving door, quick as a wink.

But not this day, Blink. You're good to go.

Just don't hurry and, Christ, don't gawk like you've never seen the inside of a hotel before.

But, oh, look at this lobby, will you? Drink it in. You want to skate across it, so shiny wide. Look at those urns with the exotic plants stuck in them and those chairs just sitting around on the thick carpet discussing important matters. Keep the jitters pressed way down in your empty belly. Stroll like you're heading up to room . . . pick a number—with your left hand holding on to an imagined key.

No one asks. No one cares. In the Blessed BU, you are a *guest*.

The elevator doors shine like they've been through the car wash.

Ding.

There's a camera in this thing, but resist the urge to wave. Look steady at your reflection in the golden door; comb back that sandy-brown hair sprung loose over your brow. Convince those brown-as-hot-tea eyes to calm themselves. You're here to eat—that's all. A boy's got to eat.

Blink. Blink. Blink. A blink for every floor.

Ding.

The carpet is like the floor of an enchanted glade, as if the sun has somehow found its way into this windowless place and seeps down the walls in thin streams. Little green bags hang from every morning doorknob, with a newspaper inside, like it's Christmas. But you aren't here for the news, my friend.

Do you remember the fairy tales Granda told you? Enchanted glades can be a problem. This one here is not as wide as the Westin, or as long as the Sheraton, where you could see trouble

11

coming a mile away. It feels more like you have stolen your way into someone's house.

You round the corner, and—ah!—a black tray with domes on it like some tiny silver city sits outside a sleeping doorway. There's a wilted carnation and a bottle lying on its side. What your stepdaddy calls a dead soldier.

What have we here? Half a gnawed pork chop, mashed potatoes with a cigarette sticking out the top like a chimney on an igloo. Hell, you can do better than this.

There—two doors down. See it, boyo?

You feel the luck oozing up from those one-size-too-small track shoes. You're just full of fairy dust, Blink. It comes on like that sometimes, the good feeling on the heels of the bad. Someone might even fall in love with a boy like you on a day this lucky.

Then you hear your stepdaddy's voice, and you wilt like last night's carnation. You shake him out of your head. You hang on to that sunny disposition, boy. You hang on tight.

Kneel silently before tray number two, like it is a prayerful thing. And, yes! Your prayers are answered. Scrambled egg, hardly touched, a couple of sausages, home fries, and—*jiggle, jiggle*—coffee still hot in the thermos. Amen.

Then the crash.

You're up off that floor like some wild thing on the Discovery Channel, eyes looking every which way, claws out, listening to . . . nothing. Nothing. You brush your knees off, like you might've picked up some enchantment, kneeling there, sniffing at the tray. You listen closely. There's talk somewhere behind a door. Not this one, the next.

But no one comes out. There's just you and this

12

seven-a-empty hallway. Your breath returns to normal.

Then — *thump* — something big falls over. Something real.

What are you waiting for, child? The next shoe to drop? An invitation to the party?

You're stiff with un-motion. But you're not brain-dead, are you? There's no shouting. No one's calling anyone a liar. No one's saying, *Why, you no-good thieving — I oughta* . . . There's no slap.

Everything you expect as a side dish to Crash and Thump — there's none of it. The Captain's listening. Down inside you in his cabin in the hold of you. For a full ticking minute there, you feel him stir in his sleep. Captain Panic. Hold him down. You're good. You can do this.

Somebody had a bad night is all. That's what it is up there, up the hall in room 16-whatever. Somebody stumbling around looking for his dick. Pick up the tray, nice and quick and quiet, and find the little room. There's always the little room with the ice machine and the soda machine, a place where a boy can eat in peace. First thing in the morning, who's going to need ice? And there it is right across the hall from the room of strange noises: 1616.

You perch the tray on the ice machine and go straight for the sausage, but before you get it halfway to your hungry mouth, you see out the side of your eye the napkin. The napkin from hell. It's all scrunched up; white linen on the outside, but inside — what *is* that? Mucus? Yellow streaked with blood. Jesus, but that's disgusting!

Your throat just bunches up at the sight of it. You want to throw up, though there's nothing in you to heave. You close your eyes — they're twitching like nobody's business.

Open them, Blink. Look straight at that sausage, eye to eye.

13

Forget the damn napkin. Oh, sure, and while you're at it, try not to think of this guy sneezing all over his breakfast. . . .

You put the fork down. Can't do it. What was that about your lucky day? You lean against the wall, exhausted from the act of holding yourself together. You got off at the wrong floor, my son—that's all. The wrongest floor of all. You don't know that yet, but you're never far from the feeling.

Shake it off, Blink. Shake it off.

Better? Good. Maybe the seventeenth? It's not like there's anywhere else you were heading today. No big appointments.

Forget about what happened at the Sheraton—put it out of your mind. That was yesterday. That's all over. Yes, one of them got a hand on you, but there's not much of you to grab, is there, and you can twist and turn when you need to—the dance of flight when the jig is up. And the thing is, you've got a day's worth of grazing to catch up on to put something on those bones of yours.

Oh, there's this fire in you that gets blown out so easy but flickers right back up again. That's my boy! Just leave the tray on the ice machine. There are more sausages in the world.

You open the door of the little room, and the door of 1616 clicks open like a mirror image directly across the hall. You step backward—fall backward—like you've been hit, fall into the low rumbling of the ice making, but you don't quite let go of the door, because something in you says that letting go is going to make more noise than holding on.

So there you are. And you hear what happens. And you see some of it, too. Three men: the big one, the wiry one, the little tough one. You name them: the Moon for the cratered roundness of his face; the Snake for the rattler coiling up his forearm;

the Littlest Hulk for his green eyes and a chest that threatens to pop the buttons of his denim shirt. Not one of them belongs here. They are no more Plaza Regent than you are the Gap. They are the Three Billy Goats Gruff coming out of the room of Crash and Thump.

The Moon rolls plastic gloves off his hands—the kind they wear at Subway so they don't have to touch your Santa Fe chicken. They're all in plastic gloves. They wait in the almost-silent morning hallway with the news hanging from every door and music that never comes to an end floating down from the ceiling. What are they waiting for?

And what are you waiting for, your hand frozen to the door? In the knife-blade of your vision, there is only the Littlest Hulk left now, leaning against the yellow wall, flexing his plastic fingers. "Come on," he grumbles, his voice all edgy with nuisance. "Come on," he calls back into the room. He holds the door open with a ragged black-sneakered foot.

"Watch it, Tank," grumbles the Moon.

"Yes, massah," mutters Tank, rolling his eyes.

Then the one they're waiting for appears. No Billy Goat, this one. He's in a shirt like a new snowdrift and gray trousers that might be cut from silk. There are tassels on his shiny black shoes and a shiny black briefcase with a gold combination lock, grasped in his right hand. There's a clean scent coming off him. He's got a trim beard and hair laced with silver. There's a bit of belly on him, like he eats regularly but takes that belly to the gym.

His type sails by you down on Bay Street all the time, like their eyes don't even register the cap in your hand. His type strides across hotel lobbies, with the future tucked tightly under their arms. He stands there filling your narrow vision, and you take in the coolness of this man with his eyes the color of water off the coast of some place people sail to in a yacht.

Has he forgotten something?

No. He shuts the door. He sails out of your sight, sweeping his hand through his hair so that his wristwatch flashes gold against skin he must have had room service iron during the night.

"Ready?" says the Moon.

"Ready," says the Suit.

"Let's get this show on the road," says the Snake.

Tank just says, "Ready, massah," under his breath with this scowl on his halfway-to-a-monster face, like he's been ready for twelve hours or something.

And you, Blink, in there with the ice machine, not breathing for fear of being sniffed out, snuffed out—are you ready? You cannot let go of that door now. So are you prepared for what comes next? Because you just stumbled into this thing, and you will need a thicker skin than the Blessed Breakfast Uniform to get to the end of it.

Chapter 2

A cell phone goes off in someone's pocket. The men in the hall play patty-cake. Tank is the winner. Except, from the look on the Suit's face, Tank just won another lap around the playing field. The Suit doesn't say a thing, just looks at the Moon, as if Tank were the Moon's little pug dog and he just peed on the Suit's tasseled shoes.

"What'd I tell you?" says the Moon, flapping his big mitts resignedly against his side, though he keeps his voice low and grave. They're all huddled together outside the door.

"You ever hear of GPS, Tank?" says the Suit.

Tank looks at the instrument in his hand like he's wondering how it got there. Like he's wondering should he answer it or just let it meow like a cat looking for a lap. Then it stops and the spell ends, and his chin falls to his chest.

"Ditch it," says the Moon, and the Suit hands Tank the room key, which is just a card, and Tank takes it in his plastic-covered fingers and sticks it into the little ATM on the door. He steps in the doorway just far enough to hurl the cell phone and leave again, stepping lively to catch up.

The Littlest Hulk is a wiseass, and this is his last foolish act—you know the type: he flicks the key card over his shoulder, and it flitters through a long slow arc to the floor at the foot of the ice-machine-room door.

You remember the first time you saw a key like this, Blink? You were with your dad, your real dad. He told you that the hotel charged in-and-out fees on the room, and you should make up your mind whether you were coming or going. You push it in, arrow first, and hear the buzz inside.

The room looks like a terrorist pajama party. There's bedding strewn every which way, a blood-colored stain on a torn sheet, a chair on its back, a lamp in shattered pieces on the floor. Magazines and newspapers have been flung from here to Sunday. The flat-screen television lies facedown on the carpet, like it's burying its head in the sand. You stand over it. Sounds come from it. "In other breaking news . . ." says a muffled voice.

You look around, waiting for a corpse to fall out of somewhere. But there's nobody—no body. Not even one floating in the tub, which is what you'd have placed bets on, if you had anything to bet with.

It's wet in the bathroom, foggy, hot. You turn to the gold-framed mirror above the sink. You can't see yourself in it. You clear a spot with your hand, and there you are, looking even more spooked than usual. And then there's the wallet. You see it as a blur in the haze on the mirror, before you see the real thing on the counter. It's leather, shiny from rubbing against a rich backside, and sitting beside a toothbrush with paste on it, ready to go.

It's a trap!

The Suit comes back for his wallet and—*bang!*—you're toast. There you are, about as far from a way out as the Lord Jesus on Good Friday. You stand there unable to move, squeezing that fool card that got you into this mess, until finally it dawns on you. The card. You're the one with the key. There could be other cards, but you don't know that. Just as well.

Breathe, okay? You know what happens when you forget to breathe.

Six hundred dollars of fresh new bills: four hundreds, the rest twenties.

There are credit cards, too, and you know that down at the squat on Trinity, there's a freak named Wish-List who messes with credit cards. For one long second, you think maybe you'll hand these cards to Wish-List—get on his good side, if he has one. Then you ask yourself why you'd want to make nice to a psycho like Wish-List.

Jack Niven.

That's the name on the cards, the license. Jack Niven is the Suit. Jack Niven of 240 Livingston Lookout, Kingston, Ontario. And there's a picture. An ash-blond woman, a honey-blond girl. You stare at the girl with her father's Bahamas-blue eyes and her mother's easy smile. They're standing on the front step

19

of a limestone house with a wood door behind them studded like the entrance to a castle with black-headed nails. A door you'd have to break down with a log.

And here she is again, the princess of the castle, standing on a lawn that slopes down to water, glinting in the sun, like someone hurled a million brand-new copper coins on the water. She's in a short white summer dress, looking back over her shoulder, the wind arguing over her long hair and lifting the hem of her dress, which she holds down as best she can with one thin hand, while the other keeps her blond hair out of her eyes.

She's a bit younger than you, Blink, by the look of it. Fifteen maybe. Long legs, small breasts, face shaped like a diamond. She's as slim as your chances of ever knowing such a girl. But for this one moment, she's smiling at you, Blink. And you smile back, like someone opened the curtains and it was daytime at last.

You shake it off. No one's smiled at you like that for a long time—maybe ever. It's her daddy she's smiling at, and he's not home: Left without his wallet. Left without brushing his teeth.

You slip the money out of the wallet and shove it into your pocket. You close the wallet and lay it down, just so, beside the loaded toothbrush. Then you breathe a bit, like you're remembering how. You pick up the wallet again and take out the picture of the girl with the lake behind her, so much lake it might be an ocean. You're greedy, son. Who can blame you? There is so much you want. You step out of the hazy air of the bathroom. You feel weak and hazy yourself. And now you lean against the door frame and look at the Crash and Thump room again closely.

*   *   *

You're back in your mother's place, out Queen Street East. It's night and you just got in from messing with your buddies, and your mother's standing in her ten-by-nothing living room — standing in the corner — like some piece of furniture, the only piece of furniture still on its feet. Then he comes into view, between her and you, with a poker from the fireplace, drunk and smiling at you like he's real happy you're home and it's going to be a lot more fun whacking you with that wicked thing than wasting it on a piece of furniture like your mother.

"Go," she says. "Just go, Brent."

"Yeah," says Stepdaddy. "We're having a little discussion."

But you don't go. Then his eyes uncross a little, and he lowers the poker. Why is there even a poker in this house? The fireplace hasn't worked for as long as you can remember. The corpse of Santa is probably stuck up there, because he sure hasn't visited this house in a long time. You stare at that poker. You stand there and it's the bravest you've ever been, but it's really just that your feet are nailed to the floor.

He drops the thing and walks past you to the stairs. He heads up, slowly, like he has to make a special arrangement with each step to stay still long enough for him to pass. It's almost like you won, but no one's going to give you a prize. Not your mother, who just looks distressed.

So you go. But not before you take a long look around that wrecked and bleeding little ten-by-nothing room. Like you want to remember what a wrecked life looks like in case you ever think maybe things weren't so bad. In case you decide some cold night to move home again. You go, because in winning that little battle with Stepdaddy, you lost the war.

* * *

A phone buzzes.

You find it in the folds of a white comforter. ALYSON, it says on the screen. And there she is on the screen—the beautiful lawn ornament! You push Talk.

"Daddy?" Electric air. "Are you there?"

You hold your breath, Blink. You're getting way too good at that.

Now there's a voice behind Alyson in whatever room in the castle she's in. The woman, you figure, the mom. "I'm not getting through," she says to the voice. "Phone me," says Alyson to you. "Just wanted to know everything went okay. Love you."

Then click, it's over. But there's a message from before. You touch the screen and hold the phone to your ear. An automated voice asks you for your password. You push the button with a little picture of a red phone on it. Silence.

You steady yourself, try to think through the strangeness of this morning; try to think through a hunger that just got worse. Like this is the sixteenth floor of purgatory, the place your mother used to talk about all the time, where you get to wait until your sins get scrubbed away. Purgatory: one floor up from hell and a long elevator ride away from anywhere good.

You look at the face cupped in your hand. Different picture. Same girl. Alyson. You just met her, and you already know her name. You even know her phone number. Fast work, Blink!

You sniff, breathe in the clammy air drifting out from the bathroom. It smells of Niven, a smell of sun-drenched rock and lime and leather. You fish out the roll of money from your pocket, stare at it a bit, and then—you're not sure why—you head back into the fog and put one twenty back into the wallet, like you're paying for the picture. Or like you're trying to balance out some of that weirdness. You pause, trying to think your way through something. Then you shove another twenty into the wallet—angry now—like you're throwing good money after bad. You're so angry you crinkle the newness right out of those bakery-fresh, hot bills. One of them flutters to the wet bathroom floor. Leave it—get out of here. You don't know what you're playing at, anyway. Then you place the wallet just so, beside the loaded toothbrush. Now you've got five hundred and sixty bucks in your pocket. And now you are truly a part of the weirdness. You bought your ticket.

Back in the bedroom, you sit on the bed and pick up the cell phone. It's a BlackBerry, slim and weighty in your hand, heavy with information. You wrap your fingers around its smoothness, then shove it in the pocket of your stolen cargos.

Time to come to your senses, child. Which is when you see the tray over on the windowsill. You step over the bedding, the toppled chair, the broken shards of lamp. You step around the mumbling television. "It'll be unusually warm in the metro area today. . . ."

You lean against the windowsill and look down at the street sixteen floors below, full of people heading to work. Dazzling car roofs glint in the October sunshine. There is a near-empty glass of orange juice on the tray, an untouched cup of coffee with cream, a banana skin, and the husks of a couple of strawberries. And one perfect golden muffin sitting on a white plate, untouched.

Breakfast at last, you think, but your eyes suddenly water and squeeze shut, as if someone turned a searchlight on you. You shield your face. You squint and look down onto the roof of the Royal Ontario Museum, across Bloor Street. The new wing—the Michael Lee-Chin Crystal, people call it—it looks like an alien crash site from here. A collision of glass and aluminum planes, flashing. And one of those leaning walls has tipped a sunbeam right up at you.

"Him!" the light says. "He's the one you're after!"

And then it's as if the whole museum goes up in flames.

Chapter 3

Caution Pettigrew waits. It is an odd kind of waiting room, concrete block, about as inviting as a tomb. Morning sifts down from grimy skylights. A thick electrical wire coils from a shadowy corner of the ceiling like some kind of industrial boa constrictor, scanning the air for prey. There's a drip somewhere, a smell of creosote in the air. She sniffs, rubs her nose with the cuff of her jacket.

If there are dentists in hell, their waiting rooms might look like this, she thinks, except there are no out-of-date magazines. Or it might be a garage for a tank. She imagines Drigo with his own tank. Soon all the drug lords in the city would want one. The turf wars would get very messy.

She pulls an iPhone from her pocket and checks the time.

She makes sure the thing is off and re-pockets it. After twenty minutes of sitting in the dank warehouse air, she's trying hard to remember what made her think this was a good idea.

There is a sixteen-foot-high garage door that takes up one whole wall. Several fifty-five-gallon steel drums stand in front of the door. From where she sits, they seem to be full of nothing but garbage. A tank could roll right over them, she figures; squash them flat. Same goes for the sitting area: this couch, the mammoth plasma-screen television, and a coffee table littered with empty long-neck beer bottles, ashtrays, and the stale remains of a pizza. There is also a pack of cards with the seven of hearts showing. A good sign? There is a carpet so worn that the backing shows through in places. If the carpet ever had a pattern, it has long since given up the ghost.

The couch is dying, too. She clashes terribly with the couch. It's plaid: all sickly greens and browns—the tartan of the McHeave clan. Caution is wearing tartan—a clingy acrylic mini-kilt in the colors of the McSalvation Army. She wears black low-tops with bright blue laces, canary-yellow socks, and plum-colored tights. She wears a short jacket made from the fuzzy pelt of some electric-blue creature tracked down in the wasteland of northern Walmartia; something that died an agonizing death, judging by the look of it—maybe in a leg-hold trap. When she saw it at the thrift store, she felt so sorry for it, she had to buy it.

For all the colorfulness of her getup, none of it is new: the shoes are scuffed, the laces frayed, the tights with enough ladders to scale a fortress.

There is a pile of DVDs beside the television. Bored, she

searches for the remote and finds it under the pizza box. She flicks the TV on. A porn movie swims into view, mid-orgy. She pushes the Pause button, and the action commences. She tilts her head this way and that, trying to figure out how the girl got herself into that position. There are three of them on the screen. They're making a lot of noise, but no one looks all that happy. She clicks the Off button.

In the gray screen, she stares at her reflection, fixes her hair. It is three degrees redder than her tights. It's cut pixie-short and held in place by seven hairpins for good luck. Her eyes are three degrees paler than the screen into which she gazes. She can see the reflection of the straps of her pink backpack, a Little Mermaid junior, just big enough for her book and, with any luck, a big fat wad of money.

She hears laughter somewhere. Drigo is doing this on purpose — making her wait like this. They wouldn't do this to Merlin. He'd cast a spell on them — turn them all into bunny-rabbits. She grins to herself at the idea: bunny-rabbit dealers. Her mood shifts, just like that. It's going to be one of those good days, she decides, and she sits up a little straighter.

She remembers sitting outside the principal's office just like this, knees tightly together, to keep from quaking, shoulders back so no one would think she had anything to be ashamed of. But this is no school, and the man she has come to see is hardly a principal. And no disgruntled teacher would send her down here. Her teachers never used to be disgruntled with her, not until last fall when everything went pear-shaped. It's an expression her English father used to use, meaning when things go belly-up. It sounds nicer, softer. But what really happened is that things went to rat shit.

The door behind the TV opens. It's Warner.

"He can see you now," he says.

"Like I was invisible before?" she mutters, but he's already turned to go.

She gets up to follow and realizes she's still carrying the remote control. She's not sure what to do with it. Then she remembers the porn movie and heaves the zapper across the room. It banks off the garage door and crashes into one of the steel drums. She pumps her fist in celebration. Three points.

"What the hell was that?" says Warner.

"Sorry," she says.

He's got his hand inside his jacket, and she thinks he's clutching at his heart. Then she realizes there is something else there he's clutching at. She catches a glint of steely blue.

"Just thought I'd better ditch my gum," she says.

He swears, tugs at his eyebrow rings. He doesn't like her. That makes two of us, she thinks.

Drigo sits behind a steel door at a steel desk the size of a pool table in an office that looks like a bunker from a war movie, the place where the Nazis wait for the poor devils about to land on the beach. He leans his bulk back in his chair, his legs splayed.

"Aren't you a sight for sore eyes," he says.

Warner glares at Caution one last time and leaves, closing the door behind him. The click is straight out of a horror movie.

"Hey, Drigo," she says.

"Caution," says Drigo.

"As in: Contents May Be *Hot*!" Caution takes in Boris sitting on a filing cabinet, leaning against a wall plastered with concert posters. He's head-to-toe leather.

"Hey, Boris," she says.

"The little engine that *could*," says Boris. He's rolling a joint. "'I think I can, I think I can,'" he says, waggling his head around. It's not the first joint of the morning, Caution figures.

"What can I do for you?" says Drigo.

"Merlin's money," she says.

"What about it?"

"I came for it," she says.

Boris starts to giggle.

"Can it," says Drigo. He turns his attention back to Caution. "And where is the magic man?"

"He's laying low," she says, "but we need the cash, bad."

Boris cups his hand to his ear. "Come again?" he says. Then he clutches his gut, he's laughing so hard.

"Oh, for Christ's sake," she says. "Get a grip."

She leans back against the smooth, cold door, folding her arms tightly across her chest.

"Enough, Boris," says Drigo, and the laughter fades to nothing, as if the big man has reached over and turned down the volume.

He sits up now, folding his massive hands on the desk, like he's a bank manager—except for the soul patch and the "I fought the bong and the bong won" T-shirt.

"And I should give this money to you, why?" he says.

"Like I said, Merlin's keeping his head down."

"And so he sent his favorite little mule?"

"Yeah," she says. "Something like that."

Boris lights up, takes a big drag, then reaches out to offer the spliff to Caution. She shakes her head, all business.

When she looks back to the boss, he's picking up his cell phone, looking for Merlin on his speed dial. He leans back, and his old-style wooden office chair groans under the weight. She swears she can hear the iPhone ringing in her pocket—prays that the ringing is only in her head.

"He won't answer," she says impatiently. "He's sleeping it off. Man, he's going be sleeping half the day."

Drigo folds up his cell and drops it on the desktop beside his packet of cigarettes. He leans back and rubs his thumb through the fuzz under his lip.

"Hey," she says. "We did this before, remember?"

He nods. "I remember. But that time Merlin, he phone me first. How I know this isn't some little scam of yours?"

She shrugs. "You don't know. But I'll sign for it—like last time. And if there's any trouble, it's not going to fall on you."

Drigo stares at her. "What's up, Caution?"

"Nothing's up," she says. "What do you mean?"

"Hey," says Boris, all animated suddenly. "Give her the rubles, man. Think about it. Caution splits. It'd be worth it just to see Merlin go mental."

Drigo holds out his hand, the first two fingers open in an inverted peace sign, and Boris jumps down off his perch to hand him the spliff. Drigo never takes his eyes off Caution the whole time. Through a veil of smoke, his eyes hold on to her, hazel eyes that always look like they're just about to cry. "Is that what you're planning?" he says.

"Splitting? What do you think?"

"You know what he do if you try something funny," says Drigo, and his gaze drifts to her right hand, which she curls up protectively in the cuff of her jacket.

"I'm not planning anything funny," she says. "Honest. It's just we don't even have coffee in the place. I've been bugging him to come see you, but he's all . . . I don't know—cagey, for some reason. I figure things are not good out there. So I just came myself."

Boris titters like a sixth-grader. "You are just Little Cat A, aren't you, girl?" he says. And she thinks how sad it is that there was once someone in Boris's life who read Dr. Seuss to him and he ended up here. Then again, so did she.

Drigo smiles, but he's not convinced.

"You come here because you're out of coffee?"

She shrugs. "I've got to do something, you know?"

"Why?"

"What do you mean, why? Because . . ."

His thick eyebrows snake up his forehead.

"Because Merlin's gone weird on me," she says. "Like his head is . . . I don't know . . . somewhere else. I can't get a straight word out of him. So I thought, I'll take charge, you know? Look after it."

Drigo chuckles—sadly, she thinks, because she is so pathetic.

"Come on, man," she says. She won't let him off the hook. She wants an answer. Drigo can boot her out if he wants or give her what she came for, but she isn't going to let him laugh this off.

"Okay," he says, finally. "Okay."

She can hardly believe it.

"Yessssss!" says Boris, holding two thumbs up, like he negotiated the deal and it's a personal victory. He bangs the heels of his biker-chained boots against the filing cabinet.

Drigo gives Caution one last sharp look, then turns to a safe built into the wall directly behind him. His wide back hides the turning of the wheels, the opening of the door. When he

31

spins himself around again, he's holding a thick stack of bills wrapped in a yellow paper band. Caution can see Merlin's name written on the paper. The bills are all hundreds. He peels off one and puts the rest back in the safe.

"Hey?" says Caution.

"This'll keep you in coffee for now."

"But—"

"Lot of coffee."

"But—"

"Until his magic self pays me the honor of a visit *in person*."

"But—"

"Or I could just forget the whole thing," he says. He never raises his voice. Never looks angry.

"Okay," says Caution. "Sorry. I mean, thanks."

He waggles the bill in front of his face with this come-hither look in his eyes. She makes her way around the desk.

"A hundred is enough to piss him off, good, if that's what you have in mind," he says.

"Why would I want to—?"

"But it's not enough for you to get very far away," he continues, cutting her off again. He taps the side of his head with a fat yellow finger. "You too valuable to Merlin," he says. "And Merlin too valuable to me. You know what I'm saying? Everything is like that. Interconnected."

Caution glares at him, but she'd need a tank of her own to intimidate the man. She wasn't thinking of running away. Why would he think that?

"Fine," she says, grabbing at the money. But despite his thick body and his soft and lazy eyes, Drigo snatches it out of her grasp. He holds up a pen with the other hand. Caution signs and dates the transaction in a little green book.

When she's done, he hands her the money. "Thanks," she says again, like a kid who's been given a carrot when she asked for cake.

He dismisses her bad grace with a wave of his hand.

She steps back to the safe side of the desk. She shoves the hundred into her jacket pocket.

"There, now," says Boris. "Everybody's happy. Right, Caution? You're happy, right?"

She nods. And when she looks at Drigo again, he's smiling, but there is this deep sadness behind the smile, like he has seen the future and it isn't good. Then she wonders what made her think that.

"You take care," he says. It doesn't sound like a threat exactly, but it doesn't sound like the good wishes of a favorite uncle, either.

"Of course," she says. "I always take care."

"She's the Cat in the Hat," says Boris. She wonders if it's the drugs that make him think of picture books. Maybe she should do more drugs.

Meanwhile, Drigo's been watching her closely, and his expression has changed, as if he's been sorting through her thoughts and come upon something interesting.

"Merlin don't even know you here, right?" he says.

She hesitates only a moment before shaking her head.

"What'd I say?" says Boris. "The Cat in the Hat!"

Drigo holds her with his gaze. "Or maybe she just suicidal?"

Caution sniffs. "Well, now that you mention it . . ."

Boris slaps his leather thigh. "You are something else, Caution."

She nods. Something else. Right. Just not sure what.

"Caution," says Drigo. "Contents under pressure."

The Boris laugh track kicks in, but Drigo isn't being funny. It freaks her out how well he knows her.

Then the big man winks, and it's her cue to go.

She turns to the door, tries the knob. It won't move. Drigo presses a buzzer and now it turns.

"Hey," says Boris. "You give Merlin our *love*, okay?"

"Yeah, right," she says. Then she turns her eyes back to Drigo. "Thanks again," she says, and means it this time. "It was true about the coffee."

"No problemo," he says.

She has almost closed the door when Boris calls her back.

"Yeah?" she says.

"You come again, okay?" he says.

She shuts the door on his smoke-stained laughter, but it follows her down the corridor, the sound of a hyena in heat.

Out on the street, the sun is shining, the air is fresh, the wind rustles the remaining leaves on the maples along this street of dilapidation. It's over. She did it. Well, sort of. She looks at the time on Merlin's iPhone. Just before eleven. He didn't get in until five or so. He'll probably sleep for hours yet, which will give her time to hit the grocery store, get home, and have coffee brewing for him when he does finally wake up. It's all going to work out fine, she tells herself.

Then the tears come, just like that. It's the tension, she tells herself—all that waiting in the cold. Testing herself, testing her mettle. Suicidal? Yeah, well . . .

"Oh, Spence," she says, looking up through the red shift of maple leaves toward the blue October sky. "What am I doing?"

She wipes her eyes. Sniffs, sucks it up. And a memory drifts down to her like a leaf that can't hang on a moment longer. A memory from Wahnapitae.

She's six and stuck in a tree house that Spence built with their cousin Wayne-Ray. She's sitting at the entranceway, her bruised summer legs hanging over the edge, looking down through her naked brown feet to where the two of them stand on the ground, a hundred miles below.

"You can do it, Kitty," says Spence.

"You got up there good," says Wayne-Ray.

Her bottom lip is trembling. It's too far down.

"Come on, Kitty girl," says Spence. He's fifteen—nine years older than her. She's an "Oops! baby"; that's what Auntie Lanie calls her.

"Ah, get a move on," says Wayne-Ray. He's thirteen and doesn't like it that Spence lets her hang around with them so much.

"Take your time," says Spence, not one bit impatient. He'll wait for her at the bottom of the tree forever. Knowing that makes it easy to shimmy her butt another inch or two closer to the edge.

"That's my Kitty," he says.

And then she just pushes off. No ladder for our Miss Kitty.

For a moment she's in free fall—terrified, thrilled—then Spence has got her in his arms and hugs her close even as he tumbles backward into the high dry grass, falling over with his little sister on top of him, screaming with laughter.

She scrambles up to her feet. "Let's do it again," she says.

Caution leans against a dusty factory wall, trying to get her balance back, trying to get her scuffed black sneakers lined up straight underneath her. Spence isn't there to catch her anymore. So why, she wonders, does she keep throwing herself out of trees?

If you could MapQuest her, Blink, on that smartphone of yours, you'd be surprised how close Miss Caution Pettigrew is. If you could Google-Earth her, you'd find she is on the same wildly spinning planet, 3.97 kilometers away: hardly any distance at all. Except for the huge distance of not knowing her—not even knowing she exists. Patience. That is about to change.

Chapter 4

Captain Panic. Oh, you are a brave sailor to have such a passenger aboard. Thinks he runs the ship. There's only so much you can take before the Captain steps in, throws one of his tantrums. He's the one who makes you blink like that, yes? He stands at the helm in your leaky skull sending coded messages out to sea through your eyes. And there's no one out there to decipher them.

You sit on a park bench in Philosopher's Walk, across the road from the hotel, shuddering a bit in the shadows. The upside-down television on the hotel room floor promised it would be unseasonably warm, but not where you are, boy. The museum looms above you, behind you—still intact. Things only *seem* to burst into flames, don't they, Blink? That's the Captain at work.

In front of you stands the Royal Conservatory of Music. Some unseen woman is singing scales; some piano player is getting the same fast passage wrong every time. In a nearby oak, a blue jay screams harshly, like he's heard enough. It's cooler down here, out of the sun, but the traffic isn't so loud, and you can almost think. While inside your head, the Captain paces back and forth in the wheelhouse.

Whoever Jack Niven is, there are a lot of folks trying to reach him. You can't access his voice mail, but you scroll through his text messages. There's Sophie, who will forward the exact wording of the injunction, whatever that is; Bernie, who wants to go over a couple things before the meeting with the minister; Sandjit, who will be joining him for lunch; and Roger, who wonders if he's still on for three o'clock. There's Clare, who's been combing through the fine print; Huraki, who says ANS will hold tight; and a reporter from the *Toronto Star* who has a couple of follow-up questions.

You look at the BlackBerry. Find Alyson in the address book. Her picture lights up the tiny screen. She's older here than in the picture by the lake, her hair shorter but filled with sunlight, as if she never goes inside. Her eyes flash like a blue jay's crest. You get an idea. You go to voice mail, and when the prompt comes for your password, you punch in A-L-Y-S-O-N.

"You have eleven new messages."

"Jack," says Bernie. "The minister is still onside, but the fucking protest is turning from media circus to nightmare."

"Jack, Sophie again. Van Luyten from the *Financial Post* has phoned three times in the last twenty minutes. He's caught wind of the creeping tender offer."

A creeping tender? You wonder at such words, Blink.

On and on like that it goes, and it's not even nine. You switch off the smartphone, shove it in your pocket, and just sit.

You slip your shoes off. They're so pretty, those spotless Adidas, but your poor toes are screaming blue murder. Something says to you, Blink, you're going to need a good pair of sneakers before this day is up.

You spend ninety of those five hundred and sixty dollars on a pair of blue high-tops that fit you like a glove. You throw in a pair of good socks, too; peel off the ones you're wearing. You need to bathe those feet of yours, Blink, and you try to think of where there's a public pond still filled up this late in October. City Hall—but that's too far. So you settle for the men's room in the Bay at Yonge and Bloor. You sit on the counter and bathe those tired, bruised feet of yours, and then clip the nails with new clippers you bought, now that you're a rich man about town. You strap on your new blue wings.

Ahhh.

You are floating, man! This is the way feet should feel. You are good to go, Blink, at least from the ankles down.

You head up to the Toronto Reference Library, and no one even looks twice at you decked out in the Blessed BU, striding with the purpose that comes with shoes that fit you right. You're some student come to work. You find one of those private reading booths and take out the money you've got left. You used five twenties to pay for the shoes and socks, because you're not even sure the hundreds could be real. You sit in that big library, quiet, and stare at those hundred-dollar bills. You've never seen one before, and for *sure* they're going to be trouble. Then you get an idea. Hey, it's a library—the place is full of ideas, and you just snagged one for yourself. You head back to the underground shopping center at Yonge and Bloor and find yourself a drugstore. You buy a greeting card and a pen, sit down on a bench, and write yourself a letter.

"Can I help you?" says the bank teller, but your clothes don't fool her one bit. Your camouflage is wearing thin. She knows you're trash, and the help she's offering is the lowest grade of stuff she has available. Her nose looks pinched as if she caught a whiff of you, too, and doesn't want another.

"I was just wondering," you say, trying to keep it cool, trying to sound the part. "My grandmother gave me this money for my birthday? But it's hundred-dollar bills? And I'm not even sure you can, like—you know—use them in a store?"

She looks suspicious, so you pull out the card in its envelope and show her the whole pretty thing. "Not so Sweet Sixteen" it says on the front, and there's a picture of this wigged-out teen, except he's cartoon cute with a skateboard, long hair, zits, and attitude. Inside you wrote in the shaky hand of some feeble old person: "To my wonderful grandson Sulley from his Granny Smith."

The teller cocks her head to read it when she picks up the bills, and her lip gloss cracks a bit in one corner.

"What denomination?" she says.

"Uh, Catholic?" you say. And now she notches up the smile.

"I meant the bills, honey: twenties and tens okay?"

"To my wonderful grandson Sulley from his Granny Smith."

Funny you'd think of *Monsters, Inc.* Sulley and Mike and Boo. You used to love that movie when you were a kid. And

Granny Smith? You made up a grandmother who's an apple! What's that about? Then you think about your real grandparents: Nanny Dee and Granda Trick. It's "Granda" not "Grandpa," you explained to some fool teacher who thought you couldn't spell. It's Irish: your dad's folks. Too bad about that. Too bad about so much.

In a fast-food place, you catch up on Jack Niven. *Whoa!* The BlackBerry is smoking. There are twenty-five calls and fifteen text messages. Seems your man never made his ten o'clock.

You eat two breakfast sandwiches and try to piece together what's going on, but there are so many players, you can't make head nor tail of it. Still, it's kind of cool, like a video game, and you're trying to figure out how to play. Like it was *Grand Theft Auto* or something.

You sit back and look at the face of that sly little machine in your hand with all its functions and all its memory. What can it tell you? Google the man, Blink. Ah, now we're getting somewhere.

Niven is the president and CEO—whatever that is—of something called Queon Ventures Development. QVD is a publicly traded company committed to the exploration and development of uranium properties.

Uranium is big again, Blink. Did you know that? Did you know it had ever been small? You know what uranium is. You weren't a stranger at school—not until now. Anyway, Queon is sitting on several large properties they have acquired 100-percent ownership of. That's what they say, anyway. But somebody else says they own the land: the Algonquin First Nations. Indians. By law, it says, the mining company has a duty to consult with them, but as far as you can figure out, this is a

41

different set of laws than the ones QVD knows. Not surprising, is it, Blink? You've always kind of suspected that there was one set of laws for one kind of people and a different set of laws for the rest. The Indians don't want QVD coming onto their property to look for or stake out anything. They don't want QVD to dig trenches or boreholes or to even so much as cut down a single blessed tree.

You wade through this stuff. Blink, blink, blink—one link leads to another. There aren't many images, but you begin to get the picture: the white guys are winning. Like in the old movies Granda Trick liked to watch. When push comes to shove, the white guys have the cavalry on their side.

The fucking protest is turning from media circus to nightmare.

The Indians have barricaded the entrance to the land. Everything is pretty peaceful so far, except a couple of people got arrested and somebody's on a hunger strike and a lot of people are outraged.

Reading this stuff makes your brain hurt. If this is a video game, you aren't scoring any points yet. But you keep going. Captain Panic's gone back to his cabin below deck. You can hear him grumbling, but you're used to that. You're all alone again, with cash in your pocket and a toy to mess with.

It's not exactly *Texas Hold 'Em,* not exactly *Doom,* but something to do with your fingers and your brain. Stepdaddy was wrong about that. You've got a brain, all right, just not one he liked to have around. You remember once trying to show him a report card—a good one. He glanced at it, glanced at you, and then handed it back.

"What?" he said. "Am I supposed to do something?"

"Oh," you said. "I forgot. You can't read. Sorry."

42

You never could leave well enough alone.

You go back to the story of Jack Niven and Queon Ventures Development. You get the gist of it, except for one thing: QVD says they have something called subsurface rights. Subsurface? As far as you can figure it, Blink, the Indians own the land, but the company owns what's under it.

Now, how does that work?

You hunker down over that smart little phone with your triple-triple coffee and try to figure out what land is—or what they mean by it here. How can you own what you're standing on and someone else can grab what's under it? Then you think of your mother's place and Stepdaddy moving in. Well, there you go.

If this were history class, you'd have given up by now. You'd be like an autumn fly on a hot windowsill, on your back, buzzing and kicking your last. But there is something about stolen knowledge that tastes different. No one is trying to spoon-feed you this stuff. It's complicated, but there isn't going to be a test. Well, not that kind of a test. Stick with it, Blink. See what you can make of it.

The Suit with the beautiful daughter claims he owns the land. The courts agree. That's what the injunction is about. QVD is suing the Indians for forty-eight million dollars—whoa! But the Indians aren't budging. QVD says it will back off if the government gives them the money. Gives who the money? *QVD*, of course. Huh. Anyway, the government's not talking. Lots of other people are joining the Indians waving signs. They're bringing in food and medicine for the folks who are occupying the land and protesting the drilling, because they don't want the uranium that'd be dug up polluting the air and poisoning the rivers.

You come up for air, Blink, and there's this maggoty-faced manager standing above you saying you've been there too long.

"You're right," you tell him, and take your coffee and your BlackBerry elsewhere.

It's hot on Bloor Street. The last of Indian summer. Ha! You never thought about that expression before. What does it mean?

And what time is it, anyway? You flick a button, and Mr. BlackBerry says it's just after noon.

You head back down into Philosopher's Walk. There are people lunching there, sitting on the grass, catching a few rays, now that the sun is more or less overhead. You find a place by yourself and check out *CityNews* on the magic machine.

Bang!

There it is: the top story.

Mining Executive Missing. Police Called In.

Jack Niven, president and CEO of Queon Ventures, did not show up for a top-level governmental meeting at Queen's Park this morning. Police were called in, and Niven's room at the Plaza Regent Hotel was found to be the scene of what appeared to be a violent confrontation. The police are keeping tight-lipped, but undisclosed sources at QVD fear that Niven may have been abducted.

Abducted?

44

The meeting he was to attend was called by the Minister of Aboriginal Affairs, the Honorable Cate McCormack, in an attempt to address the controversy over land claims at Millsap Lake in Eastern Ontario. Currently, QVD is at the center of a six-month-long standoff with more than one First Nations organization as well as local residents and several environmental groups over uranium explorations in the area. . . .

You stop reading. Look up, stunned. Laughter a little way off wakes you up: a couple sitting on the grass, laughing together. There is something odd about them, or about the woman, anyway. She's maybe thirty, pretty, but acting strangely. Then you realize she's blind. She's not wearing dark glasses or carrying a cane or anything like that; you can just tell by the way she holds her head, the way she looks, and the way she doesn't look. They laugh again. Then she reaches out and touches her friend's cheek, lets her hand linger there. He's nothing to look at, you're thinking. But she doesn't know that.

Then the BlackBerry buzzes and you look down. It's Alyson.

There have been a hundred calls and a million e-mails floating into your in-box—his in-box—but this is different.

You push the picture of the green phone.

"Dad? Daddy?"

You swallow hard.

"Are you there?"

Your heart is squirming.

"Mom called me home from school when she heard. No one can reach you, but I'm going to keep trying."

She stops again. Sniffs. You wonder if she can hear the birdsongs, the muffled traffic, the laughter so close by.

"If someone else is listening, please let me talk to my father. Please!"

You feel like some kind of Peeping Tom looking into the window at a crying girl, and you hate yourself for it, but what can you say?

Dump this damned phone before you do something rash.

"Hello?" says Alyson. "I know there's someone there. If it's you, Daddy, and you can't talk, then just be strong, okay? If it's someone else . . ."

"They didn't hurt him."

There. You've done it now, kid.

"Who is this?"

"They didn't hurt your father."

"What—?"

You lower your voice, curl in on yourself.

"I was there, okay?" you say in something just above a whisper. "I don't know what was happening exactly, but your father was . . ." You want to say "in on it," because that is what you think you saw. But you can't say that.

"Please, tell me who this is."

"He's all right, okay?" Then before she can say another word, you click the red phone because you can't take it anymore.

You look up, your heart racing, and the blind girl over by the poplar grove is looking at you.

Chapter 5

Caution will be seventeen in four weeks. She's a Sagittarius— the archer. And she's a murderer. For that, she can never be forgiven. She leans her head against the window of the streetcar, clanging down Queen Street. She has taken *Anna Karenina* from her Little Mermaid backpack. She tries to read a bit of it every day. It was Spence's favorite novel. He told her there was a character named Kitty in it. That was all she knew. She took it when she left home. She wanted to know what he found in the story. She has read 153 pages, only 715 to go. But her eyes won't focus. Her mind won't sit still.

She holds her right hand open in front of her eyes and looks at the scars there. It's as if her palm were a pond into which someone threw a hot pebble and waves of its heat have radiated out in circles. Merlin caught her at something. She can't remember what now—just something—but he was real mad. He held her hand down on the electric burner. Then he held her close and kissed away her tears.

"It was wrong what you did," he said to her, holding her weeping face in his hands.

And she nodded. She knew. You can't kill people and expect to get away with it.

She was the one who came up with the name Caution for herself. Caution, as in Slippery When Wet; Caution, as in Harmful If Swallowed; Caution, as in Toxic.

She shops at the grocery store and walks home under the noonday sun, with a plastic bag fit to burst in either hand. She thinks about a ham sandwich with mayo and cheese. She thinks about Oreos. Maybe Merlin will be up, and she'll make him a sandwich, too. She imagines them at the table with mugs of coffee, eating lunch together. In her little daydream, the table isn't piled high with dirty plates, unpaid bills, a box of Baggies, and a weigh scale.

She turns up Carlaw and there he is, up the street, looking straight at her, just as if he knew she was coming, as if he was expecting her. Drigo couldn't have reached him because she has Merlin's phone. He really is a magician.

She hauls one of her hands up into the air in greeting. It isn't much of a wave, what with the groceries dragging her down. He doesn't wave back. His hands are shoved into his pockets. And as she gets closer, she can see he's angry. He's in a white T and jeans and bare feet. There's a tat of an eagle on his right bicep, and even the eagle is glaring at her.

"Hey," she says.

Then his hand is on her arm, hurting her, dragging her toward their place, while he looks around to make sure no one is watching.

"I can explain," she says.

"I bet you can," he says.

He pulls her up the path, opens the front door and shoves her through, buzzes the inner door open and shoves her again, turns down the corridor, and shoves her so hard she almost falls.

"Okay, okay!" she says.

Then he slaps her. Hard.

She shrieks and drops the bag in her right hand to fend off a second blow. His left hand grabs her hand in a steel grip; his right hand cups her chin, lifting her face to his.

She can feel the shape of his open palm burning on her cheek and wonders if it will leave a hand-shaped mark on her face to match the burner-shaped mark on her hand.

Tears fill her eyes.

"Have you got a death wish or something?" he says.

There it is again. Isn't this what Drigo was saying? All these people that know her better than she knows herself.

"We were out of coffee," she says.

He squeezes her jaw so tight, she wonders if he might snap it right off. And it would serve her right for talking nonsense. He pushes her up against the wall.

"We may be out of coffee, but you are out of your fucking mind," he says.

She'd nod if she could.

The door to number four opens. Claudia sticks her head out, her mane all tousled, still in her nightgown.

"So you found her," she says, leaning against the doorjamb. She doesn't sound relieved.

Merlin drops his hands. Punishment is a private business for him.

Caution glares past his shoulder at Claudia. "I wasn't lost," she says.

Claudia pulls her nightgown close. "Maybe you should look into that," she says.

"Shut up, Claudia," says Merlin.

She salutes. "Yes, sir," she says, and slinks back into her lair.

In the apartment, Caution expects more but gets nothing. It's a mixed blessing. Sometimes he's loving once he's got the rough stuff out of his system. Not that he apologizes. He never apologizes. And the love, she suspects, is because the rough stuff turns him on. Except not this time.

"The money," he says. And she gives him what's left, plus the receipt from the grocery store. He stares at it in disbelief.

"It's all there," she says. "Count it."

He throws the cash on the table and walks over to the window. In the glare, he becomes a thick-shouldered silhouette. She sneaks his cell phone out of her jacket pocket and slips it down the side of the couch. It's foolish of her to think he won't know she took it, but she has to try. Pretend. Play the game, even though he always wins. She remembers a line from *Anna Karenina*. "She felt clothed in an impenetrable armor of lies." Caution wishes she were so lucky. Merlin sees through her every time.

"Never take money without asking," he says, not turning to her.

The statement confuses her. "What do you mean?"

"You know what I mean," he says.

"I don't. Didn't," she says, squinting at the white wall of light. "Take money from where?"

"Don't fuck with me, Caution."

"I didn't steal any money."

Now he turns, and though she can't really see his eyes because she's squinting so hard into the sun, she knows he's working himself up for another round of violence.

"The stash is not *our* stash," he says. "It is *my* stash."

Oh, she thinks. *He doesn't know where I've been.* She is momentarily stunned. He's Merlin—he knows everything. But not this.

"Merlin," she says. "If there's money in some stash, I don't even know about it. Count it, okay? You'll see." What she doesn't say is that if there's money in a stash, why are they living on Rice Krispies?

He pushes himself away from the window ledge and walks toward her. She braces herself for another blow, but he breezes past her to the far corner of the apartment where the painted pony stands. It's one of those rides they have outside grocery stores. You put in your quarter and let Junior have a little jiggle. She's not sure where Merlin got it, but there it is: a blue pony with a yellow mane and tail, a golden saddle, and smiley brown eyes. He cups the pony's head in both hands and lifts it up and over a foot or so. His biceps bulge from the effort. The wooden floorboards under the horse are darker. His fingers pry one of them up and then his hand reaches in and takes out a cookie tin. He opens it and removes a handful of cash, which he counts.

Caution watches in astonishment.

He puts the top back on the tin and drops it in the cubbyhole, replaces the board, then lifts the painted pony back into place.

"I told you," she says, knowing it may get her a slap but needing to say something.

He walks to the table and pockets the money left over from the shopping.

"So, are you turning tricks?" he says. "The breakfast special?"

She wishes he were angry now. She wishes that the idea of her walking the street made him furious. Instead, a smile plays across his face. He takes his long hair in his hands and pulls it into a tight ponytail. She hands him an elastic band that is lying on the table. It's instinct. He takes it and ties his hair with it, doubling the rubber band, tripling it.

"Well?"

She shakes her head. And now she'll have to tell him. Tell him what she was doing this morning. Where the money came from.

"Huh," he says, looking her up and down as if she really were a hooker and he was checking out the merchandise. He flicks the edge of her kilt with his finger.

"Maybe you should look into that," he says. He smirks. Then he gathers up his watch and car keys and looks around for his cell. She joins in the search.

"Oh, here it is," she says. "Between the cushions."

He takes it without a word, tucks it into the holder on his belt, and then heads toward the door.

"Where are you going?" she asks.

"Out," he says.

"Where?"

"OUT," he says. "Business."

"When will you be—?"

"When I feel like it," he says.

He's paying her back for . . . for what? For not being there? For showing up with groceries?

He's sitting on the pew by the door, putting on his socks and shoes. He once told her he stole the pew from Saint James Cathedral. Stole it right out from under a pack of parishioners, while they were kneeling to pray. One of his better tricks.

"Merlin," she says.

"What?"

"I'm sorry."

He stands up, tucks his T into his jeans, pats his back pocket to make sure his wallet is snug. "Good," he says.

"Don't you want to know where the money came from?"

He smiles. "You think I don't know?"

He doesn't wait for her response. He's through the door and gone. *Poof!*

Caution sits on the couch, rubbing the tops of her legs with her hands. So he *does* know. But how? They have no landline. Does Drigo communicate with him telepathically? She wouldn't put it past either of them. But, no, she thinks. Merlin doesn't know. And this is a little hard-won victory.

After a minute, she gets up and goes to the window to look down on the alley in back where his beater is parked, a rusted-out blue Nissan. She presses her nose against the glass, warm under the sun. She waits; he doesn't show. So she waits some more. Nothing. Odd. Merlin never takes public transportation. Wizards just don't. So his business must be nearby. She tries to think of any clients close by but remembers that he didn't leave with any dope.

And then it comes to her. Just like that. All of it: why he

didn't seem to care about where the money came from; where he was last night until forever; why they haven't had sex in weeks. She marches to the door, closing it silently behind her. She sneaks down the hallway to number four and puts her ear to the door. Claudia is laughing. Someone speaks in a low murmur. She laughs again.

Caution remembers how Claudia looked. Still in her nightgown but tarted up—lipstick, mascara, the whole nine yards; plucked and moisturized, her thirty-something-year-old wrinkles painted over. Caution can see her again in her mind's eye, leaning against the doorjamb, her fingernails polished.

And tuning into her very recent past, Caution pictures Merlin. She had been so frightened of him, she hadn't really noticed that he was showered and shaved, doused with L'Homme—reeking of it!

She staggers back from the door. What catty thing was it Claudia had said when Caution told her she wasn't lost? *Maybe you should look into that.* Which is the same thing Merlin had said when Caution said she wasn't turning tricks. The exact same words.

Caution stares at Claudia's door. She saw inside the apartment once when she came around to borrow something. She remembers thinking how great it looked, with cushions everywhere and Indian printed cotton flung over the table lamps. There was a beaded curtain and some kind of exotic bird in a cage, green and gold and singing.

Caution: Corrosive. May Cause Blindness.

She wants to smash on Claudia's door with her fists—knock it down. The only thing stopping her is she's not sure which of them to kill first. But even as the thought occurs to

54

her, that worst of all possible four-letter words cracks open in her skull and out flows the strong poison inside it. To even think the word *kill* is to let it loose inside her system, like some paralyzing drug. She stumbles, has to reach out and support herself against the wall. Is this what a heart attack feels like? she wonders. She starts to sob, inconsolably, burying her face in her hands to keep anyone from hearing her heart break.

She leans there for hours or minutes or until there are no sounds from inside Claudia's apartment. Then slowly she gathers herself together and makes her way back to the apartment.

Chapter 6

Caution sits in the buzzing silence of the sun-filled apartment. Apart from the sun, it is also filled with flies—filling up with flies—she isn't sure from where. Perhaps there is something dead in here, she thinks. She is sagging now—hot, worn out. She unzips her jacket. Under the fuzz, it's quilted, way too warm for this weather. She's wearing a pink tank top with a silver-sequined kitten on it. She leans back, her arms cradling her belly, though there's nothing really there to hold. She's worn out from so much weeping.

For the second time today, she is sitting on a couch with nothing before her but an oversize TV. But what is she waiting for now? Nothing, as far as she can tell.

Merlin found her on the street, sitting cross-legged behind

a fabulous straw hat she'd lifted from somewhere. It had a wide, purple polka-dotted sash and yellow feathers. He wanted to see it on her, and so she had emptied the few coins in it into her hand and modeled it for him.

"A girl should be going to a garden party in a hat like that," he'd said. She'd laughed and it hurt, like any kind of exercise you pick up again that you have abandoned for too long.

And he did take her to a party that very night, although it wasn't in a garden—it being March and freezing. He introduced her as Lalalania—she hadn't given him a name, and he hadn't asked. At that point she hadn't given herself a name—not one she could stick with. It changed with everyone she met. All she knew was that she wasn't Kitty Pettigrew. Not anymore.

He was so attentive, his arm around her as if she were his and his alone. She wasn't fooling herself. She guessed where the night was heading, knew she'd have to pay for so much attention, one way or another. She'd been living on the street for four months, after all. But that night, high, and warm in someone's eyes, she was beyond caring. It was enough to be loved. And whatever came next . . . well, that kind of fit into her plan in a way, if you could call it a plan. She was not fit to live, so this handsome man with the scar through his right eyebrow and the blond ponytail could be her private executioner.

That he wasn't a pimp was the first surprise.

He wanted her. Wanted a lot out of her. He was rough, but there was a certain sweetness to the pain. And, yes, she could help with the business, if he liked. Run errands, sure. Do the odd transaction, especially in situations when a thirty-year-old male might look conspicuous. Selling pot at high school: no problem. She was useful. She wanted to be useful. And when

57

she screwed up . . . well, the punishment was almost a relief. It was all she deserved. She remembers lying in bed one night, with him snoring beside her, while she nursed a bruised cheek with a frozen bag of peas. One of these days, he's going to kill you, she had thought. Something to look forward to.

But he loved her, sort of. Or he had loved her. Or said he had. He would set up a video camera sometimes. It turned him on to watch. He'd get the lighting just right, as if maybe he'd worked in the movies. Or maybe just done this kind of thing before.

Caution looks up at the TV, remembering the porn movie she'd seen that morning. Merlin had a few himself. Everyone did, didn't they? Guys, anyway. She pushes herself up from the couch and, kneeling by the shelf where he kept his DVDs, she looks for the one he'd made of her. She finds it and stares at the cover of the jewel case. He'd titled the little home movie. Had she ever noticed that? She doubts she had—she'd never had the slightest desire to watch it on her own. Now her hand trembles. He'd titled it "Come Again."

The scene at Drigo's office came flooding back into her mind, swamping her, drowning her. Boris's last words. *Come again,* he'd said.

It can't be. There is no way. He wouldn't.

She shakes her head, back and forth, back and forth, and even in this gesture of denial, the motion knocks the last shred of doubt from her mind. He could. He would. She may be blind, but she isn't a fool.

She gets up and finds his laptop. The top of it is covered with decals as if it were a guitar case or something. She flips it open and boots up. The computer asks for a password; she

58

types in P-A-I-N-T-E-D P-O-N-Y and waits. It had taken her a while to figure the password out—weeks, actually—but there had been no hurry. For her it had been an exercise, a brain game called "How Well Do You Know This Man?"

Not as well as she thought, obviously. In less than twenty minutes, she finds "Come Again" on the website *Amateur Whore*.

She had cleared a space at the table to set up the laptop, and now she sits there watching the video, watching them— the two of them. She makes herself watch it all the way through.

"What're you doing now?" she asks Spence.

"I'm accessing a search engine," he says.

"What's that?"

"Think of anything you want to know about."

"Hmmm. How about why Auntie Lanie has more moles than Mama."

She laughs and Spence laughs, and he types in "moles." They look at a couple of mole sites and then at a few genetics sites, and even though they never get a real answer for why Lanie has so many moles—because Spence has homework to do—she gets the idea of how a search engine works. How one question leads to another and then another, and you get closer and closer as you narrow the field of your investigation.

"Show me more," she asks her brilliant big brother, and he says, "Go brush your teeth; it's way past your bedtime."

Caution closes the movie. She sits for a moment, limp, her hands in her lap, her mind reeling. But like a spinning top, it stops eventually. Then she sits up straight, takes a deep breath,

59

and proceeds to erase every file on Merlin's laptop. She makes sure they aren't still around in his trash or on any other backup system as far as she can tell. Spence taught her a lot about computers.

It occurs to her after a while that there is a hammer somewhere in the apartment and that it would probably be therapeutic to just smash the laptop to smithereens. But the noise might travel down the hall and bring him home, and she doesn't want that. As far as she is concerned, he can stay there until tomorrow and tomorrow and tomorrow.

She closes the computer down and stares at the blank screen. She can't get rid of "Come Again." It is out there. She can't stop total strangers from seeing it if that's the kind of thing they're looking for. She can't stop friends, for that matter—people she had taken to be friends. And so shame is added to her sorrow, but that's okay. For her, sorrow is so deep, the shame is no more than a hard pebble thrown into a vast emptiness.

She closes the computer and puts it back right where she found it. She feels different. Lighter. How can that be? It may have something to do with hunger. But the ham sandwich she had been looking forward to no longer appeals to her. She is too edgy, too distracted. No, that's not quite right. Her focus has shifted—that's all. This place she has lived in all these months suddenly seems more sharply defined; there are sharper edges and contrasts. It's the light, of course—so harsh. But it's something else, something vibrating in her nerves, lifting her.

She no longer feels sorry for herself.

With the computer dealt with, she looks around the apartment to see what other surprises she might leave behind for the magic man, whenever it occurs to him to come home. She imagines buckets of pig's blood suspended above the entrance-way like in *Carrie*. She imagines hacking off the head of the painted pony and placing it in his bed, like in *The Godfather*.

The painted pony.

It stands there smiling at her. She grabs its metal muzzle and tries to lift it. Too heavy. She tries again, grunts with the effort—puts her whole heart into it. It doesn't budge. Merlin is strong, but Caution's anger is stronger. Breathing hard, her hands on her hips, she stares at the smiling muzzle. She can't just stick a quarter in the slot and expect it to trot away. She walks around it, patting its blue flank. If she could shove something under the base, make a lever . . .

She surveys the apartment. There is nothing long enough, but the idea won't go away. Outside, she thinks, in the alley maybe. She seems to recall leftover building supplies out back. She goes out and looks around, kicking through the waist-high weeds growing through the cracked concrete of what was once a parking lot. There's a rusted-out fence and metal wire looped through holes in angle irons, but the irons are stuck fast. She looks up, looks around. Down the block, she spies a Dumpster where someone is renovating. She makes her way there and soon finds an eight-foot-long piece of steel reinforcing rod. She lugs it back home, hoping Merlin hasn't returned, then thinking that if he has, an eight-foot-long rod might come in handy. Her brain is on fire. She wants to laugh out loud but holds it in for fear that once she starts, she'll never be able to stop. She is on the verge of hysteria. She imagines herself on a tightrope far above the city, holding the reinforcing rod to keep her balance.

Walking up the alley, she is suddenly aware of the line of windows only a couple of feet above her head. Stepping back, she recognizes the curtains to Claudia's place, and she has to stop herself from launching the half-inch steel rod like a spear through the plate glass. The party crasher to end all party crashers! The rod, with any luck, would pierce Merlin through the chest, pinning him to Claudia forever. Sagittarius the archer!

No. Stay focused, she tells herself.

It's something else Spence taught her.

In the end, the lever she constructs is a complicated affair. She shoves the thin-edged blade of a meat cleaver under the base of the pony, then shoves the reinforcing rod under the cleaver and uses a low stepping stool as a fulcrum. The steel is bendy and the cleaver keeps slipping, but she perseveres. She piles magazines and Merlin's CDs beside the base of the pony, and as soon as she can lift it high enough, she pushes as many of them as she can underneath the corners of the base with her toe. She likes the sound of the CD cases cracking. This allows her to take a break and move the fulcrum closer. Slowly, slowly, she tilts the horse farther and farther over. Finally gravity takes over and the thing tips until its stupid blue head is resting against the wall. She clears away the assorted parts of her machine and, on her knees, lifts the board and removes the cookie tin.

Eight thousand dollars.

They've been going without food, and he's got eight thousand dollars! She sits on her haunches, staring at the money in disbelief. What is he up to? she wonders. What does he have planned?

She hears a noise out in the hallway. Of course. It will be now that he comes back. But she makes no effort to move. The cleaver is right there within reach, but she doesn't go for it. It is easy to slip back into self-negation. He thinks he chose her on that cold March street corner, but she chose him—chose him as her executioner. And now her last appeal has been turned away and it's time. Everything has led to this moment. She has been disobedient, she has screwed up, she has talked back, but nothing has been enough for him to actually kill her, though she is sure he is capable of it. She has failed in this regard. But this . . . this should do the trick.

It's perfect, really: him walking in, her sitting there with all his savings in her greedy little hands. There's even a handy eight-foot-long steel rod for him to thrash her to death with. It has been such a long death sentence, and in the end she has had to work very hard to bring it about. If she were only braver, she could have saved them both the trouble and just offed herself. She has thought about it any number of times. But while she has prayed for deliverance, she has never been able to carry it out. This, she thinks, must be the most unconventional suicide ever.

So she waits, but he does not arrive.

And only when she feels her foot going to sleep does she decide to get up. It hurts. She has to lean on the tilted pony and shake the pins and needles out of her leg. "Owww!" she cries out loud, and then laughs. There she was, expecting to be bludgeoned to death, and here she is now, moaning about a few shooting pains.

She limps around the apartment with the money in her hands. This is called tempting Providence. This is called

63

clinging on to that death wish Merlin accused her of. Clinging on to it like a life raft. How weird is that?

At some point she is surprised to see that the sun is setting. It's after five. Where did the time go? She stops and looks around. In the falling light, she sees nothing that she cares a thing about. The cold of winter was supposed to kill her, but Merlin took her in from the cold. Merlin was supposed to kill her, but he has failed her, too. She has wondered on and off about the existence of God, and right now she is utterly convinced that He exists and has a really, really bad sense of humor. She also realizes that it is time to go, but she risks Providence one last time and sits at the messy table to write Merlin a note. She finds a scrap of paper and a pencil but cannot summon up anything to say. Then she spies her Little Mermaid backpack and goes to it. She digs out *Anna* for inspiration and flips through the pages. There was a scene with Anna and her husband. He's trying to warn her that people are noticing the way she acts around her lover, Count Vronsky. Yes, here it is. She writes as neatly as she can.

> "It may be that I'm making a mistake, but believe me that I'm saying what I am just as much for my own sake as for yours. I am your husband, and I love you."
>
> For an instant her head had drooped, and the mocking glint in her eye had died away, but the word "love" aroused her again. She thought: Love? As though he were capable of love! If he hadn't heard that there is such a thing he would never even have used the word. He doesn't even know what it is!

She doesn't bother to sign it. She doesn't bother to explain. She's not even 100 percent sure Merlin can read. It doesn't matter. She finds the DVD called "Come Again" and hacks her initials into it with a kitchen knife. This shall be her signature. She has erased Merlin's computer and stolen all his money. If he ever loved her—even for one second—he would surely hate her now.

In a matter of minutes, after all this time waffling, she is ready to go. She has her electric-blue jacket on, the zipper done right up to her chin. In her Little Mermaid backpack is *Anna*, the money, a change of underwear, a box of Oreos, and a bag of weed. She can use the weed for bartering, if it comes to that. She was going to leave her keys on the table, but she takes them just in case she wants to come back sometime and really destroy the place. Maybe light it on fire when he's sleeping off a high.

She pauses as she looks at the key ring. She's got her own key to the Nissan. Sometimes he'd sent her cross-town on deliveries. The Nissan. Now, there's a thought! But then she remembers what the car sounds like starting up. The muffler's going. Not only that, but it sometimes *doesn't* start. Not right away. She looks out the window. It's parked way too near to Claudia's window. Caution feels this shifting in her—this new kind of exhilaration. She wants out. The car might stall—it often does. She is better to leave this place the way she entered it, on her own two feet.

So she heads out, not even pausing at the door to number four. She heads down to Queen Street in the gathering dark. She walks west, checking over her shoulder for a streetcar, not wanting to wait at the stop—wanting only to put as much distance as she can between her and whatever it was she imagined had been worthwhile about Merlin.

* * *

You are on an eastbound streetcar, Blink, clanging along, filled with people going home. You hang from a strap, standing room only, in the dying light. You are so busy staring at the Black-Berry in your hand that you don't see a girl in a blue jacket look up as the car rattles by, heading the other way. It's her. A coincidence? Not at all: it would only be a coincidence if either of you ever found out that it happened—passing that close to each other. But you will meet. It's just not time yet.

Chapter 7

Backtrack this bright October Wednesday. It's noon; you are in the park. You look around and what . . . ? Is it just your imagination, or is everyone on Philosopher's Walk looking up from their sandwiches and books, crossword puzzles and cell phones — looking at you like the blind woman was?

You are in trouble. You know that much, but you don't know how much. And yet you feel good. It's as if you always knew something like this would happen to you one day. A test that you could pass because you had to. You'd stumble on to something, and instead of running away from it, you'd pick it up and run with it, follow it to the end.

You head down into the bowels of the subway and head

north. You don't know much north of Bloor—never really been there. Well, there's a time for everything.

And it's like that all afternoon. You ride around the city in no direction and every direction, while you try to think your way through whatever it is you are doing. *Ditch it, Blink. Ditch the phone.* The video game is over. You lost. QVD: forty-eight million points; Blink Conboy: zero.

What is wrong with you?

You have to laugh at that. A man across the aisle looks up from his newspaper and wonders what it is you're laughing at, what it is you're *on*.

"What is wrong with you, boy? Huh?"

He isn't waiting for an answer, but you almost want to say, Thanks for asking, *because usually he hits first and then asks those questions for which there are no answers.*

"And stop blinking at me!"

Your mother is crying at the kitchen table, either for what you did or for what he's going to do. You want to ask her if she ever imagined when she was your age that she'd spend so much of her adult life sobbing. It started with Daddy leaving. Then the pace picked up when Stepdaddy came along.

Stepdaddy's car keys sit on the table. He just found them in your jacket pocket when he couldn't find them in his own.

"Greedy beggar," he says. He slaps you then. "Little joyride, was it?"

Slap.

"Impressing your friends?" He holds the slap like maybe he wants to hear an answer this time, as if he's wondering if you've

68

got any friends. But you aren't telling him where you went, not for anything. Not for nothing.

Slap.

The day wears on and wears out. Finally you arrive back at Bloor and Yonge, near where this whole thing started. You get this idea that you might hike a few blocks west, over to the Plaza Regent—see firsthand all the commotion—the cops coming and going. But whatever anybody thinks, you aren't *that* stupid.

You catch a train east. It's clogged with homeward-bounders, hanging on to the rails and what's left of the day. You just stand there, not holding on to anything, held up by all these people with their groceries, briefcases, backpacks, and handbags. Holding on to their end-of-the-day weariness. They're all about ready to drop, but there's no room. You're all holding each other up.

You get out at Broadview. You walk south down past Riverdale Park, with the Don Valley on your right, cars bumper to bumper on the parkway in the failing light, heading north to somewhere you've never been. They're not getting there any too fast. And there is the dark river, the Don, going the other way, down to Lake Ontario, but not moving much faster than the cars. It's like the Don's going home, too, but south, like you.

You stare at the BlackBerry while you walk. You think about that river flowing south to the lake, and you think about the lake and the beach where you used to go when you were at Nanny and Granda's. There was a time you almost drowned. Funny you should remember that now. You weren't even swimming, just walking out, deeper and deeper. Kind of like today.

69

Oh, Blink, my fine feathered friend, you have walked too far out into the lake, and any minute there's going to be just water under your feet. You're as sunk as those Indians who figured that where they stood was theirs to stand upon. Except, for this: at least they *think* they have some rights. You *know* you have none. Didn't you hear that enough back home?

You have no right to talk that way, no right to come in this late, no right to joyride in your stepdaddy's Pontiac.

A Grand Prix or, as you like to call it, a Grand Prick, just like your stepdaddy.

Anyway, the only law on your side right about now is the law of survival.

You pass through Chinatown, the sidewalks piled high with crates of vegetables, people picking through them leisurely with no fear that someone might snap them up and drag their sorry asses off to jail. You cut across to De Grassi, then down to Queen. You look over your shoulder every couple of minutes. You step into the nearest shadow when a cop car passes by. You don't wait at the streetcar stop; you keep walking until a streetcar comes along, and then you hop aboard, eastbound, homeward—what used to be home.

There is a half-baked plan buzzing around in your head, and the only part of it you really understand right now is to keep moving.

You figure out how to put the phone on vibrate, and you check it with every vibration. Then just as your streetcar is nearing Coxwell, Alyson calls again. You pull the cord to stop the car and hope she waits long enough for the driver to let you off. You jump down onto the street and keep walking.

You push the green button and talk, not even waiting for her to start.

"I'm not one of the people your father left the hotel with," you say breathlessly, without introduction, your voice higher than you want it to be. You've been practicing this through two transfers now.

"Left the hotel *with*?"

"There was something weird about it."

There's a pause.

"Why haven't you gone to the cops?"

"That's not going to happen."

Another pause.

"I believe you," she says at last. "I mean, I believe you didn't have anything to do with it. Do you want to tell me what you think you saw?"

"It's not what I think I saw — it's what I *saw*. There were, like, three people with him."

"'Like' three people?"

"Three people."

"You saw them?"

"I just said that."

"Sorry."

You can feel the Captain up and about, pacing around his cabin down there in the hold of you.

"No, it's me who should be sorry," you say. "I'm just jumpy, okay? This is so fucked. Oh, sorry again."

"So he was gagged and bound?"

"No way."

"What do you mean?"

"I mean what I said."

71

"But they were in masks, right?"

"Masks? Nobody was in masks."

"Nobody was wearing a mask?"

"What masks?"

"No masks," she says. "And my father wasn't gagged and bound."

It isn't a question, so you don't reply.

There is a pause. "You stole his PDA?"

You have to think what she means. The BlackBerry. "Took it. Borrowed it."

"Whatever. But that's no big deal, right? Nobody cares about the stupid thing. So if you won't go to the cops, then that's fine, I guess. Really. But tell me exactly what you saw. Please?"

She isn't crying now. Good. You didn't want her to be hurting at her father being kidnapped. Tell her that, Blink. But you already did. And it doesn't seem to matter anymore. She's in control.

"Hello? Are you still there?"

"I'm here," you say, looking around, wanting to know where "here" is.

"What's your name?" she says, trying to sound gentle, like she's asking a child who is lost at the shopping center.

"I'll call you back."

"No, don't hang—"

But you do. You really need to concentrate. You're almost there.

Your mother always said you lived just past the Raceway. Greenwood Raceway was what she was talking about, except they tore it down the year before you were born. Your daddy worked there as a horse trainer. They closed the place, then tore it down, and there's just a fancy off-track betting place now, a movie theater, shopping plaza, and expensive condos. You used to wonder if maybe your mother didn't know they tore down the track. She doesn't get out much.

You turn up your mother's street, as the early darkness settles in and any warmth the day might have gathered around itself is sucked right back down into the ground. Most of the places along here have been gussied up. Rich folks moved in, stripping the paint off walls and putting in stained glass and lampposts and bright-colored doors with warnings printed on them about the alarm system. It would have been good to have an alarm system at your place: something to tell you when Stepdaddy was on the warpath.

But he's not home tonight, as far as you can tell. His trashed-out Pontiac isn't parked out front. He's not at supper. She's eating in her kitchen window, alone. Never did get those curtains up.

Maybe he's gone?

Oh, Blink. I'm so glad you're here. Eddy left a few weeks back, and I've just been hoping you'd call or drop by so I could give you the good news. I've stopped drinking, and I never cry anymore. Actually, Eddy died, and he even left a little money he'd been hoarding away.

Ha-ha, Blink. Nice one.

Nothing you've seen so far of life suggests there are miracles, unless this is one, this unexpected day. And so far, apart from a miraculous new pair of sneakers that fit, this one has been about 30 percent good and 70 percent weirdness, verging on dread.

73

And yet standing outside your mother's house, all you can think about is that what this day has brought you is something new. And then you want to hit yourself on the side of the head because all this day has brought you to is this.

Your gaze wanders to the blank eye of the upstairs window. Maybe he's up there, sleeping it off. Maybe he's lying dead on the living-room floor with a poker through one eye and a look in the other like, *What the fuck?*

You'd like to see that.

So, if he's not there, where is he?

You want to go in. You want to take that chance. Mostly you want out of the cold. It's way too late in the day for the Blessed Breakfast Uniform. Way too late in the year. You are shivering like nobody's business.

Look up. That's what you want to shout to your mother. *Look out your window. Your son is standing here just where the light ends. You could find me if you looked up from the table.*

Then the bitter feelings rise up in your gut, and there isn't time for this bullshit now. There isn't time for blame and anger. You need all the strength you can get to keep this thing going—whatever the hell it is. You step a little closer, anyway, until you are standing right on the bright side of the light coming through her window. You wait there, like a batter at home plate waiting for a fastball. But she doesn't look up. Maybe those muscles don't work anymore, the ones that lift the head. So you step back out of the light and start walking.

Your feet have a plan, even if you don't. Your clever feet in their fine new shoes. There's this bar he sometimes drinks at. It's him you want. Right, Blink?

And there it is, after a long cold while, the No Holds Bar.

74

You stop outside, where the Molson sign and the Bud sign in the window buzz with all that neon blood inside them.

You've seen Stepdaddy stumble out of this place a time or two. You even helped him home some nights when trying to get along still seemed like an option.

You step inside the smell: spilled beer and nacho sizzle. You hang out on the edge of the noise by the doorway in the vestibule. It's shadowy there, and the man at the bar can't see you. He's too busy, anyway, serving up brews and shots. You let your eyes go ahead of you into the room, searching out every booth and recess. The place is hopping with the after-work crowd and the slouching dregs of the no-work crowd. The no-work crowd have had such a head start on happy hour, there's no merriment left in it at all.

You move in a little closer and crane your neck to see where the bar goes when it rounds the corner. And — bingo! — there he is, the Grand Prick himself. He's drinking alone. His scuffed-up leather coat hung over the back of his chair, about as worn and torn as he is. He's got both wrists resting on the bar, with a quarter-filled beer glass between them and an unlit cigarette in his mouth. There is no smoking in the place, so he must be planning an exit.

Now what?

You hold your ground. From the look in his eyes, he's not going to be moving too fast. He talks to someone, the cigarette bouncing up and down on his lip. No one seems to be listening.

Then he pats his chest pockets, his pants pockets, and draws out a lighter. You ready yourself. He stands and wanders off toward the back of the place, to the can it looks like. Either that or he forgot the way out. He winds his way through the

75

drunken seats and the sprawled-out legs and the chatter and the clinks of glasses and outbursts of laughter, until he's gone from sight.

Move. Now!

You take a deep breath and squeeze your way down the bar to where the brown jacket holds Stepdaddy's place.

It only takes a second. You're gone before the bartender even notices your underage self. You leave, and it doesn't feel as good as you hoped it would. You wanted to close the door on him — that was all. And now it feels as if you closed it on your own hand. And there's a stab of loneliness as you step back out into the cold. You'll miss that vibrating in your pocket.

Chapter 8

"It's a Remington rimfire, bolt-action Model Five. Perfect for partridge and rabbits."

Spence sights down the barrel. Then he hands the rifle to Kitty.

"It's a .22," he adds.

She wrestles the butt up to her shoulder.

"What's 'twenty-two' mean?" she asks.

"It's the caliber."

"What's that?"

"The measure of the inside diameter of the barrel. A .22 caliber rifle has a bore of 22/100 inches."

"Bang!" says Kitty, aiming at a shiny tin can sitting on the fence. "Bang!" she says again.

"Shall we load 'er up?" says Spence. Kitty reluctantly gives up *the rifle and watches carefully as her big brother pulls the bolt back and opens the breech, places a single gold-and-silver shell inside, then closes it again. He smiles as he hands her the rifle, but he doesn't let go of it. He kneels beside her, helps her tuck the butt comfortably into her shoulder, gently pulls back a strand of jet-black hair from across her eye, and tucks it behind her ear.*

"Keep tight," he says, patting her on the shoulder. "There isn't all that much recoil from this thing, but still . . ."

"Recoil?"

"Kick," he says, and makes the rifle rear up in her hand to show her what he means.

Then he moves her right hand farther along the stock and shows her how to tilt her head just so to line up the front sight in the notch of the back sight.

She can't wait to pull the trigger, but he stays her hand.

"It's about breathing," he says. "Slowly breathe in and out, then breathe in again and hold it. This will keep you and your rifle still, right?"

"Right," she says. "Got it."

Then he shows her how to pull the bolt back to full cock.

She breathes in and out and holds it.

BANG!

And to her amazement, the first tin can goes flying.

"Whoa!" says Spence.

"Did I do that?" says Kitty.

He nods. "Rabbits, take cover!" he says.

Caution gets off the Dundas streetcar at Roncesvalles. It's night and cold—the day old all of a sudden and tired. She digs her fists deep into her jacket pockets, turtles her head down inside her collar. She's way across town from the apartment on Carlaw, but you can never tell with a magic man how far is far enough. She heads south, zipping along, half out of fear and half out of trying to keep warm, dodging traffic, zigzagging through the bustle and lights.

She does know one good someone in this city, and she knows where he lives, though she has never once contacted him. She walked by his place a couple of times last winter when she was desperate—even saw him once in his window but couldn't bring herself to ring his bell. He hates her. Still, she figures, someone from back home who hates you is better than nothing.

Oh, please be here, she thinks.

It's a rooming house, tall as a nightmare. The outside door isn't locked. The inside door isn't locked, either. It's like saying to a potential thief that there is nothing in here you want. Caution is glad she doesn't have to ring, but the unlocked doors don't comfort her. She climbs the stairs to the first landing, climbs the stairs to the next. Listens at number seven. At first she hears nothing, but when she steps back, she can see light seeping out from under the door into the dimness of the landing. She listens again and smiles nervously: someone is playing a guitar.

She sniffs, gathers up her courage, and knocks three times.

The music stops; heavy footsteps approach the door. Caution pulls back and back farther, until her hand is on the newel post, ready to launch herself downstairs if she has to.

Then the door opens.

Wayne-Ray has gotten large. Overweight. It surprises her how much he looks like Auntie Lanie now. He has his mother's deep brown eyes, her swarthy complexion, thick eyebrows, her heft.

"Kitty?"

It's taken him a long time to recognize her. She nods hesitantly. It's been a long time since she answered to that name.

He raises his hands to his head. "Jesus!" he says.

Caution glances behind her furtively, as if maybe a savior snuck up the stairs behind her. No such luck.

"Is it really you?"

She nods, a little uncertainly. She's waiting for him to come to his senses—to remember what she did. He may have identified her, but he seems to be having a whole lot of trouble figuring out who she is.

But as large as he has gotten, he is 100 percent Cousin Wayne Raymond, right down to the XXXL Toronto Maple Leafs hockey sweater, the green sweats, the moccasins.

"Hey," she says.

It isn't exactly "abracadabra," so maybe it's the sound of her voice that breaks through his confusion, takes him to the next stage.

"Ah, heck," he says, "come in here, you." He steps back into his apartment, holding out his hand. She hurries past him, and he closes the door. Next thing she knows, she is bawling her eyes out all over his big blue maple leaf.

The first thing Wayne-Ray does once she stops crying is to find his phone. "I can't wait to tell Mom," he says. "She can phone your mom."

"No," Caution says, shaking her head. "You don't understand."

"Ah, Kitty, come on. For God's sake. Everybody's been worried sick," he says. "I just want to let them know you're okay."

"I'm *not* okay."

That stops him for a moment. He puts down the phone. She looks around, finds a chair, and plunks herself down in it.

"Are you, like, knocked up?" he asks. She frowns at him. "Well, you said you were not okay. I just—"

"I'm not pregnant," she says, cutting him off. Jesus, she hopes she isn't. "There are things even worse than that," she says.

"Sorry," he mumbles. "It's just . . ."

But he doesn't finish. Then there is a long silence, which she breaks, because she owes him some kind of explanation.

"I got myself in with some bad people, okay? Really bad people." She looks down to escape the pity in his eyes. Then she thinks of something she can say. "I'm up to my neck in skunks, Wayne-Ray."

He smiles, a Charlie Brown smile. His whole face is kind of crooked. He'd broken his nose bad playing baseball when he was a kid, had a scar on his chin the shape of a ground-rule double.

"Up to your neck, eh?"

It was something they used to say, although the skunks they were referring to way back then weren't vicious, sadistic drug dealers whose stash had been pinched.

"You hungry?" he asks.

"Oh, God, yes."

He nods. "Okay." But there's a question in his eyes, and she braces herself.

"What the hell'd you do to your hair?" he says.

She sits with a bowl of stew at a tiny white table in a spotless kitchen about the size of a changing room. It's venison stew.

He was home a week or so and came back with gallons of the stuff.

The stew is hot, the gravy rich, the meat tender. Auntie Lanie never bothered much with vegetables. Caution has a hold of her spoon like she's six years old and wants the bowl to never be empty.

After she eats, they sit in his front room. She curls up on his couch with her feet under her bum. He fusses with a space heater, plugging it in so it's close to her, then switching it up to high. There's a draft coming from behind her, bringing up goose bumps on her naked neck, but it's all right. She flips up the collar on her jacket.

"You sure I can't hang that up for you?" he says.

She shakes her head, smoothing down the fuzzy blue pelt. "It's my security blanket," she says. "I kind of empathize with it, you know?"

Wayne-Ray shakes his head. "You always were wired funny."

He means it nicely, she tries to tell herself. But she's afraid it's true. Knowing that she's capable of unthinkable things.

He sits in an easy chair, a few feet away, with a cup of tea beside him on the wide armrest. She feels the nap of the cushion under her. She knows this worn fabric, knows this couch. It used to be in Auntie Lanie's parlor. She shakes her head. It's as if she's fallen down a rabbit hole. She closes her eyes. The stew and the infrared heat are making her sleepy. She can't shake the feeling that any minute her cousin is going to remember how much he hates her. It will be so bad because she doesn't think she has the energy to leave of her own volition, so he will have to drag her to the door and fling her down the stairs. She will understand.

"Have you . . . ?" he starts. "Have you been here all along?"

She shrugs. Shakes her head. "I was in Sudbury for a while, but it was too close. You know?" He nods.

"But you didn't see your dad?"

She shakes her head. "I got a job up there for a few weeks, and when I had the money, I took off again."

The only light in the room comes through the windows behind her, from a streetlight. He'd turned on the overhead, but she'd covered her eyes and begged him to turn it off again.

"So, how long since you got to Toronto?"

With her eyes closed, she can almost imagine that the warmth coming up from the heater is from a woodstove. When Spence moved to Toronto to go to school, she'd had to carry in the firewood back home. She was only nine and she'd hated it. Wished they'd had electric baseboards, like people in town. Mostly what she'd hated was Spence being so far away.

"You should've called," says Wayne-Ray. "We're family."

She nods. Doesn't look up.

"Everybody's been worried sick."

"You said that."

"Your mother—"

"Oh, jeez, Wayne-Ray. Lay off, will ya?"

"It's just that—"

"I'm serious, man. I hear you. And I really appreciate you taking me in. I promise . . ."

Where did that come from? Promise? What could she promise him?

"I promise I'll get in touch . . . when I can."

"When'll that be?"

83

"When I can."

He doesn't say anything, and she wonders if he believes her. Why should he? But if she doesn't want to talk about family, she has to say something. She props her eyes open, works up a tired smile.

"How's the . . . what's it called . . . audio engineering—how's that going?"

"You mean TMI?" he says.

"Right, The Music Institute."

He rubs his chin with the back of his hand, looks away. "I kinda dropped out."

"No way," she says. "You were so pumped—the whole recording engineer thing."

He nods. "Yeah, it was very cool. But . . . well, things got rough there for a bit. . . ."

Something in his eye finishes the sentence for him. Dim as the light in the room is, she can see it.

"Was it because of . . . because of what happened?"

He shrugs, won't look at her. "What do you think?" he says.

And what Caution thinks is that, yet again, she has made a big mistake.

Caution: Watch Your Step. She should never have come here. With all that stolen money, she could have stayed at a hotel—stayed right out of this. Wayne-Ray has been so good to her just now. Always was, once he got over her hanging around with him and Spence. Once he knew she wouldn't go away no matter how much you threatened her or cajoled her. He had become like another brother. He had been good to her, but that didn't change anything. If she stayed, she'd be waiting for him to suddenly point his finger at her, shout at her. She'd thought maybe she could tiptoe around things by asking him about school. But school ended with Spence's death. Everything ended with Spence's death. All this was just a slow dying.

"What are you going to do?" Wayne-Ray says, gentle as can be.

She shrugs. "I'd just like to lie low until all this blows over," she says.

"All what?"

"This," she says. "Life."

She hears him sip his tea, place the cup down on the arm of the chair. He is breathing through his mouth. He's so big. He was never this big.

The silence closes in. She picks at something caught between her teeth. Looks away.

He had come to the city to get into the recording business, but he'd also come to be near Spence. Spence had always been more like a big brother to Wayne-Ray than a cousin. And Wayne-Ray had flunked out of school once Spence died. Not because he wasn't good enough but because his best friend in the world had been shot and killed. Kind of hard to do your homework under those conditions. She knew that much herself.

"It's hard, eh?" he says.

And before she really knows what she's doing, Caution is on her feet, slipping into her tired shoes, grabbing up her pink backpack from where it lies at her feet.

"What're you doing?"

"I shouldn't have come," she says, pushing past him.

"Yes, you should have," he says, his voice rising. "You should have come months ago."

"It's no use," she says, shaking his hand off her arm.

"You can't go, Kitty."

"Watch me," she says.

For a big guy, Wayne-Ray is still quick on his feet. He gets to the door before her.

"You don't want me here," she says.

"Are you crazy?"

She stamps her foot. "Yes!" she says. "Haven't you been listening?"

Then she starts beating on him, punching him, trying to heave his massive frame out of the way. He doesn't even try to fend her off, just lets her go at him with all she's got, while he bars that exit, like beyond the door was some sacred shrine she planned to desecrate. And all the time he's saying, "Ah, Kitty. Ah, Kitty. Ah, Kitty."

Finally, there is nothing left in her—not one precious joule of energy, not one swear word. He guides her back to the couch, his hand cupping her elbow like she's some old lady he's helping cross the street. He gets her sitting down, then kneels, laboriously, and slips off her sneakers. When he's sure she's not going to bolt, he goes into the bedroom and comes back with a pillow and a blanket. He tries to coaxe her to lie down, but she won't. He tries to unzip her jacket, but she slaps his hand away. Puffing from the ordeal, he finally backs off.

He leaves and comes back a moment later with his guitar. He sits in the easy chair and starts playing a ballad she should recognize but doesn't. She covers her ears until he stops.

"Hate me!" she says.

"What?"

"Hate me, Wayne-Ray. It's the least you could do."

"No," he says.

"I'm not going to ever get over this."

"I know," he says.

"It's never going to go away."

"I know."

"And don't you *dare* tell me I've got to be strong."

"I won't."

Which is when she screams. She screams so loud and so long that somebody downstairs thumps on the ceiling. Then she stops.

"Sorry," she says.

"It's okay," says Wayne-Ray. "Them and I don't get along, anyway."

She chuckles. It's a sad little excuse for laughter. More like a white flag of surrender than anything else.

She doesn't lie down so much as fall over. She drags the blanket out from behind her and haphazardly flings it over her aching body. When she is next conscious of anything, the apartment is plunged into darkness and she is sore all over, as if someone has been using her as a punching bag.

Some time later, she senses Merlin hovering over her. Without letting him know she's awake, she makes her face as ugly as she can. She hopes there is enough street light in the room for him to see just how ugly she is. She hopes he finds the spittle drooling from the corner of her mouth truly disgusting. She lets herself sag into the springs of the couch, disguising any shapeliness she may possess. She even manages to snore in a most unappealing manner. Meanwhile, her hand searches under the covers for *Anna*. She was reading it before bed, wasn't she?

If worse comes to worst and he tries anything, she'll be ready.

Step one: a Russian classic to the face.

Step two: a couple of handy long-necked beer bottle empties, applied one to either ear, as if she were a cymbal player in the orchestra and Merlin's head the crash site of the symphony's climaxe.

But then she's not sure if there really are any beer bottles on a coffee table in front of this couch, or whether that was some other couch, some other place. So confusing. So many couches. Such a long day. And *Anna* is nowhere to be found. So it seems that only her ugliness can save her now. How lucky she is, she thinks, to be so deeply, profoundly ugly.

"'Everything is finished,' she said. 'I have nothing but you. Remember that.'"

The words came to her, but she had no idea why. No idea who "you" might be.

Chapter 9

You call Alyson from a pay phone a block west of the squat. You wrote her cell number down on your arm before you ditched the BlackBerry. You phone her on a ten-dollar phone card. It's eight o'clock. She answers with this annoyed voice, but you aren't upset. It's just that her caller ID doesn't know you.

"Alyson," you say, "this is Blink."

There is a pause — long enough to wonder if you just made a very big mistake.

"Who?"

"I phoned you about—"

"You!" she says. "But why aren't you—?"

"I ditched the BlackBerry. But the cops should find it soon. I didn't like chuck it or anything."

There is another pause. And you look around you as if maybe the GPS on that thing can stick to a person even when he's unloaded it.

"Why are you calling me?" she asks.

It's a good question—a complicated question. It has something to do with a picture of a girl on a lawn overlooking a lake.

"Hello?"

"I'm here," you say. "I'm calling because I want to explain what I saw."

"You said my father left the hotel *with* some people."

"Yeah. With. Not abducted or nothing."

"So you didn't see the footage?"

"Footage?"

"The CCTV footage from the hotel. Closed-circuit television? It was on the news."

"No way," you say. "What about it?"

She pauses. It's quiet right now down at Trinity and Front, which is where you are standing, shivering a little. You can hear her swallow.

"There was duct tape on his mouth," she says. "And around his wrists. And the men were all in balaclavas."

"In what?"

"Those ski masks that go right down over your whole face."

"Not when I saw them," you say. "Honest to God."

"They were holding him tightly by the arms. Real rough and kind of pushing him down the stairs . . ." She says it like she's trying to convince you.

"All I'm saying is that it didn't look like that kind of shit was going down."

You don't say more, because maybe you are crazy and this is all a crazy dream. Then she is crying.

"Alyson."

"What?" she says, angry, sniffing hard. "And how do you know my name?"

She's not thinking clearly—who can blame the girl. But get to the point, Blink. "There was three guys in the video, right?"

"*Were*," she says angrily. "There *were* three guys."

"Okay, 'were.'" Jesus. "Could you tell from the video that, like, one of them was a big dude, real tall and, you know, big like a bear. And one was real wiry, and one was short but built like a brick shithouse? Could you tell that from the pictures?"

She sniffs again. "Yeah," she says. "I guess. Yes."

"The little one, the brick . . . Well, his name is Tank."

There is dead quiet at the other end of the line.

"You got their names?"

"Just his."

She laughs, like you said something funny, but it's just this nervous thing, because there is nothing funny about her voice. "What'd you say your name was?"

"It doesn't matter. I just wanted you to know that what I saw didn't look like . . . didn't look bad. Unless they tricked him or . . ." You shut up because you're ruining it.

"Blink," she says. "Was that what you said? Is that your name?"

Now it's your turn to keep quiet.

"Blink, we need to talk."

There. Was that what you wanted, you reckless, greedy boy?

"About what?"

91

"If you know stuff—"

"I don't know squat. All I know is what I saw. These guys were with him. They were talking together. And they busted up the room—sure—but there was no yelling or anything. I was right outside the door practically."

The pause again, but this one is stiff and listening.

Then you figure out how to describe what it was you saw, the thing you want to say to her. "Your father was not their prisoner. That's all I'm trying to say."

There's no sound at her end.

"You're lying," she says. "You *are* one of them."

"No way."

"Yes, you are. You're telling me my father abducted himself?"

"That's not what I said."

"Yes, it is."

"Hey."

"This is *so* wrong, what you are doing. This is none of your business. What are you? Some freak who gets off on other people's misfortunes?"

"No! No way."

"Liar. Why are you phoning me? What do you want?"

Ah, there's the thing. What do you want, Blink? What's in this for you?

"You want something," she says, as if she's read your mind. And then while your head is reeling, she hangs up. The line goes dead. And the coldness of a late autumn night rushes into the phone booth.

Chapter 10

The squat stands on the northeast corner of Cherry and Front. It's a tired brick building—must have been an office once upon a time. The windows are all boarded up; the inside walls are falling down, smashed in. Wiring hangs from the ceiling like exposed guts. There's a vacant lot across the street surrounded by a barbed-wire fence, and you've never been able to figure out what it was they were keeping in or keeping out. On the southeast corner, there's a building sheathed in heavy plastic like it's been wrapped up. Like it's a mummy, a dead thing; your place is next. The whole area is under construction. The Distillery District. Used to be they made whiskey down here. Now they just make money.

There's this grate over a basement window in the back

corner that looks solid enough, but you can move the whole thing, drop down into the window well, and then put it back in place over your head, like you were locking yourself in jail. Then you find your way to your corner of the building with a lighter, making sure not to step on anyone. You're sharing the place with ten or fifteen people; it varies from night to night. The number of rats is higher.

You don't sleep so well, Blink. The wind comes pounding at the boarded-up windows of the squat like a wrecking ball. There's no heat, no light. And winter is out there somewhere lacing on his skates. This place is coming down. You knew that all along, but you didn't think that meant it was going to fall down all around you. That's what it feels like tonight.

Another condo will go up in its place. That's all that grows in this part of town—condos—thousands of them all along the lakefront. Like all the poor people just upped and left town, and a tribe—a whole army—of rich people moved in from who knows where to take their place. You shiver in your Sally Anne blanket. You didn't even change out of the BBU. No need to keep it clean anymore. Your breakfast days are over. Everything has changed. You pull on a ragged hoodie over your once-fancy duds, but you still shiver.

Somebody upstairs clumps across the floor, and you swear at them loudly and then cower in your blanket, waiting for the guy to come down and beat the tar out of you.

The night passes but just barely, with a D– for taking so long.

You head out as soon as it's light, looking for somewhere warm. You sit in Balzac's down in the Distillery District. You can afford to today. You're rich. You get yourself a big coffee and a Danish. You buy a paper, like you're a real person.

The story is front-page. Nothing you don't already know. If Jack Niven has been kidnapped, there's no ransom note yet. It's all speculation. There's a picture of him in his tie and jacket and his trimmed beard. Respectable.

"Whodunit?" says the headline in the *Sun*. A spokesman for the Algonquin First Nations says it isn't them.

"We have our arguments with Queon Ventures," says Chief Myra McIsaac, "but we plan on settling those disagreements legally and peacefully. This is not the way we do things."

Indians? You think of the Moon, the Snake, and the Littlest Hulk. Were they Indians? Were they militant environmentalists? That's another theory. You never saw a militant environmentalist. What does one look like?

You sit staring off into the coffee-scented air, still trying to shake the frost out of your bones. You're rich. That's what you got out of yesterday: five hundred and sixty dollars. Should have been six hundred, but you paid forty for your ticket to enter the weirdness. And what have you got left, Blink?

Four hundred and forty-two dollars and fifty-four cents. That's what's left of yesterday.

You head downtown, find a Future Shop on Dundas. You hang out in there, watching the televisions. You're definitely looking worse for wear. Everything about you is kind of dragged out and night stained, except for your new well-fitting shoes. The folks in the store watch you closely, like you might lift something. Why aren't you in school? Maybe you should scare them and buy an iPod. Make them smile at you, Mr. Money Bags and all. But you aren't there for an iPod; you're there for the news.

And there is news. You can watch it on any of a hundred screens, some as big as your mother's sitting room. You just can't hear the sounds, like the words are a secret.

You see the CCTV footage that Alyson told you about. It's on CNN every few minutes. Those shadowy men lumbering down the painted-white concrete staircase, disappearing—like they've been burned up—in the too-bright daylight of the door to the outside. They show it again: Niven with his hands duct-taped in front, his mouth taped shut. They show it again, and there's the Moon—you recognize his gut. And there's Tank; he's got the briefcase now. That big shiny briefcase. The Snake's got his sleeves rolled down covering his tat. The briefcase—was that where the headgear came from, the duct tape? They show it again: those knitted faces and Niven, his hair all mussed up, like he's been pushed around. His white-as-snow shirt torn. It wasn't when you saw it. About the fifth time you watch it, you notice the little CCTV clock in the corner of the screen: 7:16 AM.

And then there is a talking head and the words "Breaking News" tracking along the screen along the bottom. The next thing you know, there's another video and it's Jack Niven again, but now he's the talking head—larger-than-life. He's sitting looking out at the camera, and you think, they found him; he's been rescued. It's over. You move up close to the screen, but there's no sound, so you just have to imagine what's going on. It isn't long before you realize he has not been rescued. This is not TV footage from a studio. It's jiggly and jerky with a bright light in his face making him squint. He's got a Band-Aid on his forehead. Behind him there is a wall of chipboard. Nothing else. His mouth moves; his pale blue eyes try to stay calm. His eyes don't look like water off the Bahamas anymore, and the skin of his cheeks is not golden in the harsh light.

And now the newsman's talking head fills the screen, saying whatever it is that is happening, and every hair on his head is in place.

"Can I help you?" says a voice behind you.

It's a worried-looking salesman—you're standing way too close to the screen—a Pakistani guy with a turban and not much hope of getting a commission out of you.

"No," you say. "Just looking." And you leave. "No, you can't help me," you say as you push open the door, but you're just talking to yourself now.

You kick around the city as the clouds gather. Someone kidnapped the sun and is asking a big ransom. That's what was happening in the breaking news videotape. Those people want a billion dollars maybe. Something like that.

When you think she might be awake, you phone Alyson.

"I'm sorry," you say. "Don't hang up."

You cringe, waiting for her to swear at you, but she doesn't speak at all.

"I know what you think," you say. "It's not true. I'm not one of them. I don't even know who they are. I saw something on TV, though. This morning."

You stop, not sure where you're going with this.

"I'm sorry I yelled at you," she says. And her voice sounds semisweet, more like the girl in the picture in the short white dress.

"It's okay," you say. "You must be real scared."

She doesn't answer right away.

"I saw your dad talking on TV, but it was in a store and

there was no sound. So I don't exactly know what's happening."

She clears her throat. "It's an organization that calls itself SPOIL."

"SPOIL?"

"It means 'Stop Polluting Our Injured Land.'"

"Oh."

"Is that all you can say?"

Suddenly she sounds testy, or maybe she got as little sleep as you did. And then you realize that she's frightened. The abduction was real, whatever it was you think you saw.

"So do they want, like, a lot of money?"

"No," she says. "They want my father's company to drop its claim on the Millsap Lake property. Do you even know what I'm talking about?"

"Yeah, sort of."

"Blink," she says. You listen. She's switched back to semi-sweet. "I need to talk to you." Her voice is quiet. Somehow you get the feeling she's walking herself somewhere, walking from one room into another. Yes. A door closes and the sound changes. She's outside.

"What?"

"You told me you saw my father leaving with those men and he wasn't tied up and they weren't wearing hoods, right? Is that what you said, or was I dreaming that?"

"Yeah. I mean, no—you weren't dreaming it."

"So, explain to me about the hotel room. Did you see the room?"

"Yes."

"And?"

You take a deep breath. You feel this story welling up

98

in you, like you can't hold it back one more minute. "Okay. Here's the thing. I live on the street."

"Where the Plaza is?"

"No, *on* the street. You know—living on the street."

"Oh."

"Living hard." You pause, the wind spilled right out of your sails, but then you don't want to hear what she has to say about that, so you start in again. "I go into hotels to get breakfast, like what people leave on their trays outside their door when they get room service. That's why I was there. I was in the hallway on the sixteenth floor, but I ducked into this little room where they keep the ice machine. It's right across the hall from your father's room—1616. Check it out. You can ask the hotel people if you don't believe me."

"Go on."

"So when they left, the Littlest Hulk—"

"Who?"

"Tank—like I told you. He just tossed the key thing—the card—and I picked it up and went in there."

"And?"

"And it was smashed up all to shit."

"So, that's my point," she says. "Explain to me how that can be, if what you told me is true?"

You swallow hard. "Well, I heard stuff being broken. I mean, I heard a crash. Then I heard a thump. You know what I mean? Like that. But it was weird, because there was no— were no—shouts."

"So they covered his mouth."

"If you say so, but there was no bumping around. No fight, no . . . nothing."

99

"It was three on one," she says. "How big a fight could there be?"

"Okay, you got me. I hear you. Fine. Believe what you want."

There is a pause. "I'm sorry," she says. "I just don't get it."

"But . . ."

"But what, Blink? I really want to know. I'm trying to understand."

What is it you hear in her voice? There is something there. Like she doesn't want to believe you but doesn't want you to stop, either. Like she's having this fight, too, and things are crashing and thumping all around in her head, and it doesn't make sense.

"It's this feeling," you say. "It's like, in my experience, when things get broken and fall over, there has to be other things going on, you know?" Then you figure out how to explain it. "Shit doesn't happen in silence," you say.

There. You've made your best case. You listen closely because maybe there are cops there, wherever she is. Maybe they're tracing this call somehow, the way they do on cop shows. You imagine some guy with earphones. CSI. You can picture it, and you can feel Captain Panic coming on, but you fight him down. Because all you can really hear is Alyson and wind sounds. There is just the two of you. Maybe you're that big a fool, but maybe you don't care anymore. You look up and out at the world passing by your phone booth. No one so much as looks at you. You're used to that; right now you're glad of it.

"Thank you," she says.

"Don't thank me. I mean, it's so freaking weird. But I wanted you to know because maybe it's not so bad as . . . you know . . ."

100

"Maybe," she says. But her voice sounds grouchy, like she didn't really mean "thank you," but she was brought up proper and that's what you say when someone is telling you stuff you don't want to hear.

"Blink?" she says, and her voice drops to a whisper.

"I'm here."

"I want to talk to you."

"So, talk."

"No, I want to see you."

You jump back like lightning just shot right out of the phone. You jump back so far, the steel phone cable jerks your head to a stop.

"Yeah, right," you say.

"I mean it."

"Yeah, you and the cops or whatever."

"No. Just us. Here."

"Where's here?"

"In Kingston. Please, Blink, I need to talk to you."

You pause. *She is so setting you up, Blink!* You've been living on the street for near on six months now. You may be careless sometimes—you have your moments—but you aren't anybody's fool.

"No way."

"Please," she says, her whispering voice urgent. "I swear to God I won't tell anyone."

You know you want to do it. You know you want to go to her. You set this trap yourself, even if you didn't mean to. You are such a sap! You set the trap when you placed her picture in front of you on the top of the pay phone. You've been looking at her the whole time you were talking. And she's smiling at you from her lawn, in her summer dress, with her honey-blond hair and her perky little breasts and with that wide ocean of water behind her. You close your eyes to escape from her smiling eyes. Because it's not just her—that's not all of what this is about. It's coming to you now, slowly, the understanding. This greed of yours: for money, sure; but for some kind of power; attention; love.

"Why?" you say after about a million years.

"Because I have this . . . I don't know . . . Oh, this is going to sound totally whacked."

"What?"

She takes a deep breath, and her voice comes back a little shaky with excitement. "I have this idea that I know where he is."

That was not what you expected her to say.

"Your father?"

"Yes. And I can't tell anyone. Which is why I want to talk to you."

"This is so fucked up."

"I know, I know. It's a long—"

Then suddenly her voice is gone, and an automated voice is talking to you in French.

"Hey!" you shout. "Alyson? Hello?"

Now the voice switches to English, telling you that you have only one dollar left on your card.

"Okay, okay, okay!" you shout at the voice. Then the warning is over. "Alyson?" But the line is dead.

Chapter 11

Caution wakes up with Wayne-Ray hovering over her.

"I'm going to Timmy Ho's for breakfast," he says. "You want I should bring you something?"

She clutches her blanket to her and realizes there is a comforter she hadn't started out with.

She rubs sleep from her eyes. "What time is it?"

"It's seven," he says. "Sorry. I got to be at work by eight."

She rubs her face. Remembers her dream. Or was it a dream? "Kitty?"

"Oh, right," she says. "Coffee. Thanks. Double-double."

As soon as he's gone, she gets up to use the toilet. The shower curtain is still wet from his shower. She finds a clean towel on a shelf and strips down, wishing she'd thought to bring her stuff in here so she could change into fresh under-wear. But the shower is wonderful, hot, the pressure good for such an old place. The water digs into her muscles. She wants to stay in the shower all day but realizes he'll be back soon. She's dressed by the time he returns.

"Oh," he says, seeing her wet hair. "Good."

"Did I stink?" she says.

"Like someone who'd been up to her neck in skunks," he says.

She smiles and takes the coffee from him. There are doughnuts, too. She takes a Boston cream and wonders if he remembered it was her favorite. She doesn't deserve this. Not any of it. She looks up into his broad brown face. She lays her hand on his chest, at a place she remembers pounding away at the night before.

"Are you all black and blue?" she says sheepishly.

"Oh, yeah," he says, grinning. "I'm good and tenderized."

"Sorry," she says.

He shrugs. "Rage is good," he says.

Caution: Use Hand Rail. She's afraid he's going to start in on some lecture, so she makes a big deal about setting the table in the changing room–size kitchen.

He works at Long & McQuade, selling guitars. He likes it there. Meets lots of musicians, he tells her, as they sit across from each other at the tiny white table, their knees banging together. "I wanted to tell you something," he says, wiping powdered sugar off his lips, trying not to get any on his work shirt. She quakes, but it's not as if she can stop him.

"I'm going to go back to TMI. They said I could come back when I was, you know, ready."

104

Ah. "And you're ready?"

He shrugs, takes another bite of his doughnut. "Maybe next fall," he says.

Next fall. A year away. She can't remember the last time she tried thinking past tomorrow.

"That's good," she says. He nods. "Good for you, Wayne-Ray."

He glances at his watch, slurps his coffee. She can see there is more coming and that it's time sensitive.

"That's just sort of a lead-in to what I wanted to say."

Right, she thinks, and folds her hands together on the crumbly tabletop, her head bowed.

"I had to get help," he says, his voice cast as gentle and low as he can. "I couldn't, you know, do it alone."

"Yeah, well—"

But he won't let her shut him down. "I was numb. You know what I mean. I was dazed and numb. I needed someone to tell me numb was good. It serves a purpose. That's what they said, right? Gives your emotions time to . . . time to sort of catch up." He waits, and she guesses he must be looking at her, but she can't seem to raise her eyes from the gravitational pull of her coffee cup.

"The guy I was seeing. He talked about 'Life under reconstruction.' That's what he called it. I went to these group meetings, too. He talked about 'companioning.'"

"Listen, Wayne-Ray, I saw a doctor—"

"No, you didn't, Kitty. Not the kind of doctor I'm talking about. 'Less you mean you saw one here. I'm guessing that didn't happen."

She wasn't going to lie to him, but what was the point?

"Hey," he says, nudging her hand with his hand. "Sermon over. Okay?" She doesn't look up. "Okay?" he says again.

She nods.

Then he clears up and brushes his teeth and collects his phone from where it's recharging. He writes down his cell number. He has no landline, but there is a phone booth out on Roncesvalles. He tells her where. She nods through all of his solicitations, knowing this to be the price she has to pay for a roof over her head and a place to hide.

She follows him to the door, when it is past time for him to leave, and submits to a big cousin bear hug. Then he tips her face upward.

"I need to ask you a big favor," he says. "I need you to be here when I get back. You understand?"

"Why?" she says.

"I need you not to run away. I don't think I could stand losing you again."

Her throat burns. The muscles of her face contract and tighten.

"I don't deserve—"

"I don't have time to hear that," he says. "But there is something I need to tell you. No, don't roll your eyes—it's not anything you think. It's not any more sermons or like that. Promise. It's way more important than that."

His face is so serious. "What?"

"There isn't time to tell you now. That's why you've got to, got to, got to be here."

"Okay," she says meekly.

"I'm serious, Kitty. Promise me."

106

Can she promise she will still be there in eight hours? Can she even be sure she'll be alive in eight hours?

"Promise me."

"I promise."

And then he's gone. She locks the door, though it's not a lock Merlin would have any trouble destroying. He doesn't know where you are, she tells herself, and wonders why she finds this so hard to believe. But she doesn't wonder for long. She lies down on the couch. She just needs a bit more sleep. Just a bit.

Chapter 12

You race from the phone to the nearest convenience store to buy a new card. The twenty-dollar kind, and you race back to the phone, still warm from your breath on it, your hand squeezing it.

"What happened?" she says.

So you tell her. "Couldn't you hear them talking to me?" you say.

"No. Your voice cut off. Just like that."

"Sorry," you say. And then you ask her what she meant about knowing where her father was.

"It was weird," she says. "I was watching the video on the television—it must have been the millionth time—and suddenly I got this odd feeling inside. I mean, at first all I could see was that it was *him* and he was okay. He wasn't beat up . . . well, anyway." She pauses, and you imagine her shaking a bad image out of her head. "So, my eyes sort of wandered—took in the wall behind him."

"Chipboard."

"Whatever. Yes. Chipboard. And somehow I felt I knew that wall."

She sniffs. You wait patiently, but a voice inside you is saying, *This is the big news? She recognized chipboard?* She should come look at your mother's kitchen if she wants chipboard. Or your squat; every window is boarded with the stuff.

"It's pretty common," she says, as if she's reading your mind. "I know that. It's just that it got me thinking, and I looked closer. I actually stopped the recording and zoomed in."

"And?"

"And I thought I could see this stain. The outline of a stain."

Okay, you think, she's nuts. Crazier than you. The stress has got to her.

"I'm probably imagining it," she says. "That's what you're thinking, right? I know. But listen, okay?"

"I'm here," you say.

"You're the only person I can tell this to, Blink. As weird as that sounds, it is the absolute truth."

The absolute truth: something beyond just plain, everyday truth. "I'm listening," you say, real nice, because she said such magic words to you: *You're the only person . . .* So who cares if she's rowing with only one oar in the water?

"My dad goes to this hunting lodge up north. It's owned by QVD—that's the company—"

109

"I know. Queon."

"Right. So, anyone in the company can use this lodge. They have their own private lake — the whole thing. Dad goes up there to fish and hunt, when he can. He goes up with buddies or businesspeople or alone sometimes."

"And that's where he is? At a hunting lodge?"

"Just let me say this?" she says, like it's a question but snappish, too. Then, "Sorry," like she needs *you* to hear her out. You hope the story isn't more than twenty dollars' long.

"When I was a kid, I wanted so much to go up there. Some of the guys in the company would take their sons up there, and I couldn't understand why Dad never took me. So then he gave in, this one time. I was ten or eleven, I guess. It was going to be just the two of us, a little weekend fishing trip.

"We get there, and it's not very, you know, glamorous. I'm not sure what I was expecting. The lodge looks kind of grand from the outside, but it's pretty run-down. It's, like, cavernous, with log beams and rafters and all, but it's really, really basic, with no plumbing or anything. An outhouse. I mean, really basic."

You listen, enthralled, not so much by the content of what she's saying but because it feels so much like a conversation. Like you might be sitting down at Balzac's with a coffee, chatting to this beautiful girl. This was what you bought into, isn't it, Blink? All that money, sure, but the chance of something more.

"Right off I start bitching," she says. "And at first Dad just laughs because he had told me exactly what it was like and I was the one who wanted to come and . . . well, you know. So, anyway, there we are."

"And it's really bad?"

"The weather is not great, either. It's cold and rainy.

110

Suddenly this totally big-deal weekend with my dad is beginning to look like a bust. So I turn into this A1 brat. Pretty well right from the start. Dad plays it cool, trying to make it fun, but I'm just so 'Let's go home, I hate this,' until he finally gets mad. He's a sweetheart most of the time. I mean, he is so tolerant and fair and all that, but he loses it. It's not even noon on Saturday, and he just snaps—tells me to pack up."

She laughs but not much. "We had some lunch before we headed off. Lipton's chicken noodle soup. I remember *that* really well. I wouldn't eat it. Dad got severely pissed off. 'There's nothing else,' he says, 'and there's no place to stop on the way home, so if you want to go hungry, that's your business.' You know the kind of thing parents say to bratty kids."

"Right." Sure.

"And I just throw my bowl at him. Just like that. I pick it up and hurl it. Smash!"

"Wow. Really?"

"I know. Such a bitch."

"So . . ." you say, leaving lots of space for her to jump in. "So?"

"So that's why I remember that wall. The one behind him in the ransom video."

"You can see a chicken noodle soup stain on the chipboard?"

"Well, no. Not so much. Okay, not at all. But it rang a bell. And his hands are in front of him, right? Like they're resting on a table? Do you see what I mean?"

You're not sure. Is this wishful thinking or what?

"I have to find out," she says urgently, her voice dropping in case anyone else might hear her other than you. You can

111

imagine her leaning forward, clutching her cell phone tightly, her blue eyes trained on you, pleading. "I have to know, Blink."

"I don't get it," you say.

She kind of growls and then apologizes, and you think maybe you are really stupid, because this probably makes perfect sense, just not to you.

"It's what you *said,* Blink. Don't you get it? What you implied." She's whispering now. "If my daddy's in on it; if he, you know, arranged this thing; well, I can't—cannot—tell the cops."

"But why would he?"

She makes an impatient sound. "There might be a reason. Something . . . a possibility. But there's no way I can talk about it on the phone. Can you get here?"

"Where?"

"Kingston."

You don't want to tell her that you have no idea where Kingston is. You remember the license in her father's wallet, and it was an Ontario license, so—okay—Kingston is in Ontario and, hell, Ontario is only about as big as Europe. But you have money. Some. And you want to go. That's the thing. You want to. But it's still totally—

"Blink?"

"Uh, I guess so."

"Oh, great. Thank you. Thank you so much!" You can hear her sigh of relief, and it sounds real. "Oh, and Blink? You can drive, right?"

Chapter 13

*"C*ome hunting with me, Spence," she says.

"I can't," he says. "I'm busy."

"No, you're not. You're moping."

"I am not moping. And nothing's in season, so you can't hunt."

"Rabbits are in season. Nuisance rabbits. And Rory says he saw one that had already turned white. Why does that happen, Spence? Turning white when it's still summer?"

"It's called the lethal gene, Kitty. Now, will you please leave me alone?"

She backs off. He's sitting at his computer. There's a screen saver of a starry sky. She watched him go to screen saver as soon as *she came into his room. Barged into his room. "You've got to stop doing that," he'd said. He's hiding something from her, and he's never done that before.*

"You and Melody had a fight, huh?"

"We did not have a fight."

"Then why'd she leave here in tears?"

Spence turns to her. He tries to take her hand, but she pulls back. "We did not have a fight, Kitty. Just leave it alone, okay?"

Kitty's at the door now. "Are you going to break off the engagement?"

Her brother throws himself back in his chair. "Don't you ever stop?" he says.

"You are, aren't you?" says Kitty. Her hair is loose, and she has to hold it back from her face, like curtains.

"We have things to discuss. That's all. Period. Full stop. You wouldn't understand."

And that's when she knows something is really wrong. He's home from school. He just graduated. He and Melody are supposed to be getting married, and something is up he won't tell her about. You wouldn't understand. *Spence has never said that to her. Not ever—not once. She's fifteen and he knows she can understand anything. Anything he's willing to explain to her.*

When Caution wakes up this time, she is completely disoriented. She thrashes out of the bedclothes, as if trapped. Then she sits up, breathing hard, trying to make sense of this little room tucked under the eaves.

Her mouth is caked with crud. She can barely swallow. She gets up, falls back down. How long has she been out? She gets up again, more carefully, and makes her way to the kitchen.

114

Two o'clock? She's been asleep for over six hours.

She gets a drink of water from the tap. Wayne-Ray must have put something in her coffee. He didn't trust her to stay put.

It's not anything you think. It's not any more sermons . . . It's way more important than that.

She sits at the little table. There had been this brightness in his eyes when he'd said it, something that looked awfully like hope. She didn't have any faith in hope, but she had to have faith in Wayne-Ray, didn't she? Maybe not. If this thing was so important, why hadn't he told her right off? As the sleep clears from her brain, she could answer that easily enough. Maybe he'd wanted to tell her last night but didn't get the chance, what with her beating the shit out of him and all.

What could it be?

As far as she can see, she has two choices. One, she could take off for who knows where—Vancouver, maybe. Australia. That way she wouldn't have to be let down by whatever it was he had to say. Or two, she could hear him out and *then* take off for Vancouver, China, or Timbuk-fucking-tu. Her head is clear enough to know that she can't stay in Toronto. And she can't go home.

But there is something she can do. She can make Wayne-Ray dinner. He'd asked her just as he left if she needed anything, if she had any money. She'd managed not to choke with laughter. She was fine, she told him, and shoved him out the door. He told her where the nearest grocery store was as she closed the door on him. So what would she make? Steak, she thinks. Shrimp. Surf and turf, with spaghetti on the side. That's the kind of meal Wayne-Ray likes.

She kneels on the old Raymond parlor couch and peers down at the street. No magicians out there as far as she can tell. Then she takes the extra key and skips down the stairs to the outside world.

It's four by the time she gets back. Her cousin was going to be home by five thirty. And the thing is, he will be home when he said he was going to be. Merlin came and went as he pleased without a word to her. The thought of him makes her weak in the knees, and she has to sit down. Weak in the knees but not in a good way.

By five thirty she has everything ready: the spaghetti sauce is bubbling on the stove, there's salted water ready to turn on for the pasta, a green salad in the fridge. The other stuff she'll cook when he arrives.

She's excited, impatient. She finds herself kneeling at the gable window again, looking down on the street, craning her head to see out to Roncesvalles, like she's the little wifey in a fifties movie, waiting for her hubby to get home. And there he is, suddenly, filling out his voluminous white shirt, striding along the sidewalk. Her dear and wonderful cousin. And then she sees the Nissan.

"It's impossible," she says.

"You never talked about me," he says. He's sitting, holding her hands.

"Never!" She gets up to look out the window, but he stops her, pulls her back.

"He might see you," he says, and he looks instead, while Caution throws herself down on the couch, shaking uncontrollably. She swears, the same word over and over again.

116

"There are lots of blue Nissan Sentras, you know."

"Not with a rusted-out roof rack and a dent in the hood."

Wayne-Ray looks again, says nothing.

"He hit the hood with a tire iron one day when he got a flat."

Wayne-Ray grunts. "As far as I can tell, he's just sitting there," he says.

"I told you he was a magic man."

"No, he's not."

"Then how do you explain that frigging car out there?"

Wayne-Ray throws out his hands, and they flap back down against his sides, helplessly. He peers again out the window and then sits beside her.

"What does he want, Kitty?"

She shakes her head. She can't begin to explain.

"Okay, don't tell me," he says. "But he's dangerous?"

She nods vigorously. She wants to scream at her cousin. Was he not listening when she said that about the tire iron? "I've got to get out of here," she says. "I don't know how he found me, but I've got to get out of here."

She grabs Wayne-Ray's arm, squeezing it hard. She's lying to him, of course. She *does* know how Merlin found her. He was meant to find her. It was all part of the big picture in which Caution Pettigrew pays for her crime. Merlin is her death sentence. The minute she let him pick her up that freezing March day outside the Eaton Centre, with his shiny eyes turned up to ten and his cute little story about how good she looked in her fancy hat, she had committed herself to this sentence. It had all been a long, exhausting trial with the verdict already decided.

"Okay," Wayne-Ray says. "I think I've got a plan." She

117

looks at him. His face is grim. "There's a fire escape," he says, "just outside my bedroom window." She starts to rise, but he yanks her down again. "Listen to me," he says. "Listen good."

His eyes demand an answer. She nods.

"There's somewhere I want you to go. Someone I want you to meet."

She throws her head back. "I don't want *help*," she says.

"You do," he says. "You just don't know it."

"Wayne—"

But she can't even get his name out before he's grabbing her by the shoulders. "Stop it!" he says, not loud, but with every fiber of his body, every ounce of his deep goodness.

She gives in, covering her face with her hands because she is such a horrible person and does not deserve this kindness.

He gets up and goes out to his bedroom, coming back a minute later with a piece of paper. There is an address on it. He pokes the paper at her hand, until she realizes it is there and takes it from him. It's an address on Major Street.

"You know where that is?"

"The lower Annex?"

He nods. "Go there. Go straight there!"

She holds the paper with two hands. Suddenly she laughs. "I feel like we're in some war movie, and this is a safe house."

"Seems to me like this is a war," he says. "Not just him," he adds, gesturing with his head toward the window. "The whole thing."

The whole thing. Spencer Pettigrew's death, he means.

"So who is this . . . ?"

"Woman," he says. "I'll phone her and say you're coming. But I'm going to let her tell you, okay?"

"Jesus, Wayne-Ray, give me a break here."

"I am," he says. "I'm giving you the biggest break I can. And I'm not trying to be mysterious or nothing like that."

"What if she's out?"

"I'm guessing she won't be. If she is, phone me and we'll figure out something else. She'll have to decide whether she wants to tell you what she knows."

Caution laughs, but there is not a shred of humor in it.

"It's the best I can do," says Wayne-Ray. And she sees how much that is in his eyes, even if she has no idea what he's talking about. She owes him this much.

She sighs. He places his hand on the side of her face, and she rests her hot cheek against it, kissing his fleshy palm, salty with sweat.

He gets up and looks out the window. "Does this cat have a blond ponytail?" he asks.

Chapter 14

Caution moves like a cat down the rusted-out fire escape. But she didn't leave without warning Wayne-Ray how dangerous Merlin could be. He dug a baseball bat out of his closet. He used to bat in the high three hundreds in Little League. That's where he'd gotten the broken nose—sliding into home. The catcher was in the hospital for weeks.

She drops to the ground. There is a weed-choked backyard, a fence with a door that creaks alarmingly. Then there is an alley. She's out on Roncesvalles in no time. She should head north up to Bloor. Major Street is only four subway stops away on the Bloor line. But she stands on the sidewalk in the new darkness so that people have to walk around her.

"Freak," a man says, dodging to avoid making contact with her.

"You have a point," she says, calling after him. Then she turns and heads south until she comes to the corner of Wayne-Ray's street.

From behind a telephone pole, she can see the Nissan, three cars down. It's empty as far as she can tell. The sidewalk is as well. She digs her keys out of her pocket and makes her move.

The car is locked, and she fumbles with the key, drops it, picks it up again, swearing to herself. She ducks low and glances over the hood, up toward Wayne-Ray's place. Nothing.

She tries the key again, yanks the door open, and jumps in. The car starts right up. She revs too high in her excitement. Then she engages the clutch and pulls out onto the street. She cruises by the boardinghouse unseen, turns south on Sunny-side, left again at the first street she comes to, and then heads south on Roncesvalles. The car smells of L'Homme and mari-juana. That gives her an idea.

Roncesvalles ends at Queen, where she turns east. She calms herself down, concentrates on her driving; last thing she needs is a cop pulling the beater over when it smells like this. It's busy on Queen, the end of the rush hour, the start of the nightlife. She knows she promised Wayne-Ray she'd go straight to the mystery address, but she's following her instincts right now. Whatever magic might have led Merlin to Wayne-Ray's, she's pretty sure the man can't fly. So if he's going to pursue her, he's going to have to do it on foot. Might even have to rely on public transportation like ordinary mortals.

It's closing on seven when she reaches Parliament and turns

south. She pulls a U-ey south of Front and heads back, pulling over right in front of the Fifty-first Division headquarters of the Toronto Police Service. With her eye trained on the entrance-way, she unzips her Little Mermaid backpack and pulls out the Baggie of weed. She chucks the bag into the backseat, gets out, locks the car, and takes off north in a big hurry. There are no other cars parked in front of the police headquarters. It's a no-parking zone.

Chapter 15

There is something going down at the squat. There is light around the boarding covering the downstairs windows. Maybe there's a fire. Maybe it's just Thursday night—party time. You stand on the cracked concrete path and wait, your arms folded around you, shivering in the cold. Voices are yelling; things are flying. This is the second time in two days that you've stood outside a place where violent things are going on. It's like a curse. Like you carried this with you from your mother's house, and everywhere you go there will be rooms full of anger and mystery.

You stand there, shivering, because it is the middle of October, despite the warm days, and it might snow. It's so effing cold, and this piece-of-shit Gap whatever-it-is you stole from a Jarvis boy's locker wasn't really meant to keep out the elements. You had all day, Blink; you could have picked up a jacket somewhere, spent some of that filthy lucre. But you were afraid to spend anything, in case it cost a lot to get to Kingston. How would you know? But why couldn't you see as far into the future as the night?

Something big crashes to the floor, making you step back off the sidewalk right onto the street. Might be Sonya. She's sweet, mostly, but a lunatic when she goes off her meds. Or it could be Wish-List, in which case a knife is a real possibility. You are tired. Desperately tired. You just want to sleep but not in that hellhole.

You hear a siren. There are always police sirens, because the Fifty-first Division is only three blocks away, so it doesn't mean anything, except it's what they call the straw that breaks the camel's back. You are out of there, Blink, my fine humped creature. Lope down Cherry Street and good-bye. Good-bye to the few scraps of clothing and the piece of foam and the orange Salvation Army blanket. Good-bye to it all. You are back on the street. Then tomorrow you are going to Kingston, wherever that is.

A car pulls a U-ey on Parliament. You jump back, raise your fist, and swear at the driver. She doesn't even notice.

You head along Front Street, past the St. Lawrence Market all closed up for the night, past the little restaurants and bars sucking people in and spilling people out like they're breathing and their air is people. You stop in front of the dimly lit window of a photography gallery. The place is closed, but there are rich people in there, too. Tiny and framed: the children of rich people, in spotless shirts, hair mussed up on this boy here, but like they paid a hundred dollars to make it look like that. Twin girls dressed up like little ladies from some other time. A handsome Asian boy with a cricket bat resting on his shoulder. But all you really see is yourself in the dark glass; you in your breakfast clothes, which you have worn now for three days in a row and which are on the verge of disintegration. You don't want Alyson seeing you like this. You'll shop tomorrow, you tell yourself, if you can afford to after you buy your bus ticket.

You're really going through with this, Blink?

You bought that story?

Like there won't be cops waiting there the minute you step off the bus?

You pass by the Hummingbird Centre just as a show gets out. *Swan Lake*. Folks with little girls in tow — big-eyed from being out so late. They're all dressed in finery, black suits and glittering dresses under warm coats, climbing into Mercedes and Cadillacs. A little princess glares at you and leans into her father's leg.

You drift down the damp steps into the subway at Union Station and find a bathroom. You look at yourself in the cracked mirror. You push your filthy hair out of eyes steeped too long and dark, bitter. Alyson is not going to like you. Alyson is going to take one look at your collar and suddenly realize she has a ballet to go to or something.

Anyway, that story of hers . . . What were you thinking?

It's after eleven, but you phone her from the GO station. Might as well get it over with.

"Did I wake you?"

"Yes . . . well, not really. What is it?"

Her voice is soft and full of sleep. Her bed is probably like something from a movie. White. Everything white. With a soft light and a Persian cat. You imagine her in white silk pajamas. Well, too bad.

"I'm not coming."

She clears her throat, and you imagine her sitting up now.

"What do you mean?"

"What I said. I can't . . . I mean, I can't get away."

There is a pause, and you think, *Just hang the fuck up.* But you don't.

"I think you'd better," she says.

There is no sleepiness in her voice now.

"Well, that's your opinion—"

"No, listen," she says urgently but quietly. "It's for your own good."

Captain Panic wakes right up when she says that. "For your own good" is a phrase you've heard before, way too often. Usually what comes next has a buckle on it.

"What's that supposed to mean?"

"They are looking for you is what I mean."

"They who?"

"Who do you think?"

"Nobody is looking for me. And now I'm just gonna hang—"

"Brent," she says.

And you freeze.

"Brent, do not hang up," she says.

The Captain smacks his open palms against the bulkhead.

126

Once, twice, three times. You can't speak. From where you're standing, you can see a drunk in the shadows pissing against a wall. He's waggling his dick around as if he's writing something.

"What'd you call me?"

"Brent. Brent Conboy."

You look down the echoing corridor of the station past the drunken graffiti artist. There's a wind whistling down the tunnel. An underground wind. No one is watching you in the urine-colored light. No one you can see, that is. They could be anywhere.

"How'd you . . . ? There's no way . . ."

"Listen," she says. "You kind of blew it, okay? Left finger-prints all over the hotel room."

"Fingerprints? I've never been arrested. Nobody's got no prints."

"They do, Brent."

"Don't call me that!"

"Okay, Blink, if that's what you want. But they are looking for you."

"No way."

"Yes way! Listen. Your mom got you fingerprinted when you were in grade school."

The Captain is going crazy. He's charging headlong up the ladder to the bridge. He's heading for the wheelhouse, and he is going to turn this boat around!

"What are you talking about?"

"You don't remember? At school?" She's making it sound as if she were there when it happened, and it's freaking you out.

"Operation Child Find, or something like that," she says. "The cops take the fingerprints of kids in case they ever go

127

missing or whatever. My parents did the same thing with me."

You try to think. Did your mother ever care that much, Blink? How could you forget?

"Anyway, the cops have your prints, and they know who you are. They know what you look like."

The drunk turns as if he can feel your eyes on him. He's still pissing.

"No way."

"Blink, they have been to your mother's place. I'm not making this up. They've got a picture of you."

"I don't live there anymore."

"They've got a picture from last Christmas."

The drunk is smiling at you now, broken-toothed, tucking himself back in, wiping his fingers on his belly.

"How do you know all this? Is there some cop there beside you, feeding you all this crap?" You shake your head. How could these hands clinging to this phone have the same prints as a child?

"Blink?" she says gently. "There are no cops here. I'm in bed, for God's sake. But the police in Toronto are keeping us informed through my father's lawyer there. I didn't tell you before, because you were coming here, anyway, and I didn't want to . . . Well, I didn't want to freak you out."

You laugh. "Right. Nice try!" You laugh again. It's a crazy laugh. The drunk joins in, like you're sharing a joke. Like you're best friends.

"The truth is," she says, "you're probably safer here than there."

"Oh, yeah. Good one."

"Seriously. No one here is in on this. You're the only lead

128

they've got, according to Dad's lawyer, and, as far as they know, you're in Toronto."

"Until you tell them."

"*I can't tell them!*" If it's possible to scream and whisper at the same time, Alyson just did it. You feel a jolt all the way down the telephone line. "I cannot tell anyone I'm in communication with you," she says, more calmly and carefully, as if English is not your first language. Then there is a sob. "I thought I explained it to you. I guess you didn't understand."

Your new drunken buddy starts weaving his way toward you.

"I promise you it's not a trap," she says. "Is that what you're afraid of?" Her voice gets quiet, secretive. "Jesus, don't you get it? There's no way in the world I can tell the cops what I told you. If what you were saying *is* true and if my father *is* at the lodge, then telling anyone would get him in huge trouble. Think about it. Just, please—*please*—think about it. Think about my situation. Will you do that?"

The drunk has stopped as if he's forgotten something. Like maybe he pissed out his brain back there at the wall. You squint—try to read what he wrote there. It glistens but says nothing.

Think about it, she said. That's where you went wrong, isn't it? Starting to think about any of this. That's not what a thief does. A thief doesn't put money back into a wallet. He takes it all. A thief doesn't scroll through someone's smartphone. He takes it to the nearest pawnshop. A thief doesn't call a victim's daughter. But there was a reason for this, Blink. You wanted more—you're not even sure what. Just more. And that is exactly what's on offer if you're smart enough to stay in the game.

129

Meanwhile, the drunk resumes his journey, staggering toward you, closer and closer.

"Blink, I really, really need your help."

"Shit," you say.

"This is our secret," she says.

You take the receiver and bang it down hard on the ledge under the phone. "Shit!"

"Ow!" she says.

"Sorry."

"Are you coming?"

"Okay."

You hang up and step out into the cold wetness of the tunnel. The drunk smiles again, stops, scratches his head as if maybe he knows you but can't remember from where. You curl your fists in case he's got any ideas about getting to know you better. Then he melts.

Chapter 16

Caution: Contents Corrosive.

She can see in her mind's eye the little warning on the Clorox bottle with a picture of a skeletal hand. She feels the acid inside her churning. If parking Merlin's car in front of the police station is a victory, why does it hurt so much?

She walks up Parliament, her hands stuck deep in her pockets, too wired to stop for a bus or to wait for a streetcar at King or Queen or Dundas. Her crazy blue jacket is quilted under its electric blue pelt, so her torso is warm enough, but no other part of her is on this insane night. Shivering, she arrives at Carlton and digs in her pocket for change. She has enough; the first sign that anything might go right tonight. Carlton becomes College, and sometime just before eight, she pulls the cord and steps back out into the night, to find her way up Major Street.

The mystery house is semidetached, sand-blasted brick, with shutters on the lower windows and the porch light on. The door is bright yellow with a curtained window in it, but the step leading to it is tilted drunkenly. Caution looks behind her, afraid she might have been followed. The poison of anger that coursed through her as she abandoned the Nissan has left her weakened, paranoid. She can't bring herself to knock on the door. She feels as if this is just the next phase of the nightmare that began a year and a half ago, has lain dormant, malingering in her bloodstream for these past seven months but is now in full force. She has this strong feeling that she will not get through this night alive, and yet something spurs her on. If she really wanted to die, all she'd have to do is go back to Merlin. And even though she feels certain she cannot escape him now, she has her part to play in this horrible game, knowing that every minute she evades him will only make his bloodlust more virulent. He is the worst of sicknesses.

There is a knocker on the door—a lion with a ring in his teeth. She takes it in hand and announces her shivering presence.

A light comes on in the hall. A vestibule door opens, and a shadowy figure appears. Then the front door opens, revealing a slim black woman in oval glasses with silver rims. Her hair is short. She's wearing a purple shawl around her shoulders over what looks like Chinese pajamas.

"Kitty," she says, without a shade of question in her voice.

And Kitty recognizes her immediately, though the shock makes it impossible to speak.

132

"Tamika," says the woman. "Tamika Holmes. We've met."

She ushers Caution in and dead-bolts the door behind her. "Come," she says, and leads her down a narrow corridor past a steep and narrow stairway to a warmly lit kitchen and sitting area in the back. There are French doors leading out onto a deck, slippery with dead leaves in the light spilling from the house.

"Have a seat," she says, indicating a table and chairs as sunshine yellow as the front door. "Can I get you something to eat? You must be starved." Caution falls into the chair pulled out from the table for her. "I've got some lasagna I can nuke. Vegetarian."

Caution nods, swallows. "You were at the funeral," she says.

"I figured you'd remember," says Tamika, busying herself in the little kitchen. She throws Caution a smile over her shoulder. "Not too many black folk up there in Wahnapitae, far as I could tell."

There were three friends of Spence's from school: this woman and two guys. Her mother and father had been so touched that they'd driven all the way up — six hours or so. Jake and James and Tamika: her brother's closest university friends.

Tamika sets the timer on the microwave and then makes a little startled gesture as she recalls something.

"Your cousin wants you to phone as soon as you get in," she says. She takes a cordless phone from its stand on the counter and, consulting a little ringed notebook beside the phone, punches in Wayne-Ray's number.

"The eagle has landed," says Tamika, and then hands the phone to Caution.

"Where've you been?" he says. "I was worried shitless." Caution swallows, raises her hand to her throat, can hardly speak.

133

"Kitty?" he says. "What's going on?" Tamika comes to her aid with a glass of water. She drinks, while her cousin swears at her, the concern brimming in his voice. Why does she do this? she wonders. She seems programmed to bring hurt to those she loves most.

"I had some business I had to—Oh, forget it. I'm here now. I'm sorry."

He growls. A big old bear. "I was afraid he'd gotten you," he says. Then he launches into telling her what happened: Merlin out on the street, not knowing where to go, standing there with his cell phone in his hand, as if maybe there are others—as if maybe they have the house surrounded. Then, after a few minutes, he moved off up to Sunnyside.

"I can't figure it out," says Wayne-Ray. "How they could get this close and not know where you were?"

The word "they" fills Caution with new dread, as if Merlin has morphed into an army.

"I'm sorry," she says again. "I ended up cutting through a bunch of backyards and ended up on . . . I don't know. I got kind of turned around. Is Sunnyside the next street over?"

"Yeah," says Wayne-Ray. "The first block west of Roncesvalles. So you were there. Weird." But before she can say anything else, he goes on. "Phone before you come home, okay?"

She nods at the receiver and then remembers to say something. "Okay," she squeaks. "Thanks."

Home, he said, as if there were such a place.

"I just don't want you to walk into some trap," he says. "Jesus, Kitty." She can hear the love in his voice and the exasperation. She resists apologizing again. If she starts apologizing, she might never stop.

134

She hangs up, and the timer goes off on the microwave. Next thing she knows, Tamika is exchanging the receiver for a thick golden-brown ceramic plate loaded with steaming lasagna.

Caution wants to cry. The goodness of people, the badness of people. She feels like some plaything of the angels: the kind ones and the fallen.

"Eat up, sugar," says Tamika, taking a seat across from her. "You look like you could do with some comfort."

Tamika's eyes are as warm as fondue chocolate. There is a smile on her full lips, but it is tinged with sadness. This is the way Drigo looked at her yesterday morning, but there was calculation in his sad eyes.

Tamika gestures at the plate of food, and Caution manages a shaking forkful of lasagna.

Tamika leans back in her chair, her arms crossed on her chest. Her eyes ask an easy question.

"It's great," says Caution when her mouth is no longer full. And yet the word "great" doesn't seem adequate. "Thanks," she says. Then she takes a sip of water and dives back into the lasagna, somehow knowing that anything this good will not last. Cannot last.

"I liked meeting your family," says Tamika. "Your mother and her sisters, Wayne-Ray's mom . . ."

"Lanie," says Caution.

"Right. And who was the other one?"

"Dorcas. She's the youngest."

"Right, Dorcas, who married a Wayne, which is why Wayne-Ray is Wayne-Ray, is that it?"

Caution nods. "And Dorcas's husband is Wayne-Mac."

"That's it. They were all so kind. Good people."

Caution drops her head. Here it comes, she thinks: the recrimination. How could you hurt such good people? How could you destroy this good family?

She can feel Tamika's eyes on her. She's in the principal's office, waiting on judgment. But the difference—well, there are so many differences—but the big difference is that she has no idea why she is here. She puts her fork down, wipes her lips with a napkin.

"Why am I here?" she asks.

Tamika's face screws up tight, as if the easy part of the exam is over and now she's come to the essay questions.

"This is hard," says Tamika. "Wayne-Ray has kind of put me on the spot."

"If you don't want—"

"No," says Tamika, holding up her hand as if to stop Caution from speaking and stop her from fleeing, which is what Caution wants to do, despite the fullness in her belly and the warmth of this cozy kitchen.

"I don't mind," says Tamika. "I probably should have done this a long time ago, but I had my reasons for not doing it—good reasons, I thought. My intentions were good, Kitty. And I am sorry if I was wrong about that. It was hard to know what to do."

Caution is filling up with apprehension. There is to be some new twist to her nightmare—some new chasm to fall into. She can sense it and can do nothing to stop herself from falling.

Tamika folds her hands together on the table. She is wearing many rings, many bracelets.

"Spencer and I were more than friends," she says. She waits

for a reaction. Caution says nothing but nods encouragingly, though there is a fear rising slowly in her that she has no power to resist.

"Your brother was engaged," says Tamika.

"To Melody Tourangeau," says Caution.

"To Melody, yes. His high-school sweetheart. The summer after he finished his freshman year in the Big Bad City, he gave Melody a ring, knowing that despite everything, he would still be the same sweet country boy when he finished his degree." She looks down at the many rings on her own fingers. "That's the way he put it," she says. "I certainly never meant to steal him away from Melody."

Caution swallows hard, drinks some water. This is spiraling away from her. This beautiful woman is seeking pardon from me, she thinks, and seems to have forgotten why they are speaking of Spence in the past tense.

"I was one of his tutorial leaders," Tamika says. "I was recovering from . . . well, it's not important now . . . but Spence was there, this kind and loving young man—six years younger than me but so wise. You know?"

Caution's neck is too constricted to nod. Her throat is burning. There is a strong hand wrapping pitiless fingers around her heart.

"He was going to tell you—tell your family—about us when you came down for graduation, but then when your mom got sick and you couldn't make it, he knew he'd have to come home. And, of course, he'd have to tell Melody."

Now Caution nods. "They were fighting," she says.

Tamika nods sadly. "I felt so guilty. He, Spencer . . . he was such a gentleman, in the truest sense of that word. I knew how

137

hard it was for him. I told him to take as long as he needed—as long as Melody needed."

The hand around Caution's heart starts to squeeze.

Tamika is frowning now at a memory. She is staring away, holding herself tightly. "When I met her at the funeral—Melody, I mean—I could tell that she knew nothing about Spencer and me. He hadn't told her. I was a friend of Spence's from school—that was all she knew. And when I saw how nice she was, how deep her grief was, how well *loved* she was by your family, there was no way I was going to say anything to upset her. It made no sense anymore. It would only be hurtful. I had nothing to prove."

She stops and rubs her eyes. "Sorry," she says. "It's . . ."

Caution sits silently, across a table in another universe. Was this what Wayne-Ray wanted for her? To know that beyond killing her parent's beloved son, Wayne-Ray's best friend, and her own brother, she had also robbed this stranger of the love of her life? Because Caution can see in Tamika's eyes what Spence had meant to her. *How many murders have I committed?* she thinks.

Tamika takes a deep breath, wipes her face with her hands, and opens her eyes wide. They are glazed now with tears that do not fall, and they shine like jewels. "Okay," she says. "Enough already. I'm not sure how much time we have. I feel as if there is a ticking clock out there. Some trouble. Wayne-Ray didn't explain. So I had better get on with it, right?"

And it is then that it happens. The merest mention that there was more to get on with was enough to make Caution see what she had so far failed to register. The most commonplace of things. Something standing by the sink on the counter. She can see it now from where she sits. Had been able to see

138

it all along. A cup. A pink sippy cup. And the sight of it sparks a memory of something she saw in the vestibule not half an hour earlier, though it had not registered to her at the time: a folded-up stroller. And the combination of these two images—one right before her, the other recalled—suddenly explodes in her head, and she sees a hundred things she hadn't seen or perhaps hadn't wanted to see: the photos on the fridge, the bib slung over the chair to her right, a stuffed monkey on the floor.

The hand inside her chest crushes her heart, stops her breath. She clutches the edge of the table, afraid she is going to faint.

"Are you all right?" says Tamika.

And then the phone rings.

Chapter 17

"**I** think I know what's going on," says Wayne-Ray.

Caution grips the receiver tightly. She has no idea what he's talking about.

"This Merlin guy," he says. "I think he's tracking you somehow."

"What do you mean?"

"He's got a bug on you."

The bad dream is now swirling out of sense and out of mind, and Caution feels as if she's being sucked into the vortex of it. "I don't understand."

"He *wasn't* talking to someone on his cell," says Wayne-Ray urgently. "He was reading coordinates or something. Like he's got Internet or whatever."

"It's an iPhone," says Caution.

"There you go! Okay, listen, Cuz. If I'm right, then there's some kind of transmitter on you."

"What? Where?"

"Hell if I know. But it's most likely in something you have with you all the time. Your purse or something."

"I don't have a purse."

"Kitty!" he says, so loud she flinches. "*Look*. Look for something. I don't know what. Something that shouldn't be there. Do you understand?"

"I guess."

"Call me right back," he says, and hangs up.

Tamika is looking at her with worried eyes. "What's wrong?" she says.

Caution is too embarrassed to say. It's as if there is suddenly a stench in the room, and this woman doesn't know where it's coming from.

Caution feels the front of her jacket, pressing her fingers down hard to feel through the fleece, through the quilting.

"Are you all right?"

Caution shakes her head. Then she stands, unzipping the jacket, as if it were suddenly crawling with earwigs. She starts patting it, then lays it down on the table and presses her hands all over the sleeves and back of it.

"Kitty?"

"I can't explain," she says. Then she feels it. She presses hard with her index finger around the edge of some hard rectangular shape. She looks up, frantically. "Have you got a knife?" she says.

She makes a slit on the inside of the jacket and tears open

141

the lining, revealing a black box about the size and shape of a thick lighter, with a knob on the top, an antenna. It doesn't feel as if it weighs more than two or three ounces.

Caution sits down hard. Tamika takes the bug from her, staring at it with alarm.

"What is going on here?"

Caution picks up the cordless from the table and phones Wayne-Ray. He answers on the first ring. He asks her to look for a product name. She takes the bug back from Tamika, finds a name, and reads it to him. "I've got my laptop," he says. And then a minute later—"Bingo!" he says.

Caution stares at Tamika, and they share a look of incomprehension.

"Real-time GPS tracking system with enhanced cellular assist," says Wayne-Ray, but he's not really talking to Caution, just reading information on a website. "Locates via Internet . . . works inside buildings . . . low battery drain . . . A-GPS and AFLT . . . three types of locate searches . . ."

"Wayne-Ray, speak to me in English!"

"Hold on, hold on," he says excitedly, and then he mumbles to himself for another moment or so.

"Okay," he says. "This explains a lot. This thing—it's not like on *24* or anything. I mean, it's not dead accurate."

"Meaning?"

"Meaning he found his way here, but he couldn't pinpoint where you were, which is why he was waiting in the car, I guess. And it was only when you took off that he started getting a different set of coordinates."

"Am I supposed to be relieved?"

"No. Not really." He pauses, and she doesn't speak

142

because she knows he has something else he needs to say. "Kitty, whatever you're caught up in, this guy does not want to lose track of you."

There is no mistaking the tone in her cousin's voice, the seriousness or the reproach. She has been an idiot, and now she has dragged him into it. And then she looks at Tamika, and the horrible truth comes over her in a wave so icy cold she fears she will go under.

"Oh God," she says. "Oh God, oh God, oh God."

Tamika scoots her chair closer and takes Kitty's arm in her hand.

"Take it easy," says Wayne-Ray. "At least we know what we're dealing with here."

"What do I do?" she says.

"Get rid of it," he says. "But not there. Take it a long way away. You know what I mean?"

"Yes," she says.

"Good."

"Wayne-Ray?"

"What is it?"

"I'm frightened."

"Get rid of it, Cuz," he says, his voice gentle now. "And then get back to me. By phone. Be careful," he says. And then hangs up.

She puts down the receiver and stares at Tamika. There was something else. They were talking about something important. Tamika was going to tell her something. A child. There was—is—a child. There is a child, but there is no time. All of this flits through Caution's brain, followed right behind by a tsunami of nausea and guilt. On top of all her other crimes, she has robbed

143

a child of its father, and now her very existence is threatening that child and its mother.

"I've got to go," she says, jumping to her feet.

"Can we call the police?" says Tamika. She has no idea what is going on.

"I shouldn't be here," says Caution, slipping into her lacerated coat. The evil little black device is in her hand. "I shouldn't even have come."

"Oh, yes, you should have. And there is more I need to tell you," says Tamika.

"No," says Caution, cutting her off, shaking her head wildly. "Not now. Later maybe," she says, trying to imagine a later that might include her ever invading this warm little home again. "I . . . I'll get back to you . . . I'll . . ."

Tamika doesn't try to hold her back, just nods solemnly. Caution heads toward the hallway, then stops and looks back at the French doors.

"Is there a way out?" she says.

"Can you climb a fence?" says Tamika, and then a quick smile comes to her. "If half of what Spence said about you is true, you could climb the CN Tower."

She unlocks the French doors and slides one side open.

Caution wants to bolt, to disappear, to go up in a cloud of smoke. But Tamika grabs her wrist. "You don't know the whole story," she says, "and you need to."

Caution wants to argue the point. She needs to be oblivious—that's what she needs. She needs to have never existed. But she nods lamely.

"You come back to me, sister," says Tamika. "Do you hear what I'm saying?"

144

Caution nods again, not very convincingly. Then Tamika kisses her cheek, her hand warm and firm on the back of Caution's neck. "Sister," she whispers into Caution's ear. She closes the door behind her. Waves through the glass. And then Caution takes off.

There was a child's finger painting taped to the door. Red and yellow and blue handprints. There was a name in the corner: SERINA.

As Caution makes her way through the backyard and hoists herself up and over the fence, she wonders if this was what Wayne-Ray wanted for her. To know of this child, Serina, and thus to crumble the very last bit of her heart into nothing.

She knows exactly where to ditch the transmitter. She makes her way back down Parliament and finds the Nissan parked where she left it. She figured it would have been towed by now, but she's glad it's still there. Watching to make sure no cops are around—though there is a building full of them right here—she unlocks the door and throws the GPS device in the backseat right beside the bag of pot. She considers hiding until Merlin comes into view. Then she could throw a rock at one of the windows of the cop shop, raise the alarm. She imagines Merlin standing there, realizing what she has done to him as a swarm of cops comes running out to drag him away. She wishes there were any joy in this fantasy.

She phones Wayne-Ray just after eleven. Merlin has not returned, but her cousin has been on patrol. There is another dude parked on the street, he says: short dark hair, sharp beak, two eyebrow rings. "I bent down to take a good long look, smiled when the dude gave me the finger," says Wayne-Ray.

Warner, thinks Caution, and remembers the gun he had inside his jacket. In a flash, she imagines a bullet in Wayne-Ray's forehead. "Don't piss him off, okay?" she says. "Stay away from him."

"I think it's time you told me who these people are," he says.

"They are really bad people," she says. "I already told you that." She wants to say they are the fate she deserves, her just desserts—no one else's. But what she can't figure out is why Warner or any of Drigo's people would care what happened to Merlin's money, let alone Merlin's flake of a former girlfriend. "Promise me you'll be careful," she says.

"I will. And you, too, Kitty. What are you gonna do?"

She needs to go. Get away. Leave. That or maybe throw herself in front of a subway train and be done with. No. That would be too easy. She needs to make this torture last. There can never be enough of it. In fact, maybe she already did kill herself, and this is hell doing a really good job of looking like Toronto. And if it is hell, then she will be running from Merlin and company for the rest of eternity.

"Keep in touch," says Wayne-Ray. She never answered his question, which was probably answer enough. "But, Kitty?"

"Yes?"

"If you call, don't say where you are, just in case."

Just in case they've bugged Wayne-Ray's place as well; that's what he means.

"I won't," she says. "Good night."

"Good night. I wish . . ."

She waits, but her cousin can't seem to think of what it is he wishes for. She knows how he feels.

* * *

It's after midnight. Caution stands in the deep shadows of a massive tree on Major Street just down the block from Tamika's place. The street is deserted. She waits to be absolutely sure.

She makes her way to Tamika's door. The houselights are off. From her Little Mermaid backpack, she pulls the money: eight thousand dollars, minus the money she used today and enough to get her through tonight and away tomorrow—somewhere, though she has no idea where. So, seven thousand four hundred dollars she never wants to see again.

She doesn't hesitate. In the midst of her long fall into misery, what she is about to do is like a little parachute to slow her descent. She shoves the money into the mail slot, careful not to let the flap make a noise and wake the baby inside.

Then she takes off down Major in a jog, thinking about the note she has wrapped the money in.

> *Dear Tamika,*
> *This money was stolen from a criminal, so there's no*
> *use going to the police with it. You might as well keep*
> *it. It can be for Serina. I would really like that.*
> *Your sister,*
> *Katherine Pettigrew*

Tamika had called her sister. Only one other person had ever called her that. It was not a word to use lightly, and when she wrote the note, sitting in a coffee shop on Front Street, she resisted it and then gave into it. She hates the name Katherine. Not even her mother called her that, except when she'd done something really bad. But she wanted the note to be taken seriously, to be like a contract between them, or does she mean a bond?

She turns onto College and heads east, not sure where she's going anymore. She'll stay the night in a hotel—the kind of hotel that won't ask for a credit card or anything. There are places she knows way downtown that are scurvy enough to take cash and not ask any questions. She looks around from time to time and wishes she weren't so exposed. College is still pretty busy, so is Spadina. She splits off left at a side street, and then south at the first road she comes to.

She drifts southward until she finds herself in a place where there are only loud boys and girls with nothing to lose. She recognizes the type; she was one of them when she first came to the city. She walks with her head down, raising a drunken whistle, an offer, a curse or two, until she turns south one more time, and the next thing she knows there's an arm around her waist and a hand across her mouth, and she is being dragged into the shadows next to an open Dumpster.

"You must be looking for trouble, foxy lady," says a voice she doesn't recognize. It's a shaky voice on the edge of frantic. She doesn't know this man, but she knows a crystal meth freak when he's desperate for a fix. The smell of him is worse than the stink rising from the Dumpster. He just wants my money, she thinks, not struggling at all, submitting to his rough hands, letting him feel through the pockets of her jacket, slip his hands inside her bra, in case she's hiding anything there, tear open her Little Mermaid backpack. Then he's gone. And she doesn't even question the extraordinary coincidence of locating this desperate stranger. It's another chapter of the nightmare, that's all. And just her rotten luck that he didn't take her life along with her last red cent. Shaking, she bends down to pick up the copy of *Anna Karenina* from a puddle on the concrete.

Part 2

Part 2

Chapter 18

Everything changes now. The rules of the street you have been trying so hard to learn these last few months will be of some use to you, but you are entering new territory, Blink, with unknown factors. For one thing, there is somebody watching you.

You have never taken a train before. You stammer when the ticket man asks if it's a round-trip. You hadn't thought that far. Round-trip? That means you're coming back, doesn't it? How could you know that? He asks you again, this tired look on his face, even though he probably slept in a bed last night, which is more than you can say for yourself. He's bored and annoyed, and the day has only just begun. You watch his hands in case there's a button to buzz the cops. You look around, as if they might be moving in on you right now. But you are alone, except for this freakish girl in a fuzzy blue jacket. Her arms are crossed, as if you're taking way too much time. Beyond her the vast hollowness of Union Station fills your eyes and ears.

"Kid," he says.

"One-way!" you say. You yell it, like he's hard of hearing and you've been saying it over and over. One-way. Because no matter what happens, you won't be coming back to the same place you left behind.

She watches the boy take the roll of bills out of his pocket to pay for his ticket. He's around her age; a street punk—probably stole the money, she tells herself. Like the meth freak stole hers. What goes around comes around.

She sees how he holds his hand out flat to look at the money, like a child inspecting a caterpillar or some other wonder of the universe. Obviously hasn't lost enough yet to be so reckless. She can help him with that. That's just the way it is. It isn't fair, she tells herself, it just is. And now it's showtime.

"What's in Kingston?"

You look up. It's the girl in the blue jacket. You've taken a seat down in the place where the gates are. Your train doesn't leave for over an hour.

"Are you deaf?" she says. Then she makes a bunch of crazy movements with her hands as if she's talking in some kind of freak sign language.

"None of your business," you say, and her face lights up as if you handed her an engraved invitation to sit and chat.

"So it's a big secret?" she says. And before you know it,

152

she's perching beside you, her eyes big as saucers, as Nanny Dee used to say.

You get up to leave, and she stops you — grabs your sleeve. You look down at your arm, and her hand slips away. "Hey, sorry," she says. "I'm just a little wired. Bad night. Not drugs! I mean just bad. Well, you know."

She's looking at you as if she really does know how bad your night was — as if hers was bad in the same way. And her eyes — her eyes are this pale gray like early morning fog with the sun seeping through it.

He who hesitates is lost, Nanny also used to say, and you just hesitated, Blink. You sit down again.

"That's better," she says. Then she suddenly moves her face in close to yours, staring seriously into your eyes. "Have you got Tourette's?"

You shake your head, not knowing what she's talking about.

"Tourette's syndrome. All that blinking," she says, blinking herself. "It could be a symptom, especially in kids our age. So could the facial grimacing."

"It's just a tic or something."

"If you say so. But there was this guy I knew with Tourette's. It got bad. He'd swear sometimes right out of the blue — right in the middle of class. Very weird." Her hand comes up, and you pull back as if maybe she's going to try to touch your eye.

"Do you sniffle much?" she says. "Grunt?" She grunts.

"Jesus, no!" You shake your head.

"Well, good. So maybe this eye thing is just a tic."

"That's what I said."

"Okay, just checking."

Then she sits back, her hands in her lap as if the medical diagnosis exhausted her.

"What do you want?" you say to her.

She shrugs. "Apart from a house in Beverly Hills? Oh, I don't know. Some company, I guess. What do *you* want?"

You shrug. She shrugs. It's a shrug-off. You both sort of smile. But you're not buying into this con job, although she's working it hard.

"Bug off," you say.

"Hey," she says. "Give me a break. There is no one here to talk to. Just old people." You look at the lines beginning to form at the gates. "Well, okay, there are *some* young people," she says, "but it's Friday, right? They're all university students skipping classes so they can go home for the weekend and Mommy can do their laundry and cook them a roast-beef supper."

You look again, and she's right: old people and students. And some business types and a few moms with kids . . . So, she's not entirely right.

"You and I," she says. "We don't have anyone to do our laundry, do we?" You shake your head. "And when was the last time you had a nice juicy roast-beef dinner?"

Now you're suspicious. "Are you, like, a social worker?"

She laughs, shakes her head. "Do I look like a social worker?"

"So what are you? Hare Krishna?"

She rolls her eyes. "No turban," she says. "And, anyway, I look like shit in orange."

You sigh. This is too high-energy for you. You fold your arms and look straight ahead. She may be pretty, but she's wacko.

"Ah, come on," she says, punching you lightly in the arm. "Wakey, wakey."

"Cut it out," you say. "And I haven't got any spare change, so you're wasting your time."

"Huh," she says. Then she sighs. "Okay. Sorry." But she doesn't leave. And the thing is you don't want her to. You can handle this.

"You're an Aries, right?" she says. "Strengths: independent, optimistic. Weaknesses: moody and short-tempered."

You turn to stare at her. "I'm a Virgo," you say.

She shakes her head. "No way," she says. "I am, like, so good at this."

"I'm a Virgo," you say. "September fifteenth." Somehow it's important to set her straight.

"Wow!" she says. "Really?"

"Listen —"

"Okay. I hear you. I'm out of here. Have a nice day." She gets up to leave. There's a strip of lining hanging down from her jacket like a tail. You want to grab it, pull her back. If she'd just slow down a bit, a little company would be nice.

She walks about five paces away, then she spins around on her feet like an ice-skater. She plants her hands on her hips. "How about breakfast?" she says.

"I already ate."

"Liar."

You look down. She's a bully. You're too tired for this.

"You are a liar," she says.

"So I'm a liar — just go away."

But she won't. She stabs you in the leg with her finger. "Hey," she says again, her voice quiet. She's bending down, her

155

hands on her knees, to look you in the eye. "It's on me."

You look up, skeptical.

"Seriously," she says, patting her pocket. "There's a Tim Hortons in here somewhere. You know those little potato things? I *love* those. I'm going to order three of them. It's my treat. How about it?"

You haven't eaten. You were so worried about getting to the station on time, you got here way too early. You are hungry, and when you look at her, she smiles and doesn't look half as wacko anymore.

"What's your name?" she says. "I'm April."

You swallow, try to think. "Bruce," you say.

"Come on, Bruce. It's chow-time."

Next thing you know, you're in the line at Tim Hortons. You're in the GO train part of the station now, and it's crazy busy with commuters arriving in droves like cattle in a cowboy movie. She's quiet now, and you actually miss her voice.

You glance sideways at her, through your hair. She manages a tired smile. She's putting on the cheery routine. And for some reason that endears her to you. There's no way her name is April. But that's okay. She knows your name isn't really Bruce; you could tell. So already there's this thing you've got going, even if it's only a lie.

She's the only person you've really talked to in days, apart from Alyson, and that was on a phone. Oh, and you can pretend all you want, Blink, but in your heart of hearts, you know that Alyson wouldn't give you the time of day if it weren't for this thing she wants you to do.

Oh, Blink. How can I ever thank you? you have imagined her saying to you. You're out on that manicured lawn by the water. You're all in white, like she is. She's holding the collar of your shirt, her face right up next to yours.

"I'm heading to Vancouver," says April.

"What's in Vancouver?"

"My folks," she says. "I'm a 'runaway.'" She makes little quote marks in the air. "You, too, right?" You nod. "Figured. So is Kingston 'home'?"

"No."

Mr. Conversationalist. Oh, give it a try, son. Talk to the girl, why don't you? She's buying you breakfast, after all. She's a bit of a flibbertigibbet, but there's something about her, isn't there, lad? Something inside those gray eyes that you recognize. Some kind of need.

"There's this . . . thing I'm doing for someone," you say. "I'm kind of, you know, helping someone out?"

"Uh-oh," she says. "*Helping out,* Bruce?"

"It's like a favor."

She takes your arm and leans in close, her body pressing against your side, and whispers in your ear. "You're not moving drugs, are you?"

You pull your head back as if she'd shouted. "No way."

"Phew," she says. "Good one. Keep clear. Believe me. I know."

You're almost at the counter now, and you look up at the choices available on the menu board. You don't want to order too much. By the look of her, she's been living on the street, just like you. And yet she's going to Vancouver, which must cost a bundle. So you think, a breakfast sandwich and a coffee.

"Can I take your order?"

The crankcase in the hairnet behind the counter looks

157

borderline hostile. You turn to April, who nods encouragingly while she searches through her pockets. So you give your order and April adds her own, and the crankcase totes it up and tells you the price. By now April is frantic.

"Oh, no," she says. "My money!"

"What's wrong?"

"My money's gone!" She looks back as if she might have dropped it. The people in the line scan the floor, see nothing, and do not look amused. The woman behind the counter is tapping her finger on the stainless-steel counter.

"Come on, sweetheart," she says.

Now April looks at you, Blink, desperate. "I'm *so* sorry," she mumbles. "I don't know what happened."

"Move it or lose it," says the suit behind you.

April swears at him, then turns back to you. "Come on," she says, and grabs you by the sleeve. But you don't budge.

"It's okay," you say, surprised but suddenly elated by this turn of events. Then with something of a flourish, you pull the roll of bills from your pocket—the last of the windfall of Wednesday morning. "I'll get it," you say.

But you don't get it, Blink. You don't get it at all.

Before you can peel off a ten, April snatches the whole roll from your open palm and takes off.

"Hey!" you shout, too stunned to move.

"You just got took, kiddo," says the woman behind the counter, as if she sees this kind of thing every day.

You take off after the girl, but the commuter herd keeps pouring off the GO trains, and you lose sight of her in no time. You dodge through the push and hurry, catching electric-blue glimpses but nothing more. It's as if she's run into a moving, impenetrable forest. You shout her name that is not her name. You push your way through, against the flow of the crowd, the flow of everything—jostled and shoved, elbowed and insulted.

But it's no use. Give it up, you poor stupid boyo. She's gone.

It is high tide. You stop in a place where it is impossible to stand still, and soon enough the crowd carries you back like flotsam—debris from a sinking ship. That is what you are, Blink: a bit of wreckage washed up on the shore.

Chapter 19

Caution sits in the handicapped stall in the women's room, counting her take. Over three hundred dollars. How far will that get you? Someone enters the restroom, and instinctively Caution climbs up onto the seat, so her feet won't show. They're here. They're looking for her, and it isn't just Merlin. It's the others, too.

Someone tries her door. "Oh, sorry," says the someone, and finds another stall.

Another toilet flushes. Someone washes her hands and leaves. The door opens, wafting in an echoey loudspeaker voice, then shuts.

Where will she go? She hasn't a clue. Where *can* she go?

The answer to that is simpler. She can go up to three hundred and sixty dollars away. Is that far enough?

But to go anywhere, she will need to buy a ticket, which will mean venturing up into the main part of the station, standing in a line, and then standing in another line for a train. A sitting duck.

Something inside her shifts. Maybe it's because of exhaustion. She didn't sleep last night, didn't dare stop moving. Adrenaline got her through the little performance for Bruce, if that was his name. What a sap. She feels this pang of regret. It's not that he was stupid, just naive. No match for her.

He'd been wary at first, but she'd stripped him of his wariness as easily as she'd stripped him of his cash. His problem was that he had wanted exactly what she was offering—friendship and breakfast. She could see the yearning in him as much for company as for food. She knew the feeling.

She slithers down off her perch like a boneless thing until she is sitting on the toilet again, where she leans forward and rests her head in her arms. She feels empty, drained of every last ounce of spirit.

She is almost dizzy with sleep. But she can't afford it, so she drags herself to her feet, teetering like a drunk, and makes her way to the stall's self-contained sink. She turns on the water and douses her face. She grabs at her hairpins: one, two, three, four, five, six, seven—pulls them all out and throws them in the overflowing garbage bin. Then she puts her whole head in the sink and soaks her weary skull.

She looks up at the mirror, dripping wet, her eyes blinking like that unfortunate boy. The mirror is tilted forward for someone in a wheelchair. She wishes she were in a wheelchair. She doesn't want to stand up anymore. She doesn't want to be

161

on the run. She is beaten. So why doesn't she simply walk out there and give herself up?

She leans on the sink, staring at herself in incomprehension. This has to stop, she thinks. Then she says it out loud. "This has to stop."

From the restroom doorway, she can see the lines snaking toward the gateways to westbound and eastbound trains. She has formulated a plan. The end of the line for the Montreal train with service to Kingston winds its way through gate 12. The man at the gate seems only to be checking tickets, not collecting them. Nodding, pointing. A woman with a baby in a stroller is his last customer. The baby is lifted up, and the gate man helps the mother fold up the stroller.

Now.

Caution takes off across the station, running as fast as she can, running on empty, running for her life. If Merlin is here somewhere, then he will see nothing but a blue flash, a blur. There is nothing left of her but this movement toward gate 12. He will need real magic to stop her, and she no longer believes he has any. Just an electronic toy she has already dealt with.

The gate is closed when she reaches it. She rattles it like a prisoner and the conductor turns around.

"Kingston?" she says, breathing hard.

He pulls keys from his pocket as he returns to let her through.

"Thanks," she shouts, dashing past him to the steep escalator up to the platform.

"Miss!" he calls after her. But she can't stop now. She takes the escalator steps two at a time, until she is brought up short behind the woman and child. It's a narrow escalator, with no room for her to pass, but when she stares back down, the gate man has abandoned his post. The child above Caution stares down over its mother's shoulder at her, reaches out a tiny hand, says some baby word. The mother turns and smiles. "Just made it," she says.

At the top of the escalator, Caution ducks past the woman and runs to the first coach.

"Ticket," says the man at the bottom of the steps.

"I didn't have time," she says. "Can I pay cash?"

He makes a sour face but herds her onto the train, where she finds the first available seat and falls into it. By the time the train starts moving, she is almost asleep. A hand on her shoulder shakes her gently.

"Ticket?" says the conductor.

She wipes her eyes and reaches into her pocket for the roll of money. "I was late," she says. "Sorry. How much do I owe you?"

His face is stern, and she fears some kind of reprimand. She wonders if she has the energy to listen to a lecture about rules. His face is jowly and gray, but his eyes are a penetrating green. "Where to?" he asks.

"Kingston," she says.

"Student?"

She nods.

"Could I see some ID?"

She has her driver's license, but there is no way she's showing him that. She glances down at the floor, trying to dredge up some kind of ploy or scheme, but her mind is a blank. She looks up, pushes back the wet tangle of hair from her forehead.

"I don't have any ID with me," she says. "I'll be seventeen

on November thirtieth. But if you want to charge me adult fare, that's okay. I understand."

She's not sure why, but his expression suddenly softens. "Fifty-nine eighty-five," he says. "Student fare, one-way."

She hands him three twenties. He says he'll be back with the change and a ticket. "The Kingston car is two up," he says. Then he places a finger on her shoulder. "But why don't you just rest up a bit, dear? No hurry."

Her eyes won't stay open another moment. It is as if she were just waiting for permission to close them. There is a fluttering shape in her mind's eye, something primary, bright and swirling and smudged.

She marches up the hill behind the house, through the meadow to the shooting range. Her rifle bounces on her shoulder. It hurts, but she doesn't care. She's angry. Angry at Spence. First he doesn't come home from Toronto at the end of the term because he's got some kind of a job. Then they can't even go for his graduation because Mom got the flu. Finally, when he gets home, he's impossible to talk to.

"Fine," she says. "Be that way."

She is going to do some target practice. Spence helped her set up a target. He brought up some hay bales in the tractor, found a messed-up scrap of plywood out behind Dad's workshop. It's about four feet by eight feet; the bales rise above it and out about two feet to either side. They had measured out markers in the meadow to indicate 50, 100, 150, and 200 meters. They used to have shooting competitions; she even won sometimes. But that was last summer, when Spence was Spence, instead of this alien!

She pins a fresh new red-and-white paper target square in the

middle of the plywood, then trudges out to the 50-meter marker.
Beyond the target is bush, thick and overgrown. She can't see the
house from here, only glimpses of the lake. The wind is behind her,
strong. She swears and, with her rifle between her knees, ropes in
her long black hair and shoves it down the back of her sweater.

She loads up the Remington. He gave it to her for her four-
teenth birthday. It had been his, but he didn't buy a new rifle,
which is what she expected he was going to do. Another thing that
was different about him. It was as if he were leaving her, leaving
her behind. When they went hunting or target shooting anymore,
he borrowed one of Dad's old rifles.

She opens up a new box of CCI Mini-Mag cartridges.
Forty-grain solids, gilded lead round noses. Solid tip, less drag
than hollow point.

She raises the rifle to her shoulder. In, out, in, hold.

Bang!

She squints; it looks like a bull's-eye. She'll shoot twenty bull's-
eyes and take down the tattered target to show him. If she knows
Spence, he'll challenge her to a competition right then and there.
Except she doesn't feel like she knows him anymore.

Bang!

Out of the corner of her eyes, she sees a car winding its way up
Lake Road, away from their place. It's Melody in her father's truck.
There's a trail of dust behind her. She's driving fast. What now?
Kitty wonders. Did Spence tell her he's heading back to Toronto on
Monday? That's what Kitty overheard him saying to Dad.

Bang!

Well, good riddance! she thinks.

Bang!

"I don't mean that, God," she shouts into the wind. She doesn't

165

expect that God is listening. And, anyway, God probably knows. All she wants is her brother back.

Bang!

Her hair has escaped from her jacket and whirls around her face. She pushes it aside and squints again at the target. She goes to look. There's her first shot, pretty well dead center. Then there are three bullet holes fanning out across the target, as if her aim got worse with every shot. She had fired five times. There is no sign of a fifth bullet hole.

Chapter 20

You settle back in your chair by the window on the land side and watch Toronto slip away. You clickity-clack past where you slept last night on a construction site rolled in a painter's drop cloth. The train picks up and speeds past the abandoned building where you've been sleeping for the last few weeks, faster and faster, until you pass by where you were born and where you lived until May, and then the Beaches, where Nanny Dee and Granda Trick lived. Live. Lived. Your whole young life is mapped out along the edge of the lake. You are traveling backward in time. You are slipping right out of life as you know it, Blink.

Pretty soon you're speeding along the shore of Lake Ontario, and since there aren't too many people on this early morning train, you move to the lake side of the car and stare, tired-eyed, out at the endlessness of water, so wide it seems there is no other shore to it. You ride along the crest of a cliff that tumbles down into the sun-speckled water. The Scarborough Bluffs. You've heard of the bluffs, but they might as well have been the pyramids of Egypt, for all you knew.

And the lake . . . God, from up here it stretches to forever. Is this the water in the picture of Alyson? Does she live beside the same lake? You dig the picture out and hold it up to the window with the lake behind it. Could be.

You settle back in your seat. But you can't settle. The excitement of your escape and the anticipation of what lies ahead suddenly give way to the little earthquake that happened back at the train station. More like a blue tornado. If you close your eyes, you can still feel her fingernails scrape your palm as she lifts every last bill from your palm. You squeeze your eyes tight to fight back the tears.

It seems that the world is achingly full of people who want to rip you off. Pretty people, which is what makes it worse.

You have six or seven dollars in your pocket in change, and that's it. Well, if Alyson expects help, she is going to have to pay for it. Big-time. You aren't going to let anything like this happen to you ever again. And getting money out of her was always part of the plan, wasn't it, boyo?

A man comes along with a noisy cart, and you are able to afford a sweet thing that the wrapper claims to be a Danish. It's cold and hard and stale.

You close your eyes, but she's waiting there for you. April. She flits in blue across your mind's eye. Fast. Too fast for you. But you catch her, anyway, tackle her. Take the money back.

You're not sure which is worse: the loss of the cash or the burning humiliation.

It's about three hours to Kingston. You let the girl in blue go, and when you do, you feel giddy inside about what lies ahead, like when you were a kid at Canada's Wonderland, lining up for Top Gun, hoping you'd be tall enough to get to ride it this time. You are going to enjoy this trip despite what happened. You stare out across the gray-green water, the light bouncing off the steely flatness into your blinking, tearing eyes. You squint and see a sailboat. Then, even as you watch, the sailboat keels, capsizes, sinks. All hands lost.

Captain Panic is at work. He isn't happy about the incident at the train station. It confirms his most terrible fears about you. He doesn't want you to think about what might be possible. He only ever wants you to reflect on how stupid you are.

Shhh, you hear another voice inside you whisper. An Irish voice. You aren't stupid, not a bit. Forget the fact that you are heading into what has all the outward signs of being some kind of trap. You are not blind. You told Alyson you'd be arriving by bus at four. Not by train at eleven. That's how un-stupid you are.

Chapter 21

The train rolls on into overcast and leaves the lake behind. There are fields and woodlands, cows, an occasional barn, a silo. Then a glimpse of a highway to your left, clogged with cars heading west toward the city.

You close your eyes but fight off sleep. Fall asleep now and who knows where you'll end up? You rake your hands through your hair, catch a whiff of yourself, examine your fingertips, shake your head in sorry disbelief. There wasn't time for shopping this morning, let alone a cleanup. And now there's no chance of that. You have enough change to use a pay phone. That's it.

* * *

Keep on keeping on, keep on keeping on, keep on keeping on, keep on keeping on, keep on keeping on. Keep on keeping on. Keep on keeping on. Keep on keeping on.

The rhythm of this train.

There is a newspaper abandoned on the seat across the aisle from you. You pick it up, sit back down, stretch your feet out.

There have been developments in the case of the missing mining magnate. A Toronto man has been picked up for questioning. You have a pretty good idea who that might be.

You imagine Stepdaddy being rounded up by the cops with the BlackBerry in his pocket. But the smirk you had ready for this item doesn't quite make it to your face. Where did this little act of revenge get you? It turned around and bit you—that's what.

Let him go, Blink. Let Stepdaddy go. It's time to stop thinking about what you don't want in your life. Look up, out. There's the lake again. The sunshine that was glinting off the water so sharp it made your eyes hurt is gone now, and you can see rain out there on the horizon. You've never seen that before—rain a long way off. It's coming your way.

You turn your attention back to the paper. There are more serious developments. The protestors are calling for a mor-a-tor . . . a moratorium on uranium mining. You don't know what that is, Blink, but you're guessing it isn't a prize. Behind the people with their protest signs, there's a fence festooned with even more signs. There are Porta-Potties and trailers. Some kind of buildings beyond that. A tower. Flags flapping but not of any country you recognize.

You get up and head down the car toward the restroom,

swaying with the train, worse than any streetcar. You try to wash up a bit in the tiny room. Then you head back up the car and stop in your tracks.

April is in the seat next to yours.

She's got her feet up, underneath her. She's staring right at you. She holds out her hand, curled in a fist. Then she opens her fingers to reveal your money.

You sit down beside her tentatively.

"There's two hundred and ninety-four dollars," she says, dumping the cash into your hand. "And fifteen cents." She drops a nickel and a dime onto the bills with her other hand. "I owe you sixty bucks. And close your mouth, why don't you; you're collecting flies."

She turns to look out the window. You close your mouth. You look down at the ragged bills in your hand. Then she turns back to you with a snarl and closes your fingers around the cash.

"Hang on to that," she says. "People can be so wicked."

What are you supposed to say, Blink? Thank you? What are supposed to do? Punch her face in? She's looking out the window again, her arms folded tight around her. The light you saw in her eyes earlier is not there anymore. It was something she put on for her performance. Her mouth is turned down, hard. Her eyes are puffy. Her skin tired. She looks as if maybe somebody already punched her face in, though there are no bruises there that you can see. She looks entirely different from before, her hair for one thing. There had been all those hair clips.

"My name is Kitty," she says. "Not April."

You get up to find another chair.

"Sit down," she snaps. "Or I'll steal your money again."

You sit. You look forward. She's stashed your newspaper in

172

the pocket on the chair in front of you. You should just take it and move. There are lots of seats in this car. Who knows what she'll do next?

"I'm sorry," she says.

Her hands are resting on her legs, her fingers curled a little bit as if she's holding a couple of hand grenades. Then, as if she notices you looking, her hands relaxe, though the fingers are still curled. Now they look like the strong, weary hands of a fighter. The trainer has just pulled off her gloves and unwrapped the tape from her knuckles, but there's no feeling in her hands. You used to watch the boxing with your father on TV. This girl's a fighter, you think. But what fight is she in? What round is it?

"I don't live in Vancouver," she says very quietly, without looking at you. "I'm not going home. Somebody rolled me last night for every cent I had, which is why I hit on you this morning."

You used to go to confession when you were young. That's what Kitty is doing. She's confessing her sins. You wonder why. You don't trust her, but what more can she take from you?

"Well?" she says.

"Well, what?"

"I told you my name; what's yours?"

She's looking at you square in the face. "Blink," you say.

A sly smile cracks her lips. "Good name," she says, before turning away again. You hadn't noticed until then a fat paperback on her lap. Now she opens it and looks as if she's reading.

"Brent," you say. "My real name is Brent."

"Hey," she says, glancing at you. She looks pleased, and it lights up her face, if only for a second, as if knowing your real name meant something to her. Then she turns back to her novel.

173

You sit stunned for another moment and then search out the piece you were reading in the *Globe and Mail*. It's an opinion piece about how some people are "seeing red" over the protest; some people are talking about "Indians on the warpath." Some people are calling the kidnappers no better than terrorists.

"This is not how we do things in Canada," said another guy, a spokesman for whomever. "These people and their never-ending land claims," said an unidentified grouch. Then there's an editorial from the Aboriginal Justice delegation, and this guy's talking about how peaceful and respectful the blockade has been so far. How the Provincial Police have been taking "the high road" in this whole business. They've been using the Major Events Liaison Team—MELT, for short—and all you can figure is that the cops are playing it cool. Nobody's getting his head busted. The writer says that, bottom line, no Indian would be crazy enough to do something like abduct a CEO when there is so much public support for the way they're handling this thing.

SPOIL? Who are they? The whole thing is very suspicious. None of the other environmental groups has ever heard of them.

You put the newspaper down in your lap with a sigh. What is the truth of it?

You turn to your companion. Her finger is on the page, and she's sounding out a word. You look: *Che-fir-ovka*. She snatches the book to her chest. "Do you mind?" she says.

Now you can see the cover of the book: a woman's face against a dark background, ghostly clothes, downcast eyes, sad, full lips.

"The names are all in Russian," she says. "Mostly I just skip over them, but when there's a new character, I sort of try to get it into my head." She grimaces, grunts dismissively, then reluctantly opens the book again.

"Why do you keep reading it if you don't like it?" you say.

She doesn't look at you. "Because it was my brother's favorite book in the world."

Oh, you think. A flock of questions come to mind, but the questions are too jittery to land near such a grumpy girl. So you turn the pages of the newspaper, looking for something else on the story, your story, although it crosses your mind how odd this is—you and this girl reading together on a train. It reminds you of Granda and Nanny when you used to stay with them. When things started getting bad at home. Sometimes they would sit, just like this, in their living room, each in a chair, Nanny reading a novel and Granda reading the paper. You steal a glance at Kitty's face, all concentration now. You smile to yourself and return your attention to the news.

Oh, Blink, my smart friend. You have read more these last couple of days than you ever did in your life. Your brain is hurting from all the information in your brain box, flapping around trying to find someplace to roost, like pigeons scattered by a dog.

You close the paper again and watch the storm roll in. The train moves inland again, so that the lake is just something you catch, a V at a time, between the hills. You miss it already—that huge lake. In all your walking along Queen's Quay or out by the docks at Cherry Street or even out on the island when you took a ferry out there once, for no particular reason, you never knew how big this water was, how wide. And leaving it now feels as if you are leaving the last bit of your home behind. But then home kind of skittered out from under you, anyway, didn't it?

* * *

You stare out at the lake, the summer sun sitting hot and heavy on your sunburned shoulders.

"Ah, there you are, lad." It's Granda's voice, out of breath. "We were wondering where you got to." The water laps against your bare feet. You cross your arms on your skinny chest. "Nanny has made shepherd's pie," he says. "Your favorite, Brent, unless I'm much mistaken." You sniff, wipe your nose.

Granda joins you on the sand. It's a long way down for an old man.

"They just need some time, boyo," he says after a moment, his voice as gentle as the breeze. "Your folks are just going through a bad patch—that's all."

Chapter 22

She puts down her book, her eyes tearing from tiredness. The hour of sleep, two coaches back, took the edge off her weariness, but she feels as if there are months of sleep to catch up on, years.

She told the boy her name. Her real name. It was a gesture—a down payment on the money she owes him. Strange, she thinks, in seven months with Merlin, she never once revealed her real name. That first night they met, when he was taking her to the party, he told her he was Merlin and asked what her name was. Guess, she told him, which is when he came up with Lalalania. They were in a freight elevator in some warehouse—not Drigo's place, some other warehouse where people lived, as if in the parts of Toronto she knew, people were things you kept in warehouses. The elevator arrived at the third floor. He lifted the gate, and they stepped out.

They passed a door with a yellow sign that said:

CAUTION: THIS DOOR MUST BE KEPT CLOSED.

Caution. It became her name right that moment, and now she has left it behind. If Toronto had been her own personal hell, then where was this train taking her? Well, wherever it was, it was taking Kitty Pettigrew. She had dared to tell someone — a skinny street punk — her real name. She has thrown Caution to the wind, she thinks, and laughs. Then she turns, and the boy, Brent, is looking at her expectantly. He's kind of sweet, she thinks, looking into eyes, which are so vulnerable, she wants to kiss them and hold his head to her chest, the way her daddy once used to do, a million years ago when she was not a murderer. A lifetime ago.

"So, where are you really going?" says Brent.

"Away," she answers. He looks puzzled. "I'm not going *to* somewhere," she says. "I'm running away *from* something."

"Ah," he says, looking thoughtful.

"What?" she asks.

"It's the opposite for me," he says, poking himself in the chest.

"Oh, yeah?" she says.

"Yeah," he says. "I've got this plan. I'm going to make some big-time money."

She takes his pointy chin in her hand, the way Merlin used to do to her but not so rough. "Well, aren't you just the smartest thing on two legs," she says.

"Screw off," he says, pushing her hand away. She laughs. "It's true."

She looks out the window.

"Why are you running?" he asks.

"Because I killed someone."

He dismisses this with a snort. "Yeah, right," he says. She doesn't argue. She finds the button to make her seat recline, folds herself up in her chair, and gets to work on those years of rest.

Chapter 23

She wakes with a start, her fists at the ready.

"It's okay," he says.

She's breathing hard, gulping in air. "Like you'd know," she says. She swings around in her seat, scanning the aisle. In her gray eyes, he sees an army approaching. He turns to look, but there's no one.

"Hey," he says, patting her arm.

He watches her recover, calm down. Watches the danger empty from her eyes.

"I was afraid maybe you'd snuck off to tell the conductor," she says.

"About what?"

"About me being a murderer," she says. "The conductor

telephones ahead. And there's all these cops waiting for me once we arrive."

He grins. "No way," he says.

And now she's staring at him. "You're on the run, too," she says.

He shrugs, tries to look away.

She pokes his shoulder. "You are so!" she says. "Tell me." Her demand is too loud—loud enough to disturb a businesswoman, who turns and glares at them over her reading glasses.

"Sorry," says Kitty, waving to her. "My brother here is such a dick." Then they both sink low in their seats, convulsing with laughter.

Kitty turns toward him, her face only inches from his. She sniffs. "Is it you or me stinking up the place?"

He's about to laugh, but she's already tugging on his sleeve. "Tell me," she whispers.

"Tell you what?"

"What you did."

"You first," he says.

She's about to argue, but she stops, considers his face. "I did kill someone," she says.

"Liar."

"A drug dealer," she says.

"How?"

"I cut his coke with rat poison and then stole all his money."

"Liar," he says again.

"The second part is true," she says.

"But you didn't kill anyone."

"I did," she says. "But it wasn't him." And before he can ask any more questions, she squeezes his upper arm tight and says, "Your turn."

He stares at her. He looks in pain, and she wonders what it is that hurts him so much. Then she realizes it's her. She lessens the grip on his arm, rubs the spot with her palm. "Poor baby," she says.

A flicker of gratitude loosens some of the tension in his face but only reveals to her how much else he is holding in. He is not, she thinks, a boy given to secrecy. She doesn't prod him. Doesn't need to. She merely hooks his eyes and reels him in.

"I kind of stumbled into this thing. Saw something. A big-time con job, as far as I can tell. And don't say I'm making it up."

"Who said anything?"

He grabs the newspapers from the pocket on the back of the seat and shows her the stories. She reads a bit. Glances at him, then reads some more. He waits patiently.

"You saw this guy get kidnapped?"

"Yeah, except it wasn't for real. The CEO, this Niven guy, was in on it. It's the truth."

He talks. The words tumble out of him in a stream so thick and fast, she has to listen with her whole being. There is no way he is making this up—no way this boy could imagine such a thing. He may be gullible, but he seems to have a pretty good grasp of this complicated story. On and on the story unfolds, and her weariness, while it doesn't go away, backs off a bit, like crows do from roadkill when a car comes barreling toward them. He is at the wheel of this car bombing down the highway, she thinks, his eyes on high beam. She likes his brown eyes when they will stay still long enough for her to see them. She watches between blinks to catch sight of him again.

Then he stops, and though she doesn't say anything right away, he waits for her to speak . . . waits for . . . what? Approval?

"This Alyson," she says. She waggles her hand.

"What about her?"

She rolls her eyes. "She's obviously in on it."

He gets the victorious look in his eye. "That's why I'm not going by bus, see? I'm not going to play into her hands. The cops would be all over me. I figured that out, easy enough."

She punches him in the arm. Not really hard, but enough to make him wince. "You weren't listening," she says.

"Was, too."

She rolls her eyes. "Blink," she says, "I didn't mean Alyson was in with the cops. I meant she's in on the kidnapping thing. She's lured you up here to get you out of the way. Don't you see that?"

"I thought about that," he says, not very convincingly. "But it's not going to go down like that. As long as I play it my way and not hers, it'll be cool."

She wants to hit him again—hit him hard. How can he be so naive? But she stops herself. "What's she offering?"

"Alyson?"

"No, Her Royal Majesty Queen Latifah. Of *course* Alyson."

"She didn't say. But I want a lot."

"Yeah, well it had better be." Then Kitty throws herself back in her seat and folds her arms, shaking her head. "Whoa," she says.

"I'm not stupid," he says. He sounds like a ten-year-old, and she immediately feels like a bully.

"Maybe not," she says. "But you're lucky I came along."

He frowns.

"Yeah, I know," she says, before he can say anything. "And you'll get the rest of your money back. I already said that. But you see what I'm getting at? You didn't see me coming, did you? Well, did you?"

He reluctantly shakes his head.

"Well, this Alyson chick is playing for way bigger stakes."

"*If* she's in on it," he says dubiously.

"You need me, Blink," says Kitty, "even if you don't know it."

And now a shaky smile grows on his face, and to her surprise his face grows on her.

She remembers something; it comes out of nowhere. Spence staying up late waiting for her. It was when he was home at Christmas just after she turned fifteen. His last Christmas, but they didn't know that. She'd gone to a dance at the school, and he was sitting in the kitchen reading. Said he couldn't sleep, but she saw through it.

"So, how was it?" Spence had whispered so as not to wake their folks.

And she had told him — well, not everything. She imagines now that her eyes must have looked like Blink's: eager, expectant, relieved.

"I want a million dollars," he says. "To start with."

"Yeah?"

"Yeah."

"And?"

"And a place in Beverly Hills." She cocks her eyebrow. "Next door to your place," he says.

She laughs, despite herself. "Well, let's start off by trying to keep your sorry ass out of trouble." She shakes her head. Takes one more look at him grinning at her, then stares out the window. For some reason, she feels better than she's felt in a long time.

There is something totally not right about Blink's story, but her mind is unfocused, reeling a bit under the weight of all that information. Her mind wanders. She looks at him out of the corner of her eye. He's reading the paper again, squinting and blinking. She wants to push the hair out of his eyes. He needs all the help he can get. But she resists the urge. She leans her head on the seat back.

"You know where I was Wednesday morning?" she says. He looks up at her. "When you were tracking down breakfast at the Plaza Regent?"

"Where?" he says.

"I was lying in bed thinking of the best way to leave this guy who was snoring beside me."

"Your boyfriend?"

"Yeah."

"So, he snores really bad?"

"Yeah, and he cheats and lies and . . . and a lot of things."

"The drug dealer, right?"

She nods. "Except I didn't *know* I was thinking of leaving him. What I thought I was thinking was how I could impress him by getting hold of some money that was owed to us."

Blink looks confused, and she doesn't blame him. And she figures maybe if she can explain what happened to this boy here, it will make some kind of sense to her. So she tries.

"He'd gotten in real late. *Real* late. And I was lying there thinking about how Merlin—that's his name—would praise me for being so, you know, resourceful. How maybe we'd

185

get some good food and use some of the money to celebrate with — go out to a club or something."

"But you said — "

"Yeah, I know. I said I was thinking of how to leave him. But I guess what I was doing was making up my mind to do *something* — anything! — instead of just sitting around waiting for . . . I don't even know what."

He's nodding now. He gets this part, at least.

"So I go see the guy who owes us the money, and he asks me flat out am I thinking of splitting. And I swear, I hadn't been thinking of it. Not like on a conscious level. But I guess I was."

"This Merlin sounds like a real badass."

"Absolutely. Except, the thing is, I never really figured I *could* get away from him."

Blink is listening hard. "You were too afraid?"

"It wasn't *just* that. It was . . ." She pauses. Sucks in her lips and bites down hard. Looks out the window. What is she doing? Why is she spilling to this boy she only ever intended to rob?

Then his hand is on her arm. "Tell me," he says, real quiet. "I mean, if you want to."

And she thinks maybe she wants to. Wants to tell this stranger that she had stayed with Merlin because he was what she deserved. He was her sentence and her punishment. But before she can say it, the conductor's voice comes over the public address system.

"Kingston, ten minutes," he says.

Chapter 24

The sky over Kingston looks like someone stuck a giant syringe into it and sucked out all the color.

Kitty doesn't step down onto the platform right away. She hangs back and lets other passengers disembark ahead of her. You stand there looking up at her, afraid you're losing her again. Then you see the fear in her eyes. No, not fear: caution. That's all. Intense caution. And so instead of pleading with her to hoof it, you saunter down the platform, cool as all get out, checking the crowd for the kind of person to be cautious of. You're not sure what to look for. Then you realize that your job is simple: look for someone who is looking for someone. Nobody seems to be. And when you turn back, she has finally disembarked and is walking toward you. The platform is nearly empty.

"Everything's cool," you say.

She laughs and grabs hold of your arm. "Thank goodness," she says in a movie voice. "Our secret formula is safe!" She's making fun of you, but you like her holding on to you so tight, her breast pressed against your arm. Then she drops it. It was all just part of the charade.

You have to go down a set of stairs to an underground passageway that leads to the terminal on the other side of the tracks.

She stops halfway down the staircase, squats to peer along the tunnel, and you realize that no one with any brains would have waited for her on the platform, anyway. They'd be down here or in the main terminal. She'd thought of that. She's warier than you are. Remember that, Blink. And faster.

The way seems clear, but you keep your eyes peeled. You will help her escape if you have to. You imagine throwing yourself in the path of some druggie, taking his feet out from under him while she runs away.

The thing is, people do look at her — maybe it's the clothes: the yellow socks, purple tights, red and blue kilt, and crazy blue jacket. How can they not look? You can hardly stop looking at her yourself.

She gives the terminal a good once-over, twice-over — then relaxes. "I'm going to phone Alyson," you say. But she shakes her head and makes you sit down.

"Tell me more," she says.

"Like what?"

She puts her face in her hands to cover a huge yawn. She's not bored, just exhausted.

"Okay," she says. "Start with how exactly you're going to make this million dollars you're talking about."

It sounds juvenile to hear her throw this back at you. "Well, that was just—"

"Bullshit, I realize that," she says, cutting you off a little irritably. "I just want to hear how you expect to make anything out of this."

This is good, you think: put your gut feeling into words. Forget the picture of the pretty blonde on the lawn for a minute and concentrate.

"The only way to find out for sure Niven is up to something is to check out this idea of Alyson's."

"And her idea again?"

"That he's hiding out at some lodge."

"And she can't go up there herself because . . . ?"

"I'm not sure. Except it seems like she's being watched pretty closely. And, like, with her dad kidnapped and all, she can't just slip away."

Kitty nods. "And how do you turn this information into money if it is true?"

"Well," you say slowly. "If he's up to something and we know about it, then we could, like, maybe make a bundle, right?"

"Blackmail?"

"Yeah."

"Who? Alyson?"

"Well, no. She tells her dad we know or whatever."

"Or whatever . . ."

"Or we take it to somebody," you say. "The newspapers would pay for information like this, wouldn't they?"

"Would they?"

"How should I know?" You shrug again. "But we could find out."

"We?"

You blush—can't help yourself. "I mean me. I could find out."

"You're cute when you blush," she says, with this mocking smile.

"Shut up," you say, punching her arm. "Anyway, the only way we—I mean, I—can find out if there's money in it is to have the information to sell."

She's looking down at the floor. You're not sure if she's thinking or drifting off.

"Why would I want to get wrapped up in this?" she says really quietly.

"Because you owe me," you say.

She snorts and looks away, but she doesn't *go* away. She rests her elbows on her knees and stares across the station.

"Listen," you say, leaning on your own knees, so that your face is near hers and you don't have to talk very loudly. "This could be a trap. I know that. But as long as I'm calling the shots, I figure I can avoid getting caught."

She looks sideways at you. She reaches up and pushes the hair out of your eyes but doesn't say anything.

"We see anything suspicious—anything that looks bad—and we bail. We're outta there. It'll be even easier with two of us."

"Go on," she says.

"If Alyson is telling the truth and we check out this lodge or whatever it is, and we're really careful about how we do it, then we see where we stand. What have we got to lose?"

She smiles again, a faraway smile. It's as if you've finally said the only thing that makes any sense.

"We," you say. "That's the best thing, see? Alyson doesn't

know I've got someone watching my back."

"Yes," she says. She's not looking at you. It's as if she's saying yes to a voice in her head. "I guess that's why I'm here."

"I can, like, cut you in on whatever we make," you say, because you don't want to lose her now. "You're broke, right? If there's no money in it, I'll give you some of what I've got left. You're going to need something, or you might get stuck in Kingston, like, forever."

You both turn to look out the front windows of the train station, where you see nothing but waving yellow swamp grass and trees along a low hill beside a road.

"Yeah, well," she says.

"Will you do it?"

He stares at Kitty.

"Will you do it?" he says.

She sighs, hangs her head. "I don't know," she says. "I don't want to get sucked into this."

"You already are," he says.

She likes the pleading in his voice. She recognizes it. It's her pleading with Spence to let her do something with him, go with him somewhere. She sits up, looks around. She can almost feel him here. She wants to call his name. Spence? Spence, are you here? If he is, it's the first time. So why now? Easy: because of this fool boy who needs her.

"What've we got to lose?" he says again.

And this is the cleverest thing Blink has said so far, although there's no way he would understand why. Suddenly in Kitty's rattled and overtired brain, she sees that he has provided her with the one inescapable truth. She is already a part of this thing. She

191

did it herself. She stole this boy's money and then felt so bad about it she followed him here. She tumbled headlong into this.

So this is now part of the journey. Escaping Merlin was not a complete escape, just a stage. There are some insects that go through a whole bunch of stages before they finally reach their final shape. Something else she learned from Spence. That's what is happening to her. She has left behind the ugly slug of a larva-type thing she had become, and now she's some kind of other creature. She's not in the muck anymore but in this murky water. The sky is yet to come. It's as close to rational as she can get.

"I owe you fifty-nine bucks and change," she says, "not a jail term for aiding and abetting."

He grins at her. He can tell from the tone of her voice that she's not really turning him down.

"Half and half," he says, the big businessman all of a sudden, dividing up his millions. "Not counting the money you owe me."

She punches his arm. It's as close to a "yes" as he's going to get.

You phone Alyson from the train station.

"You're early," she says.

"Just smart," you say.

"I'll come for you," she says.

Funny, your father used to say that, didn't he, Blink? He'd phone out of the blue and say, "I'll come for you." And you'd wait and wait and wait.

"Blink, are you there?"

You want to say okay, but you're holding the receiver so

192

Kitty can listen in, and she's shaking her head.

"No," you say, as coolly as you can. "Where's someplace we could meet downtown? *Is* there a downtown?"

She chuckles. "There's a coffee place on Princess called the Sleepless Goat."

"The what?" you say.

"I didn't name the place," she says. "That's what it's called."

"Okay. Is that far from here?"

"Let me pick you up," she says.

"Just answer the question. Is it like an hour away or what?"

She makes an irritated sound; she's not used to being bossed around.

"It's probably under ten bucks by cab from the bus station," she says, "if that's what you mean."

"What about the train station?"

She pauses for a moment as she takes in the implication of what you're saying.

"You're right," she says. "You are smart."

You beam at Kitty, who makes like she's going to shove her finger down her throat.

"The cab fare is about the same," says Alyson. "I could meet you in half an hour. Say, midday?"

Kitty is shaking her head, mouthing something at you, holding her hand to her head like a phone.

"Uh, no. I'll call you back," you say to Alyson. Kitty nods. "We can figure out when we're going to meet then."

"Stop playing games with me, Brent." She says your name as if it's something she noticed on the bottom of her shoe.

"Forget it," you say. "See you around."

"Okay, okay, okay!" she shouts. "This is serious. That's all I'm saying. I have to know that you understand that."

"I'm here, aren't I?"

"Yes," she says. "But you don't seem to get that this isn't funny. Not for me."

"Getting arrested wouldn't be so funny, either."

"I *told* you. There's no way I can let anyone know that I'm even talking to you."

"That's right," you say, cool as spare change from a businessman's hand. "That's what you told me."

She sounds like she's going to start up again. Then she backs off. "Okay," she says reluctantly. "We'll do this your way."

"Excellent."

Chapter 25

And so Kitty Pettigrew commits herself to Blink. His plan is foolhardy at best, disastrous at worst, but there is nothing new in that. It is the way she has lived her life since last winter. Only now there is someone else to live for. This brown-eyed boy full of spark no matter how smudged around the edges he is—he will be her reason to go on. She can feel Spence beside her, feel his hand on her shoulder, steadying her, preparing her for the recoil.

She borrows some quarters from him to phone Wayne-Ray.

"Who's he?"

"Never you mind," she says, and pinches his ear.

"Owww!" he says. "Jesus."

She pats him. "He's about the only guy in the world I trust right now," she says, owing him some kind of explanation.

"You can trust me," he says, rubbing his ear. "Jesus."

"Sorry," she says. "Apart from you."

Wayne-Ray is at work. He can't talk for long, but she can tell he's glad to hear from her. She remembers not to tell him where she is.

"I'm out of the city," she says.

"Are you heading home?" he asks.

"Not exactly," she says. "Not yet."

"Kitty—"

"I just want to know everything is all right," she says, cutting him off.

"Those people haven't been around, if that's what you mean."

"And Tamika?"

"She phoned me first thing. She's freaking out about . . . you know."

"But nobody's been around her place? No one's hassling her . . . them?"

There. She has told him, just in case Tamika hasn't. She knows about the baby. Knows about Serina, her niece.

"As far as I know, it's cool," he says. "But that money, Kitty . . ."

His voice is reduced to a strangled whisper.

"Tell her I'm sorry," she says. "Tell her to do whatever she wants with it. Burn it if she wants. I gotta go. I love you, Wayne-Ray."

"I love you, too, Cuz."

"Take care." Then she hangs up before he scolds her, before he gets into trouble with his boss. Before she falls headlong back into the mess she left behind her.

196

Blink is waiting for her, looking sullen, as if his ear is still hurting.

You pay the cab fare, and Kitty swipes a five right out of your hand to give the driver.

"Stop doing that," you say as the cab pulls away.

"What? Giving the guy a tip?"

"Not *that*. Stop grabbing money out of my hand."

She just laughs.

You're across the street from the coffee shop Alyson told you about and right in front of a clothing store: Army Surplus & Adventure Outfitters. A good sign. You head inside and start cruising the aisles.

"So, now we're on a shopping spree?" says Kitty.

"I'm not going anywhere looking like this," you say. And she nods as she checks you out.

"You do look pretty preppy," she says, hooking her finger into the filthy and torn cuff of your red full-zip.

"You should get something, too," you say. Her eyes light up. Then she frowns. "Seriously. That thing you're wearing is kind of—"

"Watch it," she says. "I love this jacket."

"It's great," you say. "It's beautiful. But it's kind of like a flashing light, if you know what I mean. You don't exactly blend into the crowd."

She looks down at the fuzzy blue jacket. She runs her hands down the front. It's the first time you've really noticed she has a great body. But the jacket—it's matted, losing fur. It looks like some blue cat with mange lying on the side of the road.

"I guess you're right," she says.

197

You turn your attention to the shelves. Next thing you know, she's calling your name.

"Check it out, Blink," she says. She's modeling a wet suit—holding it up in front of her and doing this catwalk routine. Then she's trying on ball caps and triple-X-size hunters' jackets, and you're laughing despite yourself.

"Can I help you?" says the manager.

You settle on some Sly Gear camo pants and a forest-green fleece hoodie. She finds a denim gaucho jacket, a brown turtleneck sweater, and some jeans. You put them on in the changing room.

"Very camouflagey, dude," says Kitty, snapping off a sales tag. "I can hardly see you at all."

She models her new gear, which gives you the opportunity to look her over. She's skinny but not everywhere.

"Easy, fella," she says.

You pay for the duds and head out onto the street, where you find the nearest trash can. You ball up your filthy clothes and throw them out. The Blessed Breakfast Uniform is no more.

She stares at the blue fuzzy jacket. She shows you the torn lining.

"What happened?"

"Some guy put a bug on me," she says.

"Why?"

She makes a face, like she's trying to figure it out herself. "I guess because he thought he owned me," she says.

"The drug dealer?"

"Right. I worked for him sometimes."

You nod. She may be a good liar but she's a good truther as

198

well, and you're pretty sure by now you can tell the difference. She shoves the jacket down into the trash, then she leans on the can, her hand on either side of the hole as if maybe she's going to barf. But, no, she's just saying good-bye to the jacket. Then she turns to you.

"Ready?"

And you remember something Granda used to say, when you were itching to go to the beach and he was taking too long. "Are you ready, Granda?" you'd ask him, and he'd say, "Ready as I'll ever be."

But Kitty is shaking her head. "I don't know how much money you've got left, but we'd better buy ourselves some toothpaste."

He sniffs the air. "Maybe some deodorant, too, huh?"

You call Alyson again from a phone booth and arrange to meet her at the Sleepless Goat.

"What do I look for?" she says. "Are you going to have a sign or something?" She sounds like she's still pissed.

"I'll do the looking," you say.

"I'll be wearing a peach-colored leather jacket," she says. "I'll be driving a yellow Jeep Wrangler. You want me to wear dark glasses, too, a funny nose?"

"If you want."

"This may be a game to you, Blink, but it's really serious to me." And then she hangs up.

"'I'll be wearing a peach-colored leather jacket. I'll be driving a yellow Jeep Wrangler,'" says Kitty, snapping her hand open and shut like a yapping puppet. "Give me a break!"

You laugh, but it's more nerves than anything.

199

Next thing you know, Kitty is herding you back into the Army Surplus store.

"What?"

"Let's make sure she arrives alone," says Kitty, and finds a place where you can both look out onto the street through the crowded and dusty mannequins in the window.

The Jeep arrives and zips into a parking place just up the hill. You watch as a woman opens the door. It's not her. This woman has jet-black hair. Then you see the short, belted leather jacket. It's pinky-orange colored, all right. And there couldn't be two people in this city with that bright yellow vehicle and that jacket. She beeps the door locked and heads down the street in long-legged designer jeans and high-heeled boots. She must be at least eighteen. Not exactly Daddy's little girl anymore. Funny how you hadn't thought about her aging.

Kitty whistles. "Hot stuff," she says.

Alyson stops outside the Sleepless Goat, looking up and down the street, her arms crossed, her head tucked low into a cream-colored scarf, and tapping the toe of her boot on the sidewalk. She shrugs and heads inside.

"She used to be blond," you say, without thinking, and next thing you know, Kitty's swinging you around to face her, her hands grasping your arms really tightly.

"How do you know what she *used* to look like?"

Her eyes are buzzing accusingly. Like maybe you've been playing her along, holding out, setting her up.

Sheepishly, you pull the photo out of your pocket. "It was in his wallet," you say.

She relaxees her hold on you. "So, now I get it," she says. "Blink's in love."

You feel stupid. Transparent.

"Don't screw around with me," she says.

You look down. You're not sure anymore what you're doing. It's all way harder than you thought.

Then Kitty gives you a playful shove. "Buck up," she says. Then out on the street, she adds, "Go do your stuff, lover boy."

"How'll I know if something's up?" you say, suddenly nervous.

Kitty shrugs. "I'll create a disturbance," she says. "Light myself on fire. Take off my clothes."

You pause outside the café. You look up the street and down, trying to figure out if you'd even know an undercover cop if you saw one. Truth is, suddenly everyone looks like a cop: the brother with the fall-down pants talking on his cell, the fat bearded guy looking in the window of the bookstore, the blue-rinse lady picking up after her beagle. You shake your head. Just go. Kitty is watching out for you. How weird is that — somebody covering your back?

Go on, Blink. Stop stalling. Get yourself arrested.

Chapter 26

There's no way you're staying in that coffee shop. It's nice and cozy, people playing board games. It smells fantastic, but there's no back door that you can see. You are not going to risk getting cornered like that, guard or no guard. How much do you trust Kitty, anyway? Except you do. You will never understand why she came after you. Why she gave you back your money. It's not as if anyone like this has ever happened to you before. There is something about Kitty, an idea inside you trying to peck its way out of its shell, and while you can't exactly see what this creature of an idea might turn out to be, you know that it will have beautiful plumage.

Alyson has beautiful plumage, but she isn't really beautiful herself. She's pretty—that's all. Your stepdaddy used to sing this song to your mother when he was drunk. "She ain't pretty; she just looks that way." That's what you think about Alyson. Funny how that is.

With the introductions made, you head off down Princess again with her by your side. You insist. She is peeved at the "secret-agent game," as she calls it, and you're still checking over your shoulder and looking down every street you come to. Kitty makes funny faces at you whenever you catch her eye. She's about thirty steps behind you.

"Are you sure you're old enough to drive?" Alyson says.

"Trust me," you say.

"I haven't got much choice," she says. "But for Christ's sake, don't walk so fast."

You slow down. A voice is telling you you're crazy to listen to this girl, but it's not Captain Panic's voice anymore. It's Kitty's. It's as if she's beaming warnings at the back of your head.

Alyson stops walking. "Can we just do this?" She's looking at you, hard. She's angry but also nervous.

"Sure," you say.

By now you've walked all the way to the waterfront. There's a little park and a bench tucked between some droopy evergreens looking out over the harbor. A ferryboat slides into view on the green water. The overcast sky is deepening like bruises.

"Okay, enough of this, double-oh-seven," she says. "You said 'trust me' a minute ago. Well, you're going to have trust *me*, as well."

You nod. You almost say, *Yes, miss.* She sits, and you take one last look around. Kitty is sitting on a low parapet keeping guard. Your own personal guardian angel in a denim gaucho jacket.

You plunk yourself down beside Alyson—but not too close.

"Okay, shoot," you say.

She sits with her long legs tight together, her back straight, her black-gloved hands together on her lap, her left hand in her right. She's not looking at you; she's looking out at the water.

"I've got to explain some stuff," she says. "About my father." She pauses, takes a big breath, like this is going to take some time. "He's the president and chief executive officer of this business."

"I know that."

"But that's not who he really is," she says. "I mean, he didn't used to be this big high-powered business type. He studied geology in college and became a prospector. He loved that, I guess: the whole outdoor thing, alone in the woods for days on end. That was before I was born. He spent a lot of his time up north and a *lot* of his time with First Nations people."

She glances at you now, to make sure you're clocking this. You nod for her to go on.

"So all the stuff in the papers about him being dismissive, hostile, arrogant, and not giving a shit about their land claim— that is so not true."

"If you say so."

"I do," she says, and her voice isn't hard anymore. "The court injunction against the Indians and everything? Dad felt really bad about that, okay? Because he has no axe to grind with them."

You nod once and wonder if there's something else you are supposed to do, like maybe take notes. It feels likes a lecture.

"So, anyway. The land legally belongs to QVD. But Dad

hates the press that makes him seem like this tycoon who doesn't give a damn about people's rights. He does. Give a damn, I mean. If it were totally up to him, I think he'd be happy to take an offer from the government."

"Forty-eight million."

And it's as if she suddenly remembers you're there, the way her head snaps back in surprise.

"That's what your dad asked for," you say, because you remember reading it.

"Right," she says. But she's looking at you differently now, kind of calculating, like she's wondering who you really are. Good. Up to now she was looking at you like maybe you should be raking her lawn or something—picking up after her dog.

"That was the initial offer, yes. But I think Dad was going to come down from that. That's why he was in Toronto on Wednesday. He was supposed to meet with the minister of Indian Affairs. Just from stuff he said at home, to Mom and me, I think he wanted to make an offer that showed, you know, a spirit of goodwill or whatever. Something that paid for the investment QVD put into this claim so far but that showed they weren't, you know . . ."

You're not entirely sure what she means, but you don't want to show it, so you nod slowly, and her face lightens a little.

My, my, my. When was the last time a rich girl like this gave you the time of day? You're only half listening. Her face intrigues you. The sculpted eyebrows, the sheen of makeup properly applied. There's a hardness around her mouth. Maybe just stress. She's high class, that's for sure, with her diamond-shaped face, Hollywood teeth, and jewelry-store eyes.

"Are you listening, Brent?" says Alyson.

And you nod, like you knew where this was heading all along.

"I'm sorry," she says. "I just need for you to understand the background a bit."

"Uh-huh."

"So, the thing is, that's what I think Dad would do. And it *is* his company and all, but when they went public—I mean, when they started selling stocks in order to grow the company . . ."

"Grow the company?"

"By selling shares, they could get investments in order to, you know, get bigger. Do more."

"Right."

"Then Dad and his partners suddenly had all these other people he had to satisfy. It's not just his company anymore. And the stockholders, they want a profit on their investment—well, obviously—and so does Dad, of course, but . . . Is any of this making any sense?" she says.

"Yeah, sort of. But why don't you just cut to the chase?"

She smiles back. It's a tight smile, not much twinkle to it, but some of the ice melts in her eyes. "Right. Okay. And this is just . . . I don't know . . . just an idea based on what *you* told me *you* saw." She emphasizes the word "you" both times, as if she's saying that whatever is going to happen is your fault.

"I'm wondering if the pressure from the board was just too much," she says. "Maybe Daddy realized he couldn't do what he thought was right, so he decided to . . ."

"Get creative?"

Her head swivels around to look at you, and there is something like respect in her eyes, or at least she's dumped some of the condescension.

"You could put it that way. Get creative. Exactly."

She takes off a glove and rubs at her temple with long pale fingers, like maybe she's fending off a headache. Then her hand flops down onto her lap again, one white hand in one black-gloved hand. She looks as if she's said as much as she can right now and you're going to have to take over.

"And you think he's up at this place, this lodge?"

"I don't know," she says. "But if he is hiding out, it would be a good bet. And if he is, that means he's okay. Then Mom and I can breathe easy and just cross our fingers and hope this all turns out right."

"So you want me to drive up to this place?"

"Yes," she says. "I'd go myself, but my mother would freak out. I had to beg her just to let me go out this afternoon to meet you." She glances at her watch. "I'm amazed she hasn't phoned yet. She's afraid I'll be next—to get kidnapped, I mean. We've got security guards at the house right now. But I pulled a scene, and she let me go as long as I got back soon."

Then she looks at you—really looks at you like she's trying to decide whether you pass the grade or if this is the stupidest idea she has ever had in her life. And then suddenly she starts to cry.

You stare at her. Those are real tears.

"I'm sorry," she says, sniffing. "I love him so much."

You'd touch her arm if you weren't afraid you'd dirty her peach leather jacket.

She sniffs again, finds a tissue in her purse, wipes her eyes carefully, so as not to smudge her makeup.

"It's about two hours north of here," she says. "There's GPS in the Wrangler. I've already set it for the trip."

You try to think clearly. She's wearing some perfume or it's her shampoo, maybe, but there's this vanilla smell wafting off her, and it is messing with your brain.

"You're the only person I can trust, Brent," she says, mistaking the pause for a change of mind.

"That's okay, but how are you going to explain about the car—the Jeep, I mean? You show up home without it. How do you explain that to your mother?"

She gets this shrewd smile on her face. "I'm on the university newspaper. Queen's is playing U of O, and I'm supposed to cover the game up in Ottawa, but I had to back out because of . . . well, you know, all of this. So I told Mom I was going to lend Jason the Wrangler to cover for me. Jason's another guy on the paper. He doesn't have his own car. Mom's fine with that. Just as long as I'm staying put."

You nod. Good plan.

"So?" she says. And she looks straight at you, her eyes glassy from tears. There is no way she is lying.

You hug your arms to your chest. You're trying to take in the fact that she's in college. You kind of guessed that when you clapped eyes on her, but the fact of it disturbs you for some reason. This was all easier when you thought you were dealing with another kid.

"I don't know," you say, shaking your head.

"Please don't do this to me, Blink."

"What am I supposed to do about gas, food—that kind of thing?"

"Expenses?" she says. You nod. "Obviously, I'll pay for fuel," she says. "And I'll give you money for, you know, food and all that. But, like, you could be there and back tonight, right?" She looks at her watch. "It's only two o'clock. You

208

could be back before it gets dark."

"Yeah . . . but then what?"

"Right," she says. "You'll need a hotel or something. Sorry. I hadn't thought that far. But I'll pay for it," she says. "I'll pay you for you doing this. Is that what you're getting at?"

You nod, but you wish Kitty were here. You wish you could consult with her. But Kitty is your secret weapon—your ace in the hole. Alyson can't know about her.

"I really, really appreciate you doing this," she says. She sniffs again, wipes her nose. "It's a lot to ask. And I'm sorry I was so bitchy. I'm finding this whole thing really hard, okay?"

You nod. "That's cool," you say at last. "But how do you know I'm not going to steal that nice yellow Wrangler, huh?"

She laughs.

"I'm serious. Here you are, handing over your new ride to someone you don't even know, but who you *do* know is a thief. Maybe I deal in stolen Jeeps."

She nods. Then she stares closer at you.

"How come you blink so much?" she says.

"Don't change the subject."

"Sorry. Right. That was rude of me." She taps her brow with one long white finger ending in a perfectly manicured fingernail and says, "GPS works both ways, right? What you did with my father's BlackBerry—planting it on somebody else. Slipping it into your father's pocket?"

"Stepfather."

"Whatever."

"You know that?"

"I told you, Dad's lawyer has been relaying us all the news from the cops—whatever he can get out of them. When it turned out the guy with the BlackBerry was the father—excuse me, *step*father—of the one whose prints were all over the room at the Plaza, well . . ."

You nod. Right. "Don't rub it in," you say.

Just then her cell phone rings.

"What'd I tell you?" she says as she reads the caller ID.

She answers, and it must be her mother. She turns away to talk and leaves you with your own thoughts. You don't know if she can track your journey herself or how that works exactly, but the cops sure could. But if there were cops involved, they'd have jumped you by now. It would be a heck of a lot harder to nab you in a car than out in the open on foot in a city you've never been to before. And so maybe she's telling the truth, but if she doesn't want the cops to know about her daddy's scam . . .

You glance back at Kitty. She gives the peace sign.

Can you do this? Drive up north somewhere, check out whether Jack Niven is hiding out at this place of his, and if he is, then beetle on back? And if he isn't, well, then maybe he has truly been kidnapped. Sure, she'd want to know that. And it is true she can't tell the authorities, because if this is a con game her father is playing—if that's what's going down—he'd be in big trouble.

Besides, Blink, admit it—you are *dying* to drive that Wrangler.

"Okay, Mom. Yes. I will. Love you. Love you. Promise."

She flips her cell closed. "I've got to go," she says. "She's totally freaking out."

She's done all the talking she's going to do and lets her eyes take over. They're on you now, and even you can't blink away this alien tractor beam.

You snap back to consciousness and then, picking up her

arm gently, twist it in order to look at her watch. Heading on to two thirty. Everything goes all right, you could be at this place by five — six at the outside. Sun won't go down until six thirty or so. You know that well enough. So the drive back would be in the dark, but what the hell. There's just one thing left niggling inside you.

"Okay," you say. "But I still want to know — "

"How much?" she says.

You nod.

She stands up. "Let's talk about that," she says, "while we walk back to the Jeep."

Chapter 27

He sits in the driver's seat, with Alyson leaning in the open door, showing him what's what. Kitty situates herself at the corner of the intersection half a block away. When she thinks Blink is looking, she points to the left down a side street. Blink nods, but then he's nodding away as Alyson indicates this and that, and Kitty has to hope that one of those nods is intended for her.

She waits at the corner of Wellington and Queen, leaning against a telephone post. As soon as the Jeep turns the corner onto Wellington, she crosses Queen and starts heading up the street. A moment later, he makes a left turn onto Queen and pulls over, and she heads around to the driver's door. He rolls down the window.

"What are you doing?"

"I'm driving," she says.

"No way!"

"Yes way," she says. "Because I've actually got a driver's license."

"So do I!"

"No, you don't," she says. "You're not old enough."

"I'm sixteen."

"As of last month. Your birthday is in September, Mr. Virgo."

She's got him, but he won't give up. "So? I got my license right away."

"Oh, really? You've been living on the street for six months, and you just show up at home and borrow the car to take your test? And how did you pay for it?"

"I'm driving," he says, gripping the steering wheel with both hands, like a toddler who won't get off the merry-go-round.

"Fine," she says. "And when we get pulled over, you say, 'Oh, Mr. Officer, sir, stupid me. I forgot my license at home, which, by the way, no longer exists. But that's okay, right, Mr. Officer?'"

"I know how to drive. I'm not going to speed. We won't get pulled over."

"The cops don't need a *good* reason to pull over a couple of ugly, screwed-up teens in a brand-new hot yellow car. Now move it, or we're going to be here all night."

He stares at her.

"What?" she says, not exactly pleased to be standing there arguing.

"You aren't ugly," he says.

He gives in. But he won't talk to her. She can feel the heat

213

of his resentment. He's a funny boy, she thinks. She adjusts the rearview mirror and takes the opportunity to look at herself. Doesn't he see how ugly she is?

They head northwest up Princess and north on Highway 38 out of Kingston. It's all mapped out. There's a voice coming out of the dashboard to tell her what to do and when. It's dead easy. But kind of strange, too, because the voice doesn't tell you any place-names, just gives you directions.

"Turn right in five hundred meters."

"Thanks," says Kitty. "What's your astrological sign?"

"You're talking to the dashboard," says Blink.

"Oh, good, you're still alive," she says. And he goes all-over sullen again.

Fifty bucks an hour, plus expenses, plus the cost of his trip from Toronto, the trip back, gas, food, and the hotel for tonight. That's what Alyson offered him. She told him which hotel to go to, said she'd book a room for him. He told Kitty when they first started out, before he clammed up on her.

"Where does she get money like that?"

"That's what I said. And she said it was her university fund."

Kitty shakes her head. "This stinks," she says. "She's got it all worked out. Doesn't that seem a bit unreal?"

"Drive straight for the next forty-five kilometers." The dashboard voice is English. Some Englishwoman.

"I'll think about it," says Kitty.

The money obviously doesn't include her. So, assuming this all goes well and Alyson keeps her side of the bargain, they're going to end up with something like three hundred dollars, split two ways. That was what Blink told her, kind of proud.

"Not exactly a million," she says.

214

"That comes later," he says, but she can hear the reservation in his voice. The reality of the thing is not living up to his daydream. Lucky he has her along, she thinks, and then hopes that she's right about that. Maybe she'll end up screwing things up even worse.

She sighs.

"You okay?" he says.

She smiles at him. "I'm as nuts as you are," she says.

How far will one hundred and fifty bucks get her? Kitty wonders. Back to Toronto, sure, but is that wise? Hardly. And yet there is unfinished business there. Important business.

You come back to me, sister. Do you hear what I'm saying?

Then she remembers that she owes Brent sixty of those dollars. So where will ninety dollars get her?

You are angry at this brash girl. Mostly you're angry because you wanted to drive, but you know she's right. Any run-in with the law would be disastrous. But you *can* drive—you've been driving since you were fourteen. Taught yourself in Stepdaddy's Grand Prick.

It was a time when he was working. Took the subway every morning and didn't get back until after six. So there was that ugly old Pontiac sitting out front, collecting bird splatter all day long. And there were his keys just lying around in an ashtray in the front hall. It was a happenstance waiting to happen.

But you weren't joyriding with your friends. You were looking for someone, weren't you, boy? Up to Woodbine Racetrack, just west of the city; down to Flamboro Downs outside Hamilton; out to Mohawk Racetrack in Campbellville. Looking for a trainer by the name of Ginger Conboy. Little bandy-legged

Irish fella, former jockey, who still had the Old World accent—or at least he could put it on when it served his purpose. He had a gift with horses but not much of a gift with fatherhood. Still and all, he was a better man than Stepdaddy. And what better way to find him than in Stepdaddy's own car?

Except you never did. People knew of Ginger. Somebody told you he'd headed west—maybe California. Somebody else thought maybe he was dead. You never found him. But you did learn to drive.

It was Ginger Conboy who took you to a hotel, just that once. He would show up sometimes out of nowhere. This was before Stepdaddy moved in. And there he was one bright Saturday morning, like a leprechaun springing up out of the ground, wanting to see his one and only, all cheery and full of blarney. Your mother didn't want to have anything to do with him, but she was glad enough to see the back of you, Blink, my lad, for a day or two, and so off you went with Da. That's what he wanted you to call him: "Da."

He took you to the Delta Chelsea. He'd come into some money, he said, and you wondered—prayed—that this meant he and your mother could get back together now. But all it meant was the one night at the Delta Chelsea. You never saw any money after that. Never saw much of Ginger again, either. But what a night it was, flipping channels, watching a movie, right there in the room. You could order anything you wanted from room service, and they brought it right up, all nice on a trolley with the silver cover over the hamburger to keep it warm and the ketchup in a little bowl with its own little silver spoon and all. And when it was done, you just shoot the tray out the door into the hall and let someone else take care of the dishes.

So these are the things you learned from Ginger: how room service works and how to drive a car to try to find a father.

"Bear right at the next intersection."

"Oh, I was thinking maybe I'd just crash into the yield sign instead," says Kitty. "Thanks for the suggestion."

"Stop doing that," says Blink.

"I hate her know-it-all voice," says Kitty. "And she's English. What's with that? They drive on the opposite side of the street."

"You can change it," he says. "You want a guy's voice? You want it to speak to you in French? German?"

"It can do that?"

"That's what Alyson said."

"Hmmm." She thinks a minute. "How about Bart Simpson? No. How about Homer Simpson? Even better."

"Then we'd have to stop at every donut place," says Blink.

"Like, you see any donut places?"

"Well, I can't help it if we're in the middle of frigging nowhere."

He's not really angry anymore, she figures. They're on a road trip. Who can stay angry on a road trip? And even though she knows that the GPS means that someone can track where they are, she finds it hard to believe anyone could find them out here.

She had almost forgotten this feeling of being out in the larger world. Which is funny, because when she was at home and tried to imagine Spence at school in Toronto, she always thought that the city was the larger world—a heck of a lot larger than Wahnapitae. But driving on this winding highway, heading north, catching glimpses of lakes and distances, she wonders. Her time in the city seems like a trap to her now. A nightmare. She has the urge to turn off this wooden woman's voice doling out directions and just keep on driving, heading north until she finds the Trans-Canada. It must be up here somewhere. Find the Trans-Can and head west. Let them try and keep track of her! There are places, she knows, that are beyond the range of satellite signals.

She glances at Blink. He's looking out his window. He feels distant, although he's only an arm's length away. She wants company. So why does she jump all over him whenever he says anything? If she's going to watch his back, she could at least try being a bit friendlier.

"We had this dog," she says. "Scooter. He was a Lab. He was really nuts. And he kept getting lost. So, Spence—he's my brother—suggests we look into getting a dog-locator device. It's this thing you attach to the dog's collar. And if he runs away or gets stolen, you can just track him down."

Blink has shifted in his seat. Out of the corner of her eye, she is aware of him looking at her.

"I really wanted us to get it—this dog gizmo. I loved Scooter, and I was afraid he'd get so lost we'd never find him again. Or maybe, you know, wolves would get him. Or a bear. But the thing is I got kind of mixed up. I thought that this thing would guide him home, you know?"

She glances quickly at Blink. He nods.

"I thought it would guide *him* home," she says again. She wants him to say something, laugh—anything. "Pathetic, huh?"

"Not really. I mean, you were like this kid, right? What do kids know?"

She doesn't answer. There is no answer.

218

The forest is pimped up with fall colors, ludicrously bright. Over-the-top bright, even on this mostly sunless day. The leaves seem to exude their own light. She imagines they might actually shine at night, though she knows well enough that that isn't so.

The trees are barer than back in Toronto, Kitty thinks, but there are so many more of them. It feels a bit like home, although the maples back home hardly ever amounted to much. She almost wants to pull over and turn off the engine and listen to the sound of nothing. Of air and birds.

"It's kind of beautiful, isn't it?" she says.

"No way," he says. "It's freaky. I've never been out of the city until this morning. Not ever."

"Sometimes in Toronto, I'd go out to High Park or the Forest Hill ravine and close my eyes and try to pretend I was home again," she says. "Out in the country again. But even with my eyes closed so I couldn't see the joggers and dog walkers, there was always the hum of it. The city. The machine— that's what I called it."

She glances at him.

"For me, it was this huge machine that never got turned off. I kind of loved it at first. The worst thing in the world is silence," she says. Then she stops, because without really meaning to, she's gotten too close to the truth.

"What do you mean?" he asks.

She shrugs. "Nothing."

In silence she had to face the screaming in her head. That's what she meant. The city was like a drug that took the edge off the scream, hid it at least. Her scream merged with a million other screams. On the street, pretty well everybody she met looked as if they had some major scream going on inside their skulls. There was this thin wall of bone holding it in. She could see it in their eyes. She wondered what would happen if all the lonely people let it out at the same time. She imagined the city quaking, collapsing like in some apocalyptic movie—*The Day After Whatever.* She remembers expecting it to happen any day. Waiting for it. But now, up here, driving north, she wonders if the scream she took with her to the city is even in her anymore. In her hurry to leave, did she leave it behind?

"I've never seen so many fucking trees," says Blink.

She laughs. It explodes out of her, too loud in this enclosed place. It makes him jump.

"I'm not kidding!" he says. "There's nothing *but* trees."

"I was born in the country," she says.

"So, not Vancouver?"

"I already told you that was a lie."

"Oh, right. But I'm supposed to believe you were born in the country?"

She nods. "An ant fart of a place called Wahnapitae, up near Sudbury."

"Where there are wolves and bears," he says.

"Yes." She's pleased he remembered her saying that. "I grew up on a little farm on a lake. Not a real farm. I mean, we grew stuff, but Dad had a full-time job as a mechanic and Mom was a preschool teacher."

He's watching her again. She glances his way, slips him a smile. Is this her way of trying to convince him she's telling the truth?

"So what happened?" he says.

"What do you mean?"

"Why'd you leave?"

She grips the wheel tight. "I already told you. I murdered someone."

"Now you're lying again."

"I am not."

"Yes, you are. I can tell. All that stuff about your mom and dad sounded like the truth. The murder sounded different."

"Well, what do you know about it? Somebody got killed. I killed him. How does that sound?"

He doesn't say anything for a bit. Maybe because you bit his head off.

"I believe you," he says.

"Thanks."

"But those are two different things."

"What do you mean?"

He lifts his feet up and puts them on the dashboard. He wraps his arms around his knees.

"If I killed my stepfather," he says, "*that* would be murder."

She waits, but he doesn't go on. She wants him to complete the equation, but when she thinks about it, he doesn't really need to. She knows what he's saying: that you can kill someone by accident; that it's only murder when you mean to do it. And she *didn't* mean to kill Spence. It *was* an accident. Everybody *told* her it was an accident. Nobody *blamed* her. Nobody but herself.

"Was it your brother?" says Blink.

She can't think how he figured that out. She wonders, suddenly, if this is just the next stage of the nightmare. The part that seems like escape but isn't. Because you can't escape. Not ever.

"Yes," she says.

Chapter 28

The sun dips below the cloud cover, the first you've seen of the sun since early this morning. There are people out on a lake you pass by, people fishing. Sitting on top of their reflections, on a lake so green it makes your eyes water. Green and burning in the sun trapped between the clouds and the earth.

You're tired, Blink. Reluctantly you admit to yourself that it's lucky Kitty is driving. You glance at her. She's closed up again. When she said that about her brother getting killed, you wanted to reach out and touch her, but you were afraid to. Afraid of what she might do. But maybe you could say something.

"I'm sorry," you say, and immediately wish you hadn't.

"Not as sorry as I am," she says. "I am the sorriest excuse for a human being who ever walked the earth."

"That's bullshit."

"Yeah, thanks but—"

"No, I mean it. I don't know what happened—how it happened. And you don't have to tell me or anything—I'm not asking you to. But it was a mistake, wasn't it?"

"Was it?"

"It must have been. I know it was."

"You do, huh? Suddenly you're Mr. Know-It-All."

"Yeah, I am." You swallow, rub at your eyes. "I'm not stupid. I know you think I am, but I'm not."

She frowns. "I never said you were."

"You don't have to. I can tell. But I don't care. Because I'm not stupid."

"Okay, okay, you're not stupid. And I'm not the sorriest excuse for a human being. There, are you happy?"

"No."

"No?"

"No. I'd be happy if you let me drive."

She laughs, and you like the sound of it. You settle back into your seat. You didn't get much sleep last night in your drop-cloth bed. And today has been like no day you've ever even dreamed of—the third day of the weirdness. You yawn—a big one—but keep your eyes on the road, just in case she decides to veer off it and plunge the car into a lake and kill you both.

"Turn left at the T intersection coming up in two-point-five kilometers."

"Anyone ever tell you you're hot?" you say.

"Go back to sleep," says Kitty.

"I was talking to Direction Lady," you say. "And I wasn't asleep."

223

You feel good. Where's Captain Panic? Must have jumped ship. You don't feel one bit of badness inside you out here on this winding highway heading north.

"You are pretty hot," you say.

"Shut up," she says, laughing.

"Just not as hot as Direction Lady."

She laughs. That's what you wanted. To hear her laugh.

You've got this little job to do, right? You get to this place, park the Jeep, make your way down this private road until you get to the end of it, and there's the lodge. See if anyone's there, and get the hell out. Done. And, best of all, there's two of you.

"What if, like, somebody else is there?" you asked Alyson.

She shrugged, and her eyebrows came together, what there was of them, because she's plucked them right down to narrow gashes. "I don't know," she said. "Keep watching, I guess. You know what he looks like, right?"

"Your father? Yeah."

"Well, if he is there—and if I'm right—he won't be a prisoner. He's bound to make an appearance sometime."

You nodded. Then you remembered something. "Right. He'll have to come out sometime to use the can."

"Right." She frowned, looked away, as if the memory of that outhouse haunted her all these years later. Then she snapped out of it. She looked at you like you were smart—like you'd been paying attention. Hell, yes! You'd been listening and looking and reading the signs like never before.

The T intersection turns out to be pretty well the end of Sharbot Lake, even though Kitty didn't exactly remember the beginning of it. There is no place to eat except a Petro-Can station at the junction of Highway 7. She pulls the car into the lot, and they get out to stretch and use the restroom. Inside, they stock up on chips and chocolate bars and sodas.

The air is clean out here, even on a major thoroughfare. It's been a while since Kitty has smelled clean air. But there isn't time to stop now. Blink is antsy to get going. He pleads with her to let him drive, but she's not taking any chances. They head off again, west like the lady says. It's less than an hour away.

"Turn right, two hundred meters."

"You got it, lady."

There's a big stop sign at the corner of Highway 509, and somebody's attached a yellow balloon to it. The balloon bops around in the wind.

"Huh," says Blink. He's looking at it, too.

"Somebody's having a birthday party," says Kitty. "That's how folks know where to turn. Hey, why don't we crash the party?"

"Very funny," says Blink.

Above the yellow balloon is gray-green rock face, a craggy bit of cliff with a ghost-eye tree on the top of it.

This is the last leg, and in between mouthfuls of Doritos and slurps of Cherry Coke, Blink has started talking excitedly.

"Where are you going to go with your half of the take?" he says.

"Moscow," she says.

"No, seriously."

"Who says I'm kidding? What about you?"

"I don't know. Hey, maybe I'll go to Moscow, too. Maybe we could keep the Wrangler and, like, drive there." Kitty's mouth gapes. "Kidding," says Blink.

"Mr. Geography," she says.

He's rocking back and forth in his seat like some kid on his way to a paintball competition.

"Knock it off," she says. But she's picking up on his excitement, pressing down a little too hard on the accelerator. She catches a look at the speedometer and pulls back to the speed limit, which is good, because it means she doesn't have to squeal to a stop when three deer burst from the bush at the side of the road. She swerves, and the Wrangler shimmies a bit as the brakes do their thing. Then she swears a whole lot.

"You are so strung out," says Blink.

"I am not!" she says.

"It's cool," he says. "No one got hurt."

This new enthusiasm of the boy's is maddening. She liked it better when he was half asleep.

"Are deer always that dumb?" he asks.

"Always," she says.

Then suddenly he's yelling. "Look at that!" And she almost slams on the brakes again, but he's only pointing at a sign: a road to some settlement.

"What about it?"

"It wasn't like a town or a village," he says. "It was a 'settlement.' Like we've gone back in frigging time or something."

She lets out her breath in a long, slow exhalation. She is getting more and more nervous. Less than half an hour ago, she had been feeling good about being out in the open again. But now she feels a bad case of paranoia coming on — the playing out of the nightmare. She feels herself reverting to the girl she became in Toronto. Caution: Watch Your Step.

226

"A settlement," says Blink, shaking his head.

"Yeah, and next we'll be seeing ox carts," says Kitty. "And guys with flintlock rifles."

"Whatever."

"That's what I'm afraid of," she mutters.

"Flintlock rifles?"

"No!" she says. "Whatever. This whole setup. It stinks. You do know that, don't you?"

He stares at her. "Chill out," he says.

"No!" says Kitty. "Blink, I'm not sure about what you think is ahead, but I've got this really bad feeling it might be . . ."

She can't think of what to say.

"A chance to make a million dollars?" he says.

"Ha! I was thinking more along the lines of a Date with Destiny." He doesn't say anything at first, but she can almost hear him thinking. "What?" she says.

"You didn't see her," he says. "Up close."

"I saw enough. She's in on this."

"You didn't see her when she cried," he says.

"You think a girl can't fake cry? A girl can fake a lot of things if it gets her what she wants. What she thinks she wants."

"She wasn't faking. I trust her."

"You trusted *me*," says Kitty. "Look where that got you."

"Here," he says.

"You know what I mean."

"Okay," he says. "I trusted you. And I was right."

She doesn't know what to say to that. But it doesn't matter because suddenly Brent is yelling at her again. "Stop! Holy shit! Stop!"

She slams on the brakes, leaving a trail of rubber on the blacktop. Luckily no one is behind her. She eases the car onto the shoulder. "Are you trying to get us killed?" she says.

"Look."

She looks, sees nothing. He jabs the air with his finger. She looks again, squints. There is a road sign. He's pointing at the road sign. She reads it. Conboy Road.

"I don't get it," she says.

"Conboy," he says. "That's my name. Brent Conboy."

"So you've got your own road," says Kitty.

He nods. "I've never seen my name anywhere," he says. "It's, like, so cool."

She wants to say, *So this is why you nearly gave me a heart attack,* but she holds her tongue. She looks at him, sees his eyes shining as if that stupid tilted road sign was an omen or something. And she sort of gets it. "It's like there's this place in the world where you've got a name they put up on signs."

"Yeah," he says.

She stares at his profile until he looks at her. "Sorry," she says.

"For what?"

She shrugs. She leans her forehead on the steering wheel, closes her eyes. She wills Spence to come down out of the sky and comfort her, lay his hand on her shoulder again. Then suddenly there *is* a hand on her shoulder.

"You okay?" says Blink.

"What do you think?"

He squeezes her shoulder. "I think we don't have much choice what to do. You know?" She nods. "Like, we've come this far."

She nods again. And she thinks just how far she's come.

How far back in time this car ride into nowhere really began.

"Nothing's going to happen," he says. "Trust me."

"Oh, good," she mutters. "Now I feel a whole lot better."

She checks over her shoulder, puts the car in drive, and pulls back onto 509. She concentrates on the road. This boy has such faith, she thinks. She doesn't. She can only see that it is going to go badly. And here she is chauffeuring him to whatever badness lies ahead. How has this happened? Why has she crossed paths with this odd blinking boy? Then the answer comes to her: to tell him. To tell someone.

"After what happened . . . after what I did . . ." She finds her mouth is dry. She remembers her soda, takes a swig.

"I'm listening," he says.

"After that . . . what I was talking about . . . I felt like nothing was real. It was"—and this is new to her, the first time she's thought of it—"it was as if I were the one who was dead. I killed my brother. But I killed myself, only I didn't know it. And all this—everything that has happened since then is just . . ."

"Purgatory?" says Blink. She glances at him nervously. "Right?" he asks her. She shrugs.

"My family wasn't all that religious," she says. "I sort of know what purgatory is, but . . ."

"It's like this big chill-out," says Blink. "God is so pure, he can't look on any evil—not even the tiniest of sins. That's what my mother used to say. So even if you've been this totally good person all your life, you're probably not good enough for heaven. So you have to hang out in purgatory for whatever— a million years or two—to clean up your act."

A weak smile lights up his brown eyes. "Just because I

didn't pay attention in geography," he says, "doesn't mean I don't know where purgatory is."

"Yeah?"

"Grew up there. I mean, my mother was living in it already. And I guess the idea rubbed off on me."

Kitty doesn't speak. There was more to say . . . or was there? What good was talking, anyway? Then she feels his eyes on her again and realizes that she likes it. Likes him checking on her, like a patient in a hospital who wakes up from time to time and there's someone sitting beside her bed.

"Is that sort of the place you feel you're in?"

"Maybe," she says. "Walking around, waiting for someone to tell me, *Oh, by the way, you're dead.*"

She glances quickly at him, her eyes uneasy, as if maybe he's the messenger with the news. But instead of saying anything, he reaches out and touches her again, softly on the arm. And this time she places her hand on his, squeezes it but not too tight.

There is kindness in his face: all that hope brimming in his eyes! But then the person who would finally tell her she was dead probably would be an angel, she thinks.

"Are you the one?" she says.

"What?"

"You know. Like I said."

He screws up his face. "The one who's going to tell you you're dead?"

She frowns. "I guess not," she says.

"Well, don't sound too disappointed."

She smiles and lets go of his hand.

"I'm sort of in the same boat," he says. "I mean, I feel like I'm not anywhere."

He tells her how he felt up there on the sixteenth floor of the Plaza Regent, as if none of what he was seeing was really happening—none of it real.

"I had this dream the other night that instead of throwing me the room key, the guy named Tank actually noticed me standing in the ice room and shot me."

"Exactly!" says Kitty. "That's what I meant."

"And everything after that was just trying to, you know, come to grips with being dead."

"I know. Which would explain why we'd come across a road with your name on it," she says. "If it were true, I mean. Like we're actually driving to somewhere that doesn't exist on a mission that can't be completed. That's purgatory maybe."

Then Kitty slaps the steering wheel. "Welcome to my world," she says. They bump fists.

"So we keep going, right?" he says.

"Why?" she says.

"Until we find a road with your name on it."

A road with her name on it. Right. Keep your eyes peeled, she tells herself. But instead of Pettigrew Road, there don't seem to be any more roads at all, other than the one they're on.

Then the voice of the dashboard lady startles them both.

"Bear left, five kilometers."

Chapter 29

Highlands. The word comes to you, like a word you know but never had the chance to use before because there aren't any highlands in the city. And so even though the sun is halfway down the western sky, you feel that as long as you keep climbing, it will never get dark. You can see so far. And there's another word that you never had much use for in the city. Far.

But the dashboard lady is finished now. She's given her last directive. There are no maps of this place in the GPS unit. Probably no cell service, either. You're on your own. And even though Alyson warned you this would happen, it feels spooky, after the discussion you've been having with Kitty.

The forest seems to close in, and those highland glimpses of a far horizon are soon enough lost.

"About twenty minutes after we pass through Snow Road, we're supposed to come to this broken-down log cabin on a rocky rise high up on the right."

"There are tons of broken-down log cabins," says Kitty.

"Yeah, but this one has a tree growing right through the middle of it."

Kitty starts to slow down. "Whoa, what did you say?"

"Alyson told me there's a tree growing through—"

"I heard that. But she hasn't been here since she was—what'd you say? Eleven?"

"I know. That's what I said—'You remembered this from when you were eleven?'"

"And she said . . ."

"She got all kind of shifty looking, then told me she had been here again. This summer. On a little adventure—that's what she said—with some guy."

"Ah, poor Blink," says Kitty. "You're taking it pretty well."

"Cut it out," you say. "She's so not my type."

You both laugh.

"A total Ice Queen," you say, and are about to go on when Kitty interrupts you.

"There," she says. And up on a rise is the landmark in question: a cabin pierced by the thick trunk and heavy branches of a giant oak.

"Okay," you say, excited now. "It's about five hundred meters on the left." You sit forward, your hands on the dash. "And we're supposed to take it really slow when we turn off, because the entrance dips down real steep."

"Got it," says Kitty, "and there'll be this small army waiting for us."

You peer to the left and right. "They must be hiding real good."

She slows down but doesn't stop—drives right by the turnoff.

"Hey!" you shout.

"Shh!" she says.

"But you missed—"

"I didn't miss anything," she snaps. She's crawling now, her eyes flitting to the rearview mirror, although there hasn't been any traffic for ages.

"What are you doing?" you say to her, looking back as you round a long, slow bend. Your turnoff disappears behind you.

"I thought you said you were going to play this your way," she says. "So that's what I'm doing. We'll find our own place to park, okay?"

You nod. Alyson had told you exactly what to look for, exactly where to go. And you'd trusted her because she had cried. You're still sure she wasn't lying to you, but Kitty is right. You know that, as well.

There is another turnoff on the left not so far along. She pauses at the lip of the hill, surveying the scene before her. You want her to hurry up, but you know she's right. Be patient, boy.

She groans. "Well, here goes nothing," she says. Then she eases the Jeep down the steep and rutted entranceway.

There is a sign nailed to a tree: TUMBLE ROAD.

"Hey," you say. "It's the same name she told me. Weird."

"Yeah, so that other turnoff and this one are the same road, which is good. Because we're like a good country mile from where they're expecting us."

"No one is expecting us."

"Fine. But I'm a lot happier here, if that's okay with you."

She isn't really asking, so you keep your mouth shut.

She drives slowly now, looking for someplace to pull off. Light glints through the trees in an eerie way—too bright— like there's a *Close Encounters* mother ship over there, just landed in the forest. It's not sunset yet, but the two of you are wrapped in shadows. Then you come to a rough cleared place, and she veers right into the brush, so that it rubs against the sides of the car. You instinctively pull your arms in tight against your sides. It's like panhandlers all around the vehicle bending down to look inside.

She maneuvers the car until it is facing out onto Tumble Road but pretty well hidden. Then she stops and turns off the ignition. You catch the time on the dashboard just as the lights go out.

"It's not even five," you say. "We've got lots of time."

"I hope so, because there's not going to be any moon."

"Really?"

She shakes her head. "Trust me. And you're not going to want to be stuck in bush this dense after dark."

You stare straight ahead at an impenetrable wall of green. "So we'd better get a move on, right?"

She nods, her face all business. But neither of you move. And the quietness rushes into the Jeep.

"No army," you say, but you whisper it.

"Not so far," she says.

You climb out, close the doors quietly. She pockets the key.

235

"No one should be able to see the car," you whisper.

"I guess," she says. "But I wish the damn thing were green."

You're still a ways from the turnoff, and then it's another kilometer to the lodge, according to Alyson's directions. You walk in the eerie silence along Tumble Road. Then you stop and without saying a word point ahead. Kitty nods; she's seen it, too, about a hundred meters ahead: another turnoff. And beyond it is a clearing where an old tractor sits. The tractor is ancient, with metal wheels and spokes—an overgrown antique sitting in a clearing. That's where you were supposed to park. She pulls you into the bush. You watch and wait. You make a move to go, and she stops you, her finger on her lips. You do as she says. You are in her territory now.

Finally, she gives the go-ahead. You make your way to the new road that goes off to the right.

PRIVATE ROAD says the sign nailed to a tree trunk. NO EXIT. It has no other name. The road is downhill, a long, slow decline. There are many turns, a winding path, sandy, with soft-looking grass growing between the tracks and everything covered with pine needles. There are alien fluorescent orange toad stools.

Kitty suddenly stops.

"What?" you whisper. But she doesn't answer, just stares into the bush and up into the canopy. You follow her gaze. See nothing.

You remember what she said about wolves and bears up where she was from. You're not sure how far that is from here, but these woods look like they're jam-packed with carnivores. Who knows what's in there, you think: cougars, wildcats, a madman with a hockey mask and machete.

You want to get this job done, climb back into the safety of that yellow Jeep, open up a bag of SunChips, and beat it back down to Kingston—mission accomplished. Instead, you pick up the pace. You have no idea how long this road is, but before you know it you're running.

Suddenly you're aware of being alone.

You stop and turn around. Kitty has fallen behind. She's leaning against a tree, not casually but as if the tree is holding her up. You head back. She's breathing hard.

"Are you okay?" you whisper right up close to her ear.

She shakes her head. "We could lie," she says. "We could just turn around and head back. Tell the Ice Queen the place was empty. Take the money and run."

You think about it. Now that you're here, the whole thing is a lot scarier. But you shake your head. "Yeah, but then there's no way we can make any *big* money. We only get three hundred measly bucks."

"Don't be so greedy," she says. She's looking scared, and that scares you because she doesn't seem the type.

"What is it?" you say. Something is eating her.

She looks around. She rubs her hands up and down her thighs.

"This place," she says. "I don't know . . ."

"If we see anything, we split," you say.

"It's not that," she says. "Listen."

So you listen. "I don't hear anything," you say.

"Exactly," she says. "No birds. No animals. Nothing."

You touch her arm, and she shrinks from you. "Kitty," you say, pleading a bit. "Don't cack out on me now. We've got to find out for sure." And right then—right that very instant—

237

you think you hear laughter. You listen hard. You're sure you heard something.

Was it your imagination? Or was it the Captain, having a good laugh? Funny how you haven't thought about him in . . . well, pretty much since you met Kitty. But now that she's gone all psycho on you, he's back, just like that.

"It's not natural. The quiet," she says. Then she seems to snap out of it. She stares hard at you, and then she smiles. The fear is still there, but she's smiling through it. "I won't let you down," she says. And for some reason, that only makes it worse. But you nod.

"I'll hang back," she says. "But I won't desert you."

You feel weak. You hadn't realized how much you were depending on her. Breathe, Blink. Get on with it, boy.

You wipe the hair out of your eyes and head down the road. When you've gone another fifty strides or so, you look back and she's following at a distance. Covering your back.

You round a bend, and there it is. You see it, kind of blurred, through the trees, just the jutting angle of the roof at first, a glint of last sunlight off a window. Then the road rounds one last bend, and there's this big clearing and the lodge about sixty meters down the hill over on your right. You pull back into the shadows. Hide behind a tree.

The lodge is massive, two stories high, built from dark logs with white caulking between them. The roof is steeply pitched, and there are three, four, five gables on this side and a tall stone chimney stack but no smoke coming out of it. Beyond the lodge there's a bay with a thick fringe of bulrushes, the dark green of water. The bay opens up onto a wide lake, almost black but with long smears of orange-and-pink sunset, and beyond that, a long way off, the silhouette of the far shore.

You pull back behind a tree, hold your breath. There's noise down here, the wind, the lapping of the water.

You lean into the tree out of sight and close your eyes the better to concentrate. You want to hear voices. Or if not voices, then something human: music, hammering, a window opening.

You open your eyes again. You want to see a door open up right now and see Jack Niven step out onto the hard-beaten dirt to cross the yard to the outhouse over there on the left, clear across the yard. There are another couple of sheds there, too, and a van.

A van!

There's a van parked in the shadows behind the shed. But it's pretty old looking. Could be abandoned. You turn to Kitty and point toward the van. But from where she is, she can't see it and she shakes her head. Her eyes are wide, her face angry. Stop looking at her, you idiot! That's what she's trying to tell you.

Right. Best to act as if you're on your own, in case . . . Well, you don't want to think about what might happen.

You kneel and peer out from behind your cover. Take it all in. A red canoe pulled up on the shore, a narrow dock leading out into the bay, an aluminum boat sitting in the water at the end of the dock, rocking ever so slightly up and down in an onshore breeze. You can feel the breeze off the water, just a tendril of it, all the way up here in the trees at the very edge of the clearing. It cools the sweat on your face and makes the branches above you stir and crack.

The outboard motor is tipped up. Fishing rods stick up from some holder contraption on the rail of the boat.

Fishing rods?

People might leave a boat in the water—how would you know? But fishing rods? Would there be fishing rods left out like that if there wasn't somebody here? And the canoe: it's just sitting there on the beach.

You risk a glance back toward Kitty, but she's gone. Nowhere to be seen. Vanished.

Your heart is beating like a jackhammer. *She did desert you!* No, you don't believe that. You can't believe that. She's taken cover—that's all. But a part of you wishes you had those car keys.

You turn your attention back to the clearing. Someone *is* here. No one is supposed to be, as far as Alyson knew, but someone *is* here. She was right. Alyson was right. *You* were right, too. Her daddy wasn't kidnapped. He's hiding out. He's here! This comes crashing into your brain all in a rush. You could go now, you think, but then you imagine the look Alyson would give you if you didn't do the job right. You've done a lot of lying in your life, but you're not sure you could get away with lying to her. She'd have some test, anyway. She'd know. You need to clamp your eyes on him.

So you move from tree to tree, around the clearing, your eyes peeled. You wait. You ignore the Captain, who is yelling at you at the top of his lungs, deafening you. You take your time. The upstairs gable windows are shuttered, which is good because it means no one can see you. The downstairs windows, however, are not. What does that mean?

It means be careful!

That's what the Captain screams. But those naked windows mean something else, too, just like the fishing rods and the canoe and the van.

You watch the dark of the windows for anything like movement. There are no lights on inside. You move with stealth, staying close to the trees, every nerve and fiber tensed. You watch your tread so you don't step on some damn branch. You are thirty, twenty, ten meters from the place, sneaking up toward the back of the building as far away from any window as possible.

You want to get close enough to look in just one window.

Then without warning an enormous pair of arms wraps around your chest and holds you tight.

"Where the heck you think you're going?" says a voice you almost recognize. You struggle without any chance of getting away, but in your squirming you catch a glance of the man who has soundlessly stalked you and now has you bound tight to his chest.

It's the Moon.

Chapter 30

Down there in the hold of who you are, Captain Panic has found himself a fire axe, and he's swinging it around like crazy, screaming "Bitch" and less savory words he picked up along the way, some of them from your stepdaddy. But you say nothing, Blink. Instead you yowl and groan in agony and try to tear yourself from the Moon's huge embrace.

"Whoa, there!" he says. "Take it easy, kid."

He crushes you against his massive chest. You groan not from pain but treachery.

Alyson did this to you!

She was in on it, just like Kitty told you—warned you. Alyson sent you here to this, and you came like the fool you are—the fool your stepdaddy always said you were and beat into you lest you failed to see in yourself what he saw.

"Calm down," says the Moon. "No one's going to hurt you."

You moan and twist and jerk, because what does he know about hurt? You are hurt—mightily injured. Not by his hold on you, but by life with its never-ending snares and pitfalls and dire consequences.

You try to elbow the man, but your arms are pinned to your sides. You kick back at him hopelessly. Your blows might as well be aimed at a tree. You fling your head around, arching your neck back, teeth bared, like a dog wanting to grab any part of him and tear it out by the roots. But by now the pressure on your skinny chest has forced most of the air from your lungs, and you can hardly breathe.

Finally, you stop. Your chin falls forward. The Moon lessens his grip, enough to let you breathe, but not enough to wriggle free.

It's only then, winded, close to fainting, that you remember Kitty. You fight hard against the instinct to look back to see if she, too, has been grabbed. You resist the temptation. You'll know soon enough.

"What you got there?" says a voice from across the yard. You lift your eyes enough to see Tank coming from behind one of the sheds, wiping his big hands with an oily cloth. He's wearing jeans and a white sleeveless T-shirt, as though it's the middle of summer.

The Moon frog-marches you out from the shadows at the back of the lodge, into the dying light of the yard.

Then a door in the lodge opens, and Jack Niven steps out. He's in khaki canvas flight pants and a checkered shirt, with the long sleeves rolled up. His neat beard has filled in a bit, so that his clean, tanned cheeks are a patchwork of salt-and-pepper bristle. His hair is mussed. Except for the casual shirt, he looks just like he did in the video: the captured man—the prisoner of SPOIL. Except the prisoner has a coffee cup in his hand and a pissed-off look on his face that has everything to do with you.

"What the hell is this?" he says.

The Moon half shoves, half carries you over to be presented to Niven, who stands just out of kicking range, guarding his coffee cup. Tank grins crooked-toothed at you as if the Moon just fished you out of the lake and they're about to fry you up for dinner. Niven is the one who does the talking.

"You are trespassing," he says. "Didn't you see the sign saying this was a private road?"

It's not what you expected him to say. Is he playing a game with you? Does he really not know who you are?

"Son, I asked you a question."

"I'm sorry," you say. You clear your throat, try to shake the Moon off you. He loosens his grip. You could still get out of this. "I was just, you know, tooling around, and I didn't know what was down here."

"Yeah, right," says Tank. "Maybe thinking of breaking in, huh? Making off with some stuff?"

"What do you mean tooling around?" says the Moon. "You got a car?" He turns to look back up the road. *You idiot, Blink.* You try to think of an explanation and then realize anything you say will only make it worse. "I'm sorry," you say again. "I'll just head out, okay? I didn't mean to trespass or nothing."

"Yeah, I'll bet," says Tank.

"What do you say?" says the Moon to Niven.

Niven is looking at you hard. He steps closer. He reaches out to grab your chin; you turn away. "You see this?" he says to the Moon.

"What?"

"The way he blinks like that."

"Well, I'll be," says the Moon.

"It's that kid!" says Tank. "The one that—"

"Shut up!" says the Moon.

You try to take off, but he wraps you up again.

"Brent?" says Niven. "Was that the name? Brent Conboy."

You collapse a little inside, shrink a little bit more. "My name's not Brent. My name's Bruce." You're blinking like crazy. Is this what the blinking is about? Have you always looked out at the world, never quite able to make sense of it?

"Well, Bruce, I don't know how you got here," says Niven. "But we don't want to hurt you, okay?" His voice is business-like. "Are you listening?"

You look at him, wondering if it would be a good idea to spit in his face. But you're not sure you have that much juice left in you. And, besides, you are one squeeze away from a broken rib.

You nod.

"Good. Have you got any ID?"

You shake your head. "I left it at home. I live up 509 a piece," you say, nodding your head in some direction—it doesn't matter which.

The Moon slackens his hold a little. You don't thrash about. You're innocent, just this country kid messing about. You don't so much as fidget or give him any reason to tighten

245

his grip again. You sag, defeated, take deep breaths. Wait.

"So, no driver's license?" says Niven.

"Sure," you say, feeling a little more confident. "Not on me, though. Like, who's gonna check out here?"

Niven nods. He wants to believe you. He doesn't want you to be who he thinks you are. You'd like to help him out.

"This is a cool place," you say, looking around.

There was a fourth guy, the one with the snake on his arm. You keep half expecting him to make an appearance, dragging Kitty with him. Maybe right now he's chasing her back up the road. There's nothing you can do about that. Look after yourself. Like always, Blink: it's you alone.

"It is," says Niven. "A cool *private* place, Bruce." He grins at the Moon as if things are looking up, except that there's a lot of grimace in that grin. "So what do you think we should do to convince you not to trespass here, even when there's a sign?"

"Don't worry, I won't do it again," you say quickly. "And I won't tell nobody about it, either."

"Tell them about what?" says Niven.

"This place. That's all I meant."

Niven frowns.

"Puny son of a bitch to be causing so much trouble, huh?" says Tank, shoving the dirty rag into his back pocket.

Niven looks irritated. Then he glances at the Moon.

The Moon speaks into your ear, nice and soft. "I'm just going to ask you to lean up against the wall here, son."

"Why?" you say. "Hey, what is this?"

"Can we do this nice?" says the Moon.

You nod reluctantly. And feel him lessen his hold on you slowly, carefully. You swallow hard. But Tank must have read the look in your eye, a shifty look you couldn't hide, and he maneuvers his brick shit-house body into position, arms out in case you try anything funny. From the look on his face, he'd love you to try something funny. You look beyond him toward the sheds and the van on the sundown side of the clearing, already dense in shadows. The Snake hasn't made an appearance. There's just the three of them so far. Hold fire, Blink. Assess your odds. It's how you face every day. If there's going to be a chance to make a break, this is not it.

The Moon makes you spread your legs, and he pats you down, just like in the movies. He digs out your cash, hands it to Niven.

"My, my," says Niven. "Planning a night on the town?"

Then the Moon digs out the picture of Alyson that you stole from Niven's wallet. "Oh, boy," he says. He hands it to the boss.

You glance sideways at him. He stares at her picture, stares at his daughter, and when he looks up, his face is filled with distaste. "Hell," he mutters. His face hardens. "What are you doing with this?"

"I found it."

"In my wallet," he says.

"So, it's him," says the Moon.

You're about to say something, but Niven raises his hand, ready to strike you, and you hold your tongue. The jig is up. Don't get him angrier than he already is. "I don't know how you got yourself into this mess," he says, "but it looks as if we've got some damage control to do, gentlemen. What we do depends on you. Do you follow?"

You nod slowly. There's not much good about this except for one small thing. *Alyson didn't set you up!* Somehow that seems to matter, although you're not sure why.

"The man asked you a question," says the Moon, his voice even.

"Okay. I follow."

"So, where did you get this picture?"

"Like you said. It was in your wallet."

"In my hotel room?" You nod. Niven shakes his head. "And how the heck did you get into that hotel room?"

The Moon stands back so you can stand up straight again, turn around, and answer the question face-to-face. You tip your chin toward Tank.

"Smart ass there handed me the key."

You don't know what pain this may end up bringing down on your head, but it's worth it right now to see the look on the Littlest Hulk's face.

"What the—?"

"Can it, Tank," says the Moon. Then he looks at you, Blink, his eyes asking a question, and you answer it, because you don't want trouble with this one.

"He threw away the key after he chucked the BlackBerry back into the room."

"Bullshit!" says Tank.

You just shrug.

Niven doesn't look at Tank. He never looks at Tank. He didn't up there in the hall of the hotel, and he doesn't now, as if the sight of him is painful or maybe only irrelevant. Instead, he looks at the Moon, his eyes questioning, his chin clenched tight as if to say, *Do we really have to put up with this?* You glance nervously at the Moon.

"You gonna believe this little asshole?" says Tank.

"Pipe down," says the Moon. He doesn't raise his voice. Doesn't need to. Then he sniffs and looks at you. "Are you alone?"

You nod. Don't even have to think about it. Right now you are totally and utterly alone.

Niven places the photograph of Alyson in his breast pocket and pats it. "How did you get here?" he says. You shrug. "We're miles from anywhere, kid. I asked you a question, and I want an answer."

"Hitched," you say.

"Bullshit," says Tank.

The Moon waves his head at Tank.

"What?"

"Go take a look," says the Moon.

Tank makes a face, like a kid whose mother has just sent him to bed.

"Go," says the Moon.

Tank spits, then heads across the darkening yard toward the shed. There's an ATV parked in the shadows behind the van. In another moment Tank straddles it, starts it up, flips on the headlight, and after a brain-jarring few revs, tears out into the yard and up the road. The sound of the machine shatters the silence, which seems to fall in jagged pieces all around you, Blink. You want to duck, afraid that you might get pierced by this sharp-edged falling dark.

You think of Kitty out there somewhere. At least there's no chance of her being surprised by Tank.

"Bring him in, Wallace," says Niven, and turns toward the lodge.

So now the Moon has a name.

You stumble forward, with Niven leading the way toward the door, Wallace right behind you.

You have to time this just right.

The instant Niven turns and reaches for the doorknob, you spin out the other way, like a crazy dancer, ducking as you go, feeling the breeze of Wallace's arm pass over your head—and you are gone, running down toward the lake.

Scamper! Don't look back! Straight to the dock and that boat tethered at the end. The deck shakes and rattles under you, and then you jump.

Chapter 31

She watches Blink's capture from high in the branches of a white pine. She sees the big one moving in on the boy and wants to yell out, only stopping herself when she realizes that giving away her position won't help anyone. So she lies flat on a thick branch, like a large cat, and takes it all in, feeling as though it is she who is being dragged, kicking and screaming.

They empty the boy's pockets, and then the short one is sent off for the ATV. She wonders how tough Blink is. Do they know about her yet? They haven't had much time. Is the little one heading after her? All the more reason to stay put. All the more reason for this bird's-eye view. She sees the one who is clearly the boss and knows now, for sure, what she had suspected all along. It was a trap, and Blink has walked right into it.

She tried to stop him, didn't she? But did she try hard enough? Why does it all seem like fate, as if it were meant to happen? But there isn't time for such speculation now.

The ATV flies up the road, passing underneath her and out toward Tumble Road. The sound diminishes to nothing, but she is not sure whether the little one—what did Blink call him? Tank. Yes, that was it—whether Tank has stopped the machine, or whether he has driven out of her range of hearing.

The Jeep. That's where he must have gone. It won't be where he expects it to be. There may be a chance he'll miss it. Right: a yellow Jeep. Damn!

They turn out Blink's pockets and don't find a key, because it is safe in her pocket. The doors of the Jeep are locked. What will they make of that? Will that give them more reason to suspect an accomplice? Or will Blink think of something? If they do manage to pry the information out of him, then she will need to make herself scarce. It disturbs her that she has seen only three people. She's sure Blink said there were four in all.

And now there is a shout. He's gotten away! He's heading toward the dock. As she watches, clinging to her branch, he jumps onto a boat that's there, waiting. And suddenly a part of her cracks wide open, letting out an animal cry of pain and sadness all wrapped up together that she can't begin to understand. She presses her face against the bough of the tree, shaking, holding on for dear life.

Chapter 32

You land in the aluminum boat and lose your footing, tumbling forward over the middle seat, landing painfully on your shoulder, and lying there like a fish in the bottom of the boat, gasping for air. You stumble to your feet, adrenaline charged, only to lurch forward as the boat comes to a juddering stop at the end of the line securing it to the dock.

You fall again, but you're up in a flash, scurrying to the bow to untie the taut yellow rope connecting you to the land. You shove yourself off, putting water between you and them.

You're floating free.

You stand as the boat drifts outward into the still black water of the little weed-choked bay. You are breathing hard, bruised and hurting, but triumphant! Your mouth hangs open, gulping at the cool air. Niven and Wallace just watch you like someone pushed the Pause button on them. Then click—Wallace moves. You've got more of a head start than you'd have ever dreamed. It's eerie. You turn sharply to look behind you out onto the bay, half expecting to see a gunboat approaching—an armada. But there is nothing out there but the dusk.

You put your hands on your hips. Now what? You stare at the outboard. You have no idea how that works. It's tipped up, the propeller out of the water. You step over the seat and give it a shove. It doesn't move. Locked in position somehow. But lying in a rack attached to the inside of the boat is an oar. You grab it and stick the business end straight down into the water until it hits bottom, which is not deep. The bottom gives, you push down hard, and the boat shoots back end first out into the bay. You dip the oar in again and shove with all your might. The boat starts to come around, and you realize that this is a good thing, so you shove that oar down into the muck and push again so that the prow of the boat is now facing out into the lake, the way it ought to be. You're a good twenty meters from shore now, and Wallace is only just reaching the dock. He's got his hands in his pockets. He's not in any hurry.

"Where you heading?" he says, standing at the end of the dock.

He doesn't sound concerned, which immediately makes you worried. But you aren't about to launch into any discussion about your immediate plans. It isn't about plans is it, Blink? It never has been. Life is about reacting. When you end up in a mess, you do something about it. You beat them at their own game, didn't you, boy? They only lowered their guard for a split second, and you were gone, ducking and weaving out of there.

You stick the oar down one more time into the murk, and you almost follow it overboard as the blade catches on something—a submerged log maybe—something that moves but not much. You reach out to grab the side of the boat, drop the oar into the drink. You fall to your knees to drag it out, wet and slimy.

You push again more carefully, and now the water is getting too deep to pole the boat away. Your eyes fix on the oarlock. You've never seen one in your whole life, but you know what it's for, all right. You sit and slam home the pin attached to the oar into the lock and then stare into the boat for the other oar. But there isn't one. Where the other oarlock should be there is a rubber holder with a couple of rods stuck in it, standing straight up like car antennas.

You pull on the oar anyway, and the boat starts veering right.

"You aren't going to go far like that," shouts Wallace. There is a bit of laughter in his voice. "Why don't you just bring it back, son," he says. "It's a lot shorter distance to here than it is to there."

You pull the oar out of the useless lock, shimmy your butt across the seat, and with two hands dip the oar into the water on the other side, using it like a paddle.

"I've got a canoe over here, Brent," says Wallace. "I can reach you in about three strokes. I'd rather you saved me the trouble."

You shut him out. You paddle on the right until the boat starts heading left into the thickest of the bulrushes, and then you shimmy back to the left again and paddle there a bit, bring-ing the boat around, though you are now moving ever so slowly in a dry jungle of rushes. Up close, you can see that their brown heads are busted open, spilling out guts like the stuffing of a chair. You paddle hard, the best you can, with those reeds battering against the hull, while the prow piles up dead and shriveled lily pads.

The exhilaration of escape seeps out of you. An endlessly long day catches up to you. You sit. You turn and stare at the outboard as the boat comes to a dead stop out in the reeds. You are baby Moses in his basket. Except this Moses isn't going to escape the pharaoh.

You are so tired. You are tired to death.

You turn your back on the shore and look out across the lake. And that's when you notice the fishing tackle box. You don't know for sure that's what it is, but when you open it, you can see well enough. And what you see first is the white cross and the bright red of a Swiss Army knife.

You sit up straight, glancing back toward the shore, hoping Wallace didn't see you make this discovery. The big man's back is to you. He's walked up the deck toward the shore, where Niven is coming to meet him.

Quickly you slip the pocketknife into your left running shoe, pushing it down under your arch, wiggling your foot to make it as comfortable as possible. Then you sit there waiting for a second wind, but all you get is the cold breeze coming up off the water, pushing the boat into the shallows. Even in your snug new hoodie, you can feel October close its fist around you.

The water stinks. Something died here. Out there, beyond the bay, the water still holds long gashes of setting sun. In here the water is brown and turgid like a plugged toilet bowl.

"There's nowhere to go, boy," says Wallace. He's back at

his spot at the end of the dock again, and Niven is standing at the foot of the dock, his arms crossed. "Out there is just bush and wetland," says Wallace.

You turn to look out toward the "there" he's talking about.

"You head out onto the lake, and you make our job easy. Nobody's going to see you for a good long time, my man."

You are "boy" one minute and "man" the next. And right now you're not sure what you are.

He lets his news sink in.

"Now, there's wetland at the south end of the lake," he says. "With a bit of luck, you might find a channel through it. In a day or two, you might even find your way out to the Mississippi."

He doesn't say it nasty. He even sounds a little encouraging, as if he's giving you a chance — a head start. But by now you can hardly imagine getting out of the bay, let alone all the way to some river. Did he say the Mississippi? How far is it you've come, anyway? Does that legendary river come all this way? How little you know about the world, Blink.

The darkness is coming on, and Wallace doesn't have to say anything more to convince you that it's over. There are no roads but the one behind you. The road ends at this nameless lake.

"Mr. Niven was right, Brent," says Wallace. "We aren't going to harm you. We just gotta talk, eh? I know you don't want to believe that. Why would you? But it's the truth. The only truth you've got right now."

Not the only truth, you think. You've still got Kitty. She might have already beaten it back to the car. All you've got to do is hold on.

257

Captain Panic retires again to his deep room inside you. The dread recedes. You look down into the gloom on which the boat sits and see no reflection in it. You could just tip yourself over into it, into this brown nothingness. Which is exactly what you do. You stand and just step right out of the boat. You hit bottom, thigh deep.

The cold makes you catch your breath. Then you grab the yellow rope and lead the boat back to the dock, like it's some big dumb animal that made a break for freedom and you're this patient farm boy who has to bring it back to the barn.

Chapter 33

She clings to the tree, her eyes tight shut, her face wet with tears. It no longer matters if anyone heard her strangled scream. In her mind's eye, she sees him jump from the end of the dock to the boat, sees the boat shoot out onto the water to the end of its rope. The end of the dock, the boat, the end of the dock, the boat, the end of the dock, the boat. He escapes and doesn't escape. He is gone forever and never leaves. He only passes from one state of being to another. A floating brother in a dark floating world.

The ATV returns, and the noise passing under her perch brings Kitty back. Shakily, she wipes her face, slick with tears and snot.

She sniffs and raises herself to a sitting position, straddling the branch. What now?

She shinnies down the tree, scraping her arms and legs, liking the pain of it—good, clean pain. Distracting her from the pain inside. So much for her brand-new threads, her cute little gaucho jacket.

There is a window of opportunity here that might not come again. She races up the road, now deep in shadows. She reaches the Jeep and curses the beep it makes when she unlocks it. She climbs in and sits behind the wheel out of breath.

But what is she to do?

The police? After she and Blink left Sharbot Lake, they passed through nothing but a village or two. Settlements. Sharbot Lake itself wasn't all that large. The man at the Petro-Can had been friendly; she could ask him where the nearest police station is.

And yet . . .

There is something wrong with the idea. And foremost of what is wrong is the idea of the police. She has spent the last seven months on the other side of the law. She has become the kind of person who crosses the road to avoid passing a cop on the beat. She has been a person whose eccentric pink Little Mermaid backpack has often contained restricted substances. The police, she has come to think, are not her friends.

She shakes this off. She is not on the wrong side of the law right now. She has nothing on her and nothing to hide. She has no record. And she has witnessed a crime—seen it with her own eyes. Those men did not give Blink a talking-to for trespassing. She could convince the cops of what she had seen, she's sure of it.

But . . .

Even if they came, even if they took her seriously, it would be hours before they got back to this place, and what would they find? A trio of guys at a hunting lodge. That's what. There would be no trace of Blink. Even if they weren't expecting trouble, there would be time enough to stuff him in some closet somewhere once they saw the cruiser entering the clearing. Or stuff him in a grave, for that matter.

No. It wouldn't be a trio of hunters the cops would find. The businessman . . . what was his name? Niven, Jack Niven would make himself scarce, since his face would be too well known. So he would hide, and no matter what she tried to tell the cops, they'd look at her as if she was delusional or a troublemaker or some hopeless freak trying to get her face in the newspapers.

As she sits there in the Jeep, her thoughts become clearer and clearer, and she realizes that even if she were able to convince the cops to come, there would be no one here by the time they arrived. They would find a boarded-up lodge, with no recent signs of habitation. Jack and his men would have split. They'd have had all the time in the world.

And finally Kitty realizes that at this very minute, those men may be torturing Blink to find out where the key to the Jeep got to. They could be screaming up that road anytime now—and not in an ATV, but in the van she saw parked behind the outbuildings. She could take off now, but they could be on her tail in minutes, and there was nowhere to go on 509 but south again—not if she was trying to go for help. She has no idea where the two-lane goes as it meanders north. Somewhere called Ompah. And beyond that? It is essentially a deserted road. They passed little more than a handful of vehicles in the forty-five minutes they drove after leaving Highway 7. Two of those were logging trucks. And there she would be tootling along in a bright yellow Jeep Wrangler—not exactly camouflaged.

So she will stay.

She sniffs, wipes her face again, pinches her cheeks. Of course she has to stay. Burned into her brain is that image of Blink jumping from the dock to the boat. Blink, not Spencer. She cannot rescue Spencer. But she can rescue Blink. If it's the last thing she ever does.

So she must watch and wait. She climbs out of the car into the coolness of the evening. Somewhere far off she hears the drone of a truck changing gears on a long hill. All around her are the sounds of the bush at night. These are not alien sounds to her. She has no fear of this. She locks the car, pockets the key.

She heads back down the road. It is just light enough that she would see someone approaching. She will need all her hunting smarts. What was it Spence had taught her about moose hunting? You don't look for moose; you look for something that doesn't look right.

She must keep her eyes and, more important, her ears alert for something that doesn't seem right.

None of it seems right, really. She thinks back to the discussion she'd had with Blink about purgatory. Not just a place but a state of mind. And as she walks down the road toward where it ends at the lake, she realizes that this is purgatory's end.

There is a low rumble of thunder.

Chapter 34

By the time you've waded to shore dragging that fool boat behind you, you're about as tired as a human can be. It's a deep tired, deeper than your bones. It's a give-up kind of tired. The Captain must have drowned out there in the bay, because you don't feel him inside you anymore. There is no alarm left in you, Blink. The battery ran out. Surrender has sucked the last drop of juice right out of you just like the mud of the bay is sucking the last bit of strength out of your leg muscles. You hang your head in defeat.

If there is any hope left in the world, it is in that girl with the dove-colored eyes, Kitty Pettigrew.

You hand the end of the yellow rope to Wallace, still standing at the end of the dock. He squats to tie the boat back up again while you wander those last few feet to shore, your legs heavy now from the soaking and growing cold as the night air gets at them. For one brief moment, you think about making a run for it in your mud-heavy sneakers, but the knife hidden in your shoe isn't going to make running any too easy. And when you look up toward the lodge, you realize that Niven is standing there, and you can hear the whine of the ATV getting louder as Tank makes his way back. With Kitty? You send up a soggy prayer to the God you knew as a boy that she has not been captured. You remember her escape from you at Union Station with all your money in her hand. Was that only this morning? You recall how quick she was. How quick her mind is. This is all you can hang on to.

You stand on the silted shoreline, looking at Wallace, wavering a bit as if you might collapse. He is coming, and for some reason you want him to be the one to claim you as his captive. He takes you by the arm and leads you up the hill toward the lodge. He must feel the breakdown of your spirit, for he barely holds on to you at all.

"You're limping," he says, staring down at your left foot.

"I twisted my ankle," you say.

Niven wrinkles his nose and waves you away. "Show him the shower, for Christ's sake. I'm not going to talk to him in that state."

One of the sheds turns out to be a sauna with a shower in it. Wallace points at something on the roof and explains how they run the generator and fill the drum up there with water from the lake, and then heat it with a woodstove in the sauna.

You look at the bay. "I'm going to wash in that shit?" you say.

264

He chuckles. "The line goes way out to where the water is fresh."

You aren't about to argue with him because Tank is back, his ATV rumbling and grumbling as he brings it around to the back of the shed. He's alone; good. But his face is clouded, angry. So you head into the shower house quickly, and Wallace doesn't follow you, which is also good. There's a little front room where you strip down, palming the knife before you enter the sauna. There is a shelf of towels where you find a place to hide the knife for now.

The stove has made the whole place warm, and the smell of cedar, pungent and soothing, fills your lungs. The water from the shower scalds until you get the mix right and then washes away the muck of the bay, the muck of days and days. When was the last time you washed? You feel your muscles relaxe. You look down at your skinny self and see a new batch of bruises blossoming, ones you got from your daring escape. The *only* thing you got from your daring escape. Well, other than the knife.

You wash your hair with some lemon-scented shampoo. You wash it twice, putting off what is coming, though you don't really know what is coming.

When you finally step out of the shower and into the little front room, there are ironed and laundered clothes waiting for you: jeans, anyway, and a thick plaid shirt. No underpants or socks but a pair of moccasins for your feet. They've taken away your beautiful blue two-day-old sneakers and your brand-new gear from the Army Surplus. There's some ornate stitching on the back pockets of the jeans, and you guess they must have belonged to a woman, though you haven't seen one around.

They've put your money back in your pocket. How weird is that? The pants are loose on you. There is not much of you left, child.

There's a little mirror lit by a battery-operated lamp. You comb the tangles out of your hair and recover your hidden weapon from its hidey-hole. The knife fits better in the moccasin than it did inside your sneaker. Then you step outside to face the music.

Tank is standing next to Wallace, steaming.

"You think it's funny wasting my time?" says Tank.

You do what Niven does and ignore him. You stare straight at Wallace, as if Tank is speaking in some other language and you need a translation.

"Tank here says he couldn't find no car keys."

"I hid them," you say.

"They're nowhere on the Jeep," says Tank, his voice raised as if this is an insult directed at him.

You shrug and he makes a move toward you, but Wallace stops him. Then Tank points his finger at you, like it's the barrel of a gun, and pulls the trigger.

There's more trouble with Tank when you get to the lodge. Wallace sends him away.

"What?"

"Get back to the camp," says Wallace.

"Jesus, Wally," he says, shaking his head, his teeth gritted. Then he looks at you, Blink, as if yet again you've screwed things up for him. You can't help it: you give him a wave. He doesn't lunge this time. He smiles the wickedest smile you have ever seen.

"You have rubbed me the wrong way one too many times, punk," he says.

He throws up his hands to stop Wallace from scolding him anymore and heads off back across the yard, still shaking his head and rolling his shoulders like a heavyweight going to his corner but dying for the next round.

The door into the lodge leads through a kitchen area, where something is bubbling on a gas stove. Wallace looks you over in the light and then finds some thick string in a kitchen drawer and hands it to you.

"You're going to need this to hold your pants up, eh," he says.

You pass it through the belt loops and tie it. "Thanks," you say. You want to keep this one on your side as much as possible.

Meanwhile, he has ladled out some soup into a big bowl. You can see beef and potato in a rich broth. The savory smell makes your knees weak.

He indicates the table. "Take a load off," he says. He shoves a spoon into the chest pocket of your oversize shirt.

You carry the soup in two hands toward the table. You recognize it. There is the chipboard wall from the video. The table in front of it is enameled white metal, with benches on either side. You remember Alyson trying to tell you that she saw a stain on that wall when she saw the video. How many stories did she have lined up to tell you—how many layers of lies— until she convinced you? Except that they really *didn't* know who you were at first, you remind yourself. It wasn't a setup. Well, it hardly matters now. Your street smarts are no match for the games these people play.

When you're finished, Wallace leads you through a long dining room that opens up into a huge living room. There is a fireplace in the center of it, big enough to stand up in. It's built of pink and yellow and deep gray stone and rises into the darkness of varnished yellow-gold timber beams. There's a rustic stairway of thick planks notched into a single, central tree trunk, with branches forming the balustrade leading up to a gallery that looks down on the living room. The lights are low and solar powered. That's what Wallace tells you, like you are a tourist or in the market to buy the place. The fire is bright and crackling. There are stuffed deer heads on the walls, a couple of sets of moose antlers, long, sharp-nosed fish mounted on plaques. There's a rack for fishing rods and a gun rack with a half dozen rifles in it.

"Are we just about ready?" says Niven. You've been avoiding looking at him as long as you can. From the look on his face, his patience has worn thin.

He's sitting on a couch, working on his laptop. He's got his feet up on a wide coffee table. He closes the top of his computer, and Wallace leads you before him. Niven nods toward an ugly, old easy chair across the coffee table from him. You sink down so low, your knees stick up as high as your chin. Not something you're going to leap up from any too quickly, assuming you had any leap left in you.

Wallace takes a chair nearby, just in case you have such an idea in mind. His chair is of about the same vintage and ugliness. All the furniture is old and homey, with colorful blankets thrown here and there to cover holes and stains—that's what you figure, anyway. It's the same as your mother's idea of home decorating. The blanket on this chair doesn't do much to lessen the effect of the spring that's sticking into your backside. But what did you really expect?

The coffee table between you and Jack Niven is heavy and hokey knotty pine.

Niven looks at Wallace first. "Did he find a vehicle?"

Wallace nods. "And it's not some punk's ride."

"What do you mean?"

"It's a late-model Jeep Wrangler."

You watch Niven's face darken, his eyebrows knot. "What color?"

"Yellow."

"Really?" He glances at you, perplexed.

"That's what Tank said."

There is a flash of panic in Niven's face. "Where did you get that car?" he asks. And although his voice is not raised, there is trouble in those piercing blue eyes. There is no point in fooling around.

"From Alyson."

"You stole my daughter's car."

"No way. She lent it to me."

"Do not lie to me."

"I'm not lying. She had this idea you might be up here, and she couldn't come herself to find out. So she asked me to do it."

"Asked *you* to do it."

"To come up here. To check. She was worried about you."

He clears his throat but can't speak.

"How would I ever find a place like this in the middle of nowhere?"

He rubs his face with his hands. There are bags under his

eyes. He looks down at the table in front of him, shaking his head. You glance at Wallace. His eyes are on the boss. You turn back as Niven raises his head and looks at you hard.

"You saw something at the hotel. You saw us leave the room. Is that it?" You nod slowly, just once. "And then you contacted Alyson?"

"She phoned you. I just picked up the call."

Niven's eyes close for just a moment and then open again. "And you told her what you saw." You nod again, but the look on his face gives you a sinking feeling. "And she . . . what?"

You shrug. "She didn't believe me. I was just, like, trying to tell her that you were okay. That's all I was doing, honest. I figured she'd want to know. I didn't get it . . ." You stop there. Niven's face looks gray. He stares at the fire for a moment. You can see the fire in his eyes. His hands are clenched. The room is silent but for the crackling of the logs.

He rubs his face again. "So what exactly was the plan, Brent?"

You swallow hard. "I was supposed to drive up here and check and then drive right back and let her know. She's expecting me back, like, by eight—nine at the latest." You're not sure if you should tell him this. Someone is expecting you—that should be a deterrent to him trying anything, except that the person expecting you is his daughter. His well-loved daughter. It doesn't look good.

He looks at you again, and the concern on his face melts away and shifts to a wry smile. "Do you really expect me to believe this?"

"It's true."

"Who put you up to this, Brent?"

"Listen. I've got her car, right?"

"Apparently, and you're trying to tell me my daughter — my highly intelligent daughter — just handed over her new set of wheels to a scumbag street kid — a thief, no less? Is that what you're telling me, Brent?"

You reel a bit from the force of what he's saying, but you also hate him for it — him calling *you* a scumbag. Your jaw clamps tight to hold back the rage you feel percolating up inside you. Then you look down and see a cell phone on the table in front of Niven. There are no cell towers up here, but this one has a heavy-duty antenna on it. You look right at him, eye to eye. "Why don't you phone her and find out?" you say.

Chapter 35

Niven leaves the room. He just ups and leaves. Doesn't take the phone, doesn't say good-bye. He gives no instructions to the Moon. You look over at Wallace; his hands are folded on his belly, his face giving nothing away. You lean your head back, close your eyes, and try to think what the last expression was that you saw on Niven's face. Something happened to that cool exterior. And you remember once when Da came to pick you up, out of the blue, and your mother tore into him. She still had a bit of fire in her then, and she called him a disgrace. "You're a disgrace, Ginger Conboy," she said. And Ginger, for all his smiling and winking at you, had this look—this flinching—as if she'd struck home. Was that what he saw on Jack Niven's face? Shame. Could a man like that feel shame?

You drift off to some restless turbulent place that is as far from sleep as it is from wakefulness. You're jarred back to consciousness by the sound of a door slamming. You look up, bleary-eyed, but it's not Niven returning but Tank with a tool belt on and a cardboard box in his hands.

"What are you doing here?" says Wallace.

"Keep your shirt on," says Tank. "The boss got me to take a padlock off one of the sheds. I'm supposed to put it on one of the bedrooms upstairs." He looks at you with a smile that he's been soaking in some solvent. "Seems like we've got ourselves an overnight guest." As he passes you by, he leans down to speak in your ear. "Hope you call for room service," he says.

He heads upstairs, chuckling. You close your eyes again, and even though you try not to, you fall asleep to the sound of an electric drill. Next thing you know, Wallace is shaking you awake. You look around and rest your gaze on Niven, sitting on the couch again.

"Here's what's going to happen," he says. "The cops will find the Jeep in Toronto somewhere. Stolen and abandoned."

You think about Alyson's friend Jason, who was supposed to have borrowed the car to go to Ottawa. But that's not your problem, and you've got enough of your own.

"We'll deal with that tomorrow."

"Boss, we didn't find no keys."

Niven chops the air with his hand. "We'll deal with that tomorrow, Wallace," he says. Then he clasps his hands together and examines you a moment like a man wondering whether he wants to soil his shoe by stepping on a cockroach.

"I do not appreciate you dragging my daughter into this business," he says. "Mistakes were made. That happens. We are going to clear up those mistakes. But she is never going to know about this. Ever. Do you understand me, Brent?"

You nod. You almost admire him. How amazing it would be to be loved so much.

"Good," he says. He looks down at the coffee table for a moment. When he looks up, his face is all business.

"So, Brent, what do you think is going on here?" You shrug and he leans forward, rests his chin on his fists. "This can be done quickly, or we can take all night, but I think you'll be a lot happier if you choose the quick option."

His voice is straightforward, but there's no mistaking the threat. He's not a man who has to try very hard to be frightening.

"If I say I don't know nothing, will you just let me go?"

"No," he says.

"So, why not just kill me and get it over with?"

"Not unless you really piss me off," says Niven, which makes Wallace laugh. He gets up to stretch. You look at him in the firelight. He gives you a little encouraging nod, as if maybe this thing could still get turned around.

"Brent," says Niven. "Can we just do this?"

That's what Alyson said. *Can we just do this?* Maybe it's a Niven family thing.

You look from him to Wallace, who nods at you again.

"What am I supposed to do?"

"First of all, I want to know who you've talked to about this, apart from my daughter. You could lie to me, but I'd rather you didn't."

"No one," you say.

Niven nods. "Okay, good. Now tell me what you know—what you think you know."

274

"Okay. So you own this land, and you want to open a mine on it. But there's these Indians who say it's their land, and they don't want you mining uranium because it's like a major pollutant and 'everybody lives downstream'—that's what this guy in the paper said."

Niven looks peeved. "Go on," he says.

"So, anyway, they've got this big protest happening that is getting lots of press and making you look bad, and you say you're willing to back out if the government takes the land off your hands for forty-eight million."

Niven is looking at you with interest. "Am I supposed to think you figured this all out yourself?"

"Yeah."

"No one coaching you?"

"You mean like the FBI?"

He frowns. "Don't be smart, kid."

"I told you I didn't talk to no one. You can believe me or not—that's your problem. Do I look like some undercover agent?"

"Good point," he says. "You *look* like a street punk. But you haven't exactly acted like one, and you don't talk like one."

"I had your BlackBerry. There are newspapers. I can read."

He nods. "Apparently. But I can't help wondering if you're some kind of Greenpeace troublemaker or something. Someone with a simplistic and overly emotional take on business in general and mining in particular."

You shrug. It almost feels like a compliment.

"Does that shrug mean you *are* or are *not* affiliated with some such organization?" he demands, as if he were the prosecutor in some TV drama.

"What if I am?" you say. But seeing the look on his face, you decide that playing cocky is not going to help. Your shoulders slump. "No," you say. "Do you see anyone around coming to my rescue?"

"No," he says. "No rescuers and no media so far, which is how I want it to stay. So you just fell into this thing, is that what happened?"

You nod. "Tank chucked the key thing, and I took a look in the room, found your BlackBerry, and checked it out. There were a lot of people pissed off at you."

The Moon chuckles, leans against the fireplace.

"Yes, well . . ." says Niven, raising an eyebrow at the Moon. Then he turns his courthouse eyes on you again. "So you find my phone, which is when you make contact with my daughter."

"Yes, sir."

He settles back on the sofa, his arms crossed as if he's trying to figure out how badly he's going to hurt you. You are the little piece of grit that got into his fancy machine here and maybe could bring it screeching to a halt, if you were to tell the right people what you know. Somehow you've got to make him believe you have that power, right? God, no, boy—think again! What you want to do is the opposite: try to convince him you wouldn't have a clue what to do with what you know.

"So, let's see where we are," says Jack. "You ran away from home last May; you're living on the street; you're a thief—"

"Who says I'm a thief?"

"Five hundred and sixty dollars says you're a thief, though why you left anything in the wallet, I'll never know. We have our contacts in Toronto, Brent."

"Yeah, right. Your lawyer."

"My lawyer knows nothing about this. He passes on information about the investigation to my office, and one of my associates passes on that information to me."

The Snake. He means the Snake.

"Anyway, my point is that you need money. And what I have to try and establish is how much will keep you quiet and whether I can trust you to keep quiet."

Money? They're thinking of giving you money?

Jack is looking at you, and there's a sly grin on his face, like he read you dead to right. "I'm a businessman, Brent," he says. "Businessmen trade in all kinds of commodities. And silence, non-action, compliance—these are just commodities as far as I'm concerned. Or, to be more accurate, goods and services."

"Maybe you need to say that more simple," says Wallace.

"No, I get it," you say.

"Clever lad," says Jack. "So let's say if I were to give you a thousand dollars. Would that do the trick?"

Did he say a thousand dollars? "You mean to keep me from blabbing?"

He nods. "And could I be sure you wouldn't try to blackmail me later? Threaten to take your intriguing little story to the press, see if you could double dip, so to speak?"

Your head is still reeling from the fact they're not going to kill you, so a thousand bucks catches you right off-guard. But your brain is quick, Blink—too quick for its own good—and you can't help wondering whether there is more here. Much more. Hell, he's just about told you there is.

His smile is not pleasant. He can see right through you.

"Let's play a game," he says. "You've spent your thousand dollars, and now you can't help wanting more. Stands to reason.

It's human nature. So how do you go about collecting?"

You shrug. "I don't know."

"Humor me."

Wallace puts a new log on the fire. You look at the blaze. "I'd go to the press, like you said."

"What press?"

"I don't know. The *Sun*? No, the *Globe and Mail*."

"What would you take them? They'd want proof of some kind. What have you got to show them?"

You stare at nothing, like you're trying to conjure an idea out of the air.

"Nothing," you say.

"The correct answer," says Jack Niven. "Nothing but a crazy story."

"I could bring them here," you say. "Show them this place."

"And?"

"The wall in the kitchen, where the video was shot."

Jack claps his hands. "Nice try," he says. "Assuming you could convince anyone to drive up here. Oh, and the wall would be painted when you got here, right? Maybe even done up in some tongue-and-groove paneling. So try something else."

You scratch your head. You're not sure what he's playing at. And now you're wondering if he's even going to bother giving you the money, since what he's saying is that no one will believe you, anyway. So you've got to earn the thousand dollars. Is that what this is about?

"The cops are looking for me. That proves I was in the hotel."

"So go to the cops. But they're certainly not going to pay you anything, because extortion is against the law."

"No, I mean, I'd go to the newspaper or, like, the TV, and they'd know I was the guy the cops were looking for."

Jack is already wagging his head. "You're underage. The police cannot release the name of a minor to the press. It took a lot for my lawyer to find it out. Oh, and by the way, if you did go to the cops, you'd be arrested for petty larceny and mischief, not to mention obstruction of justice."

"What?"

"Playing hide-and-seek with the police with my BlackBerry in the middle of a serious investigation. Dumping it in the pocket of an innocent victim."

"Ha!" you say. "You obviously don't know my stepfather."

"A stupid move," he says. "Vindictive. That's what got you in this mess. Revenge."

He's right. You throw up your hands. "Okay. So what am I supposed to say?"

Niven looks pleased with himself, but he gets serious again quickly. "I just want you to know that you have fallen down a very deep mine shaft, Brent. So you're best bet is to scramble back out as fast as you can. And if a thousand dollars will make the trip worthwhile, then I'm willing to give it to you. I am willing to buy your silence. But I don't want any second-guessing on your part. Do I make myself clear?"

You nod right away. The mention of the money means it's still on the table, and that's a lot better than being tossed into the lake with a rock chained to your feet. Or into a mine shaft.

"I get it," you say.

"And I can trust you?"

"Yeah."

"And by silence, I mean you can talk to no one about this. Not my daughter, not anyone."

His hands are pressed together, and he's staring at you over the tips of his fingers. You don't like it when people look at you like that. You want to look away, but you know you can't. He has to believe you. Everything depends on him believing in you. So you hold his gaze, and it comes over you that this feels like the moment in your mother's place when Stepdaddy was drunk that time and he had a poker and you stared him down. Not that you really did. What you really did was freeze. But he didn't know that. And it gave him that extra minute or two to come to whatever senses he still had in his bourbon-addled brain. So you learned something from that. You nod.

"Okay," says Niven. Then he picks up his briefcase from where it sits on the floor, the big black one he was carrying Wednesday morning in the hotel. He clicks it open and pulls out a little bundle of money. He riffles the edges with his finger and then tosses the bundle over the coffee table. You trap it between your chest and your folded hands. You were never very good at catch.

A bundle of twenties.

"Thanks," you say.

He's busy clicking his briefcase shut, placing it at his feet. He glances at you as if your thanks aren't worth much to him.

"You still have to earn that money," he says, leaning back on the couch.

"By keeping quiet."

"Precisely. And to make sure you do, I want you to stay here, as our guest, for a few days." Just like Tank said, but you don't like the sound of it. "This is not negotiable," he adds, his voice hard.

You look down at the money. You look back at him. "Why are you doing this?" The words are out of your mouth before you can stop yourself.

"I wouldn't expect you to understand."

"Okay, but a minute ago you were saying I had what it takes to be a businessman, right? So?"

Niven rolls his eyes. Wallace chuckles. "Hey, boss, maybe if you explain it a bit, it'll help him keep his promise."

Niven glares at Wallace, then leans back in his chair. "Okay." He puts his hands together again. "There are these people who want to take over my company."

"That's what Alyson said."

"Do not mention my daughter's name," he says. "Do you hear me?" He might as well add something about being a scumbag again, because that's the look on his face. He can't stand the idea that you even spoke to her.

You nod. "There was something in the paper about a takeover."

"Right. A hostile takeover," says Niven. He loses the angry glare, and his eyes start to shine as if he's thinking about Goliath, even as he's carving himself a slingshot. "Let me tell you about a hostile takeover. This big mining conglomerate from Japan called ANS has been secretly buying up as many QVD stocks as they can, hoping to gain control. They get the shareholders they can't actually buy out to come on their side by promising them a big dividend—a good return on their investment."

"And this—what you're doing—is supposed to stop them?"

281

"In a word, yes," he says. "The Millsap Lake standoff is only a battle. I'm prepared to lose that, but I'm hanging on to the company." He runs his hands through his hair and chuckles. "Why I'm explaining any of this to you, I do not know."

"I'm listening," you say. In fact, you're leaning forward in your chair, your elbows on your knees, like it was Granda telling one of his fanciful stories.

Niven throws a glance at Wallace. "A future entrepreneur," he says. "Well, I guess you've got the basic training for going into business," he adds.

"I'm serious," you say. "I mean, I read some of this stuff on your BlackBerry and in the newspapers, but I can't figure out how losing the . . . the claim? Yeah, the land claim. How is losing forty-eight million a good thing?"

Jack raises an eyebrow as if he's wondering whether there's more to you than he figured. You like that look in his eyes. You earned that.

"We may not even lose that battle—the Millsap Lake fiasco—if we can convince the government to take the land off our hands. Oh, we won't get what we want, but we could get enough to write off our losses. The government looks pretty stupid right now, the way they've handled this, so they might play ball. That way, they can sweep it under the rug. My share-holders may not be pleased, but I can handle that, as long as I can squash this takeover bid."

Jack isn't looking at you anymore. He's reopened his lap-top and is reading something on the screen. Multitasking. Mumbling.

"This mining conglomerate," he says, as if you asked a question. "They only want my company so they can strip it of its assets and then flush it down the toilet. Right now, however, QVD does not look very appetizing to them. They weren't all that concerned about the standoff: the picketers, the lunatic fringe. They're used to that kind of localized nuisance. But the media surrounding my kidnapping is not good for them. You could say that SPOIL has spoiled ANS's opportunity. I love that!" he says enthusiastically. "See what I'm saying? See how it goes?"

You sort of think you do. You nod.

"Good for you, Brent. We'll make a businessman of you yet." He squeezes the bridge of his nose with his thumb and forefinger. He's tired. The discussion is over. And it's really only then that you finally and totally get it. There is no SPOIL. Or Jack Niven is SPOIL. The whole thing is a fantasy to scare off this big Japanese operation.

"Enough," says Jack Niven. "Kiddy time is over. I've got a long night ahead, and this discussion is not on the agenda." He looks at you.

"Three days," he says. "Deal?"

You don't like the sound of it. Three days locked up, with Tank out there planning to crucify you? But then you've got the money, and you don't really have any choice.

"Do we have a deal?" he says again, his patience at an end.

"Okay," you say.

"Good," says Niven. Then he glances at Wallace, who gets up, like he's your nursemaid and it's time to get the child out of the parent's sight.

"I'll take you to your room," says Wallace.

You climb out of the chair, your legs stiff and your battered body aching. Wallace shows you to the stairs. You riffle through the money in your hands as you climb slowly up toward the darkened second floor. You count again, enjoying the crispness of the new bills. But then something makes you look closer. You stop climbing. You start adding it up.

"Got a problem, Brent?"

It's Niven looking up at you from the sofa below.

"There isn't a thousand here," you say.

"That didn't take you long," says Niven.

"But you said—"

"I'd give you a thousand dollars to keep your mouth shut? Exactly. And I'm a man of my word. I think you'll find that the bundle you have in your hot little hands is equal to four hundred and forty dollars. You've already spent the other five hundred and sixty. Is my math correct?"

"But—"

"Good night, Brent."

You swallow hard. You don't move. Then you feel Wallace's firm hand on your lower back, and you start the climb again. The stairs are steep.

As you reach the landing, the rain starts.

Chapter 36

Kitty's job, as she sees it, is to know the lay of the land, to learn as much as she can. Her main job for now is not to get caught.

Following the strains of distant music, she finds a trail behind the shed that follows the shore of the lake to a small cabin ten minutes' walk from the lodge. Tank is there, sitting in a screened-in porch with his feet up, drinking a beer, listening to heavy metal on a boom box, and staring out at the water.

She makes her way back along the trail mostly by feel, through the last of the daylight. He won't be foolish enough to take such a narrow and uneven trail without a flashlight, she suspects, but she decides to make his journey difficult and as memorable as possible, littering the trail with bits of off-cut lumber she finds behind the shed. Some of the wood has nails in it.

She has already pocketed the key to the ATV, which Tank left in the ignition. It's a Kawasaki; she has driven one of these things before, but she familiarizes herself with the model, sitting astride it, feeling where everything is. She practices inserting the key into the ignition in the dark.

It has occurred to her that they might try to leave. If they have even the slightest suspicion that anyone might follow Brent here, they might decamp. She doesn't want that. The van is old, but the license plates are up-to-date, so presumably it's active. So her next job is to make sure the van is disabled. The door is locked, unfortunately, and there are no keys handy. So she finds another piece of wood with a good-size spike in it and lets the air out of all four tires.

This is a big decision. One flat would not arouse suspicion. Four flats means that Blink has a confederate. They might threaten to kill him if she doesn't give herself up. But if they could fix the flat and take off, then he would be gone anyway.

This is purgatory, all right. And that boy she robbed this morning and then caught up with—he isn't just a boy. Not anymore. She can't quite put it into words, but Blink is a gift. A chance for . . . for something—she's not sure what. But without him, there is nothing.

The sound of the four tires hissing seems incredibly loud up close, but the wind has picked up, as have the waves, so she doubts anyone else can hear it.

The rain comes by the time she finally makes her way to the back of the lodge. She had watched the big man come up behind Blink and nab him. There is no way she is going to allow

286

herself to be trapped in the same way. She has no idea where the other two are right now, though she expects they're in the lodge. But there is still that fourth man, who could be anywhere. So she waits a long time. The rain comes, and she still waits, curled up as tight as she can in the far corner near the bush. Her eyes close from time to time, only to snap open when she realizes she has drifted off. At one point she falls deeper into sleep—deep enough for half-dreams. She sees herself holding a baby. She wakes with a start, but the baby doesn't quite dissolve.

The rain picks up. If there is someone on guard anywhere near here, she hopes the rain will drive him inside. No one comes.

She finds her way to the window nearest the bush and peers in. There is just the businessman sitting on a couch, talking on a cell phone, his face lit by firelight. His expression is serious. Then she hears footsteps inside the house and sees the big man enter the room from a staircase, she figures by the sound of it, which is just out of her vision.

He speaks to Niven, who holds up his hand to stop him, while he finishes his call. She cannot make out what is said but watches the businessman close up his laptop and put it away.

Niven places various papers in a briefcase. He seems to be clearing up. The cell rings again, but the big guy, the Moon, takes the call and nods several times. Then he talks to Niven, who nods and then swears. She's not sure—she can't actually hear him, but it looks as if he's swearing. Then he rubs his hands through his hair.

Something is wrong.

Kitty is almost out of the rain, under wide eaves. Now she slides her back down the log wall of the lodge. She didn't like having her back to the clearing while she was looking through

287

the window. She is afraid. That look on Niven's face: what did it mean? Have they killed Blink? She can't believe that—won't believe that. The Moon came down from upstairs. Maybe Blink is up there somewhere?

She dashes out from under the eaves and tries to see if there is a light on upstairs, forgetting that the windows are all boarded up. There are several gables. The place is huge, which is both bad and good. Bad, because he might be anywhere; good, because she might be able to get into the place and look around undetected, assuming there are only the two of them inside. She looks again through the downstairs window and is shocked to see the Moon's broad back less than a foot away. She makes an involuntary gasp and is glad that the clattering of the rain will have masked the noise. But she reminds herself to be way more careful.

The width of his back makes her shudder. She doubts he's fast, but she has witnessed firsthand how stealthily he moves, closing a gap of ten meters without Blink ever being aware of this giant bearing down on him.

She clears the wet hair from her face, wipes the rain out of her eyes, and risks a peek inside, more carefully this time. The Moon has been busy. Busy loading a rifle.

Chapter 37

The room at the dead end of the hall is cold and sad. You stand under the peak of the roof, which slopes down to the left and right. There's a narrow bed with a black sleeping bag and a single thin pillow lying upon a thin mattress. There's a heavy-looking chest of drawers against the far wall and no other furniture. You stare at the only touch of color in the place, a small rug braided out of rags. It reminds you of the rug Nanny Conboy had woven for the guest room at the cottage in the Beaches. You would stay with them in that tiny cottage to give your mother and father a break.

Granda was a storyteller. He worked for CN Railway as a baggage handler, and he'd tell you tales that even as a little squirt you only half believed. Truth wasn't the point of the exercise. You liked them, Nanny Dee and Granda Trick. Why didn't you go to them, Blink? Were you just too angry at your father? Or now that you think about it, was it just that you were too frightened they would turn you away? "Ah, Brent, love, it's good to have you for a weekend now and then, but look at this tiny home—a cottage, lad, little more. You go back to your mother; there's a good lad." Did they say that, or did you just imagine they would? Hardly matters now.

"It's not much," says Wallace, "but it'll have to do."

You're not sure what he's talking about. The money? Your life? No, of course not. He's talking about this bare room.

It smells of dust and mothballs and wet wood. It feels small with the rain just overhead, battering down, holding you in. Is she out there? you wonder. Has she gone for help? It's hard to really believe she even exists. You knew her for twelve hours. When you try to summon her up, all you can see are those gray eyes.

There is a large gabled window on the lake side, but you don't see night through it. You walk over and lean against the sill. Through the glass you see black-painted wood shutters, closed tight, and whatever holds them shut is on the outside. The window itself is the kind divided in half midway up, with sash cords in grooves on either side to help raise the lower half of the window. Except that this window hasn't been opened in a long time. It's been painted over, who knows how many times. Painted shut.

"I need the outhouse," you say.

"There's a potty," says Wallace, standing by the bed. He touches it lightly with the toe of his boot.

"Yeah, but I need to go bad," you say. "Really bad."

Wallace looks hard at you. He's backlit, Frankenstein's monster. You can only see half his face, but he's frowning.

"I won't try nothing stupid," you say.

He looks up. The peak of the roof is just above his head. The rain is not hard but steady.

"It's urgent," you say.

You come out of the outhouse, and he's waiting there for you, a rain jacket draped around his shoulders. There are five LED lights attached to the underside of his baseball cap. Your cap's the same. The grass feels cold against your naked ankles. Your shoulders are soon damp. You draw them in, shivering. As you near the house, you look up at the lodge, shining your light on shuttered windows upstairs. The light catches a glimmer of metal on the nearest shutter; the fasteners, two of them, as far as you can tell, one high and one low, each of them S shaped, an S turned on its side.

"What about a light?" you say to Wallace, when you are once more at your bedroom door.

"I don't smoke," he says. "Might stunt my growth." It's a joke.

"I'm"—act like it's embarrassing—"I'm afraid of the dark." Wallace rolls his eyes. "Seriously. I'll be screaming all night."

He comes toward you, lays a big hand on your shoulder. "Oh, no you won't," he says, and his meaning is clear.

"Really, man. Just a flashlight. Please?"

He stares hard into your eyes, like he's looking for something in a stuffed closet, but he doesn't want to start searching for fear of causing an avalanche. He relents. He gives you a flashlight as thin as a Magic Marker. But its beam is bright.

"Thanks."

He shakes his head. He's been good, all things considered, but he's had about enough of you.

"Sweet dreams," he says. Then he starts to pull the door shut. He stops. "I'll be sleeping next door," he says. "I'm a light sleeper."

You get the message. Now he closes the door and locks it from the outside with the padlock Tank just put on. There's only a hook and eye on your side of the door. You lean your ear against the door and listen to Wallace's footsteps recede and then clump downstairs. Now the only noise is the rain on the roof. You wish it were louder.

You go straight to work. You dig out the Swiss Army knife from your moccasin and head to the window. You set up the flashlight on the top of the sash of the lower window and you start chipping away at the paint. Paint falls like cream-colored snow at your feet.

Chip, chip, chip.

It's Tank you're most worried about. You get the feeling he'd have been happy to wring your scrawny neck and dump you in the middle of that unnamed lake. A "deep-six holiday" your stepdaddy liked to call it—liked to promise you if you didn't smarten up.

Chip, chip, chip.

The paint flakes off in cream, then blue, then green. You are an archaeologist, Blink, chipping your way down through years and years of slapdash upkeep, and even if you get this window open, there's still the shutter, and beyond that a steep roof and a rainy night.

Chip, chip, chip.

It's hopeless, and yet it is all there is. You never really got the knack of hopeless. You're too greedy for life to give up on it, aren't you, boy? Always wanting a little bit more.

You press your body against the cold glass. It wobbles under the weight of your shoulder; the sash shifts in its frame. You push up and it squeals a bit in resistance, so you stop and catch your breath and listen and try again. Bit by bit it lifts and lets in the coldness that seeps through the crack between the shutters. You shiver, but it is a good feeling. The more of a crack there is between the shutters, the more room you've got to slip the blade of your knife into it and try to loosen those outside fasteners.

Which is when you hear footsteps clattering up the stairs.

The sound is so sudden and so urgent, you jump back and the window slides down — barrels down — and you only just catch it at the last instant before it slams shut. You scrape your knuckles on the sill, sliding your hands under the falling window, pinching your hands under its weight. The steps are coming nearer, someone in a hurry. They've heard you somehow, even from downstairs. You scurry to your bed, but before you get there, the door next to yours opens. You go over to the door and lean against it.

Niven's voice calls from downstairs. "You find it?"

"Yeah," booms Wallace. "I'll be right there."

Then Wallace is in the hall again, closing his door after him.

"What's going on?" you call through the door.

"Get to sleep," he says.

You slam your hands against the door. "Tell me!"

The footsteps stop and return. "It's nothing to do with you," says Wallace outside your door. "Just another fire to put out."

"Fire? Get me out of here!"

"Not that kind of fire. Now shut up and get to bed." He goes, then he stops and comes back again, his footsteps heavy. It was stupid of you to talk to him. What if he comes in? What if he sees the mess you've made on the floor? "We're going to be gone for a bit," he says, "so your friend Tank is moving into my room to keep you company."

"No way, Wallace! He'll kill me."

"Okay, then. How about I kill you right now so you don't have to worry about it?"

"Wallace," shouts Niven from downstairs. "For God's sake, let's get going."

And that's it. Next thing you know, you hear a vehicle outside. Is it just arriving? Yes, must be. You hear the engine cut off and a single door open and shut. One person. But Wallace said they were leaving. Then you hear a car door open and slam shut again. Is it a second person who had been waiting in the car and is only now getting out? Then another door slams and another. Three people leaving: Jack and Wallace and who else? You try to put together this arithmetic of sounds. Someone came and is taking Niven and Wallace away. That's what you figure. Leaving you with Tank.

But not just Tank. Kitty is out there somewhere. You want to believe it—have to believe it.

There is also another presence: the Captain is back. He is howling. Someone has locked him in his cabin, and he is

294

beating on the door and bellowing your name, damning you and blaming you for everything—everything.

Shut up. Shut up. Shut up!

You're breathing hard now, trying to get a hold of yourself. There are footsteps on the stairs. If it's Tank, he's in no hurry. He's probably enjoying the apprehension, the terror his slow approach must arouse in you. You've met his type before; they're all about arousal, intimidation: the slap, the punch, the knee to the gut—all a kind of letdown compared to the torment leading up to it.

The steps are in the hallway now. You beam your flashlight on the mess you've left by the window. There's nothing you can do about it. You race barefoot back to your bed. You climb into your sleeping bag, open your knife, ready at your side.

He knocks. Three times. "Ready for your kiss good night, Sunshine?"

You squeeze the knife tight.

"Hey," he says, knocking again. "I'm talking to you, kid. Don't you know it's rude to ignore your elders?"

The zipper of the sleeping bag is open all the way down to your feet. You plan it out. You'll wait until he's directly above you, then fling back the top, drive the knife home, and slide out of the bed onto the floor.

"I think I'll just check this old key to see if it works good," he says.

You hear the key enter the lock, turn, click it open.

He's standing there, backlit like Wallace was, and though he is half Wallace's height, he is even more intimidating, for you can almost feel the hatred rolling off him.

"I could just kill you and make it look like you tried to escape," he says.

You don't say anything.

"Huh?" he says. "Was that the sound of you pissing your pants?"

You try to control your breathing. Use it. Use it to your advantage.

"I've got this real fine rifle here, all loaded up and ready for bear," he says. "I could just let you make a run for it and—*kapow!*—get you in the back. How's that sound to ya?"

He listens, hoping for a whimper, but what he gets is the even in and out of someone sleeping. It doesn't sound all that convincing inside your head, but it's going to have to do. Murdering you in your bed will probably not pass muster with his boss. So he's going to have to wake you up if he wants to kill you. That gives you at least some kind of chance.

You can hear him growl, low in his throat. He's not the kind of bully who likes to think he's wasted a perfectly good threat. "You ain't asleep," he says. And you know what's going to happen next—he'll come to check. But just then you hear the tinny sound of a cell phone ringing, playing some rock riff.

He swears and answers the call. He does a lot of "yes, bossing" and then closes your door and locks it, with the call still in progress.

Saved by the bell.

You wait for his return, dying to get up and get at the shutters that stand between you and the outside, and yet afraid to move. It seems an eternity before you hear him coming upstairs again and the door next to yours opening and closing. Tank has taken over Wallace's room—just one thin wall away.

Chapter 38

I am his guard, she thinks. *I am his guardian angel. And like a guardian angel, there is little I can do,* thinks Kitty. Just be here. That's all.

She had defined her job as learning the lay of the land, learning as much as she can, not getting caught. Along the way she has added to this the job of making things difficult for Blink's captors. But now her job has changed to just being here. Bearing witness. She must see what happens and faithfully record it.

This boy. He is ten months younger than she is, but he seems so much younger sometimes. So open — she'd seen that in him at first glance. She could recall him in the emptiness of Union Station waiting to buy his train ticket, pulling out that fistful of bills, his palm flat, unrolling the needed amount. He might as well have had a SUCKER sign on his back. All she'd needed to do was create a situation where he would expose himself like that again.

But there is nothing else weak about him, she thinks. He is bold—reckless, perhaps—but full of this crazy kind of certainty that is like a tonic to her. In his determination to turn things to his advantage, he seems invincible in a way. Somehow he'd convinced her, against her better judgment, to join in on this whole scheme. So she feels guilty for knowing better and yet falling for it. Falling for his eagerness, the way it lights up his eyes.

She owes him, she thinks. She robbed him and then let him rob her of her own good sense. Good sense? What a laugh! She'd spent most of the year flaunting her complete lack of good sense. A death wish? Yes. Probably. And then this desire, every bit as overwhelming, *not* to die. Was that what happened to her Wednesday morning? Waking up like that with this grand scheme to collect money from Drigo? And is this what she has collected? Or had the desire to stay alive come with this brave and foolish boy?

She remembers something Wayne-Ray said about it being okay to be numb. That being numb gave the body a chance to recover. She isn't numb anymore. Blink Conboy has woken her up. If she was his guardian angel, she'd been asleep at the wheel. That wouldn't happen again.

She makes herself as comfortable as she can under the eaves. At the darkest corner of the lodge. She is more or less dry, but shivering with a cold that has winter written all over it. Her new denim gaucho jacket is too short and not at all warm. She had chosen it because it showed off her figure. She wanted him to like her.

The rain picks up, gusting off the unseen lake, black and shifting, playing the bass note to the wind's lead. She had placed herself in the lee of that wind. She begins to think about the sheds across the clearing. Perhaps there is somewhere inside one of those small outbuildings where she might curl up small, like a sow bug under a rotten board. When the lights go off in the lodge maybe. When everything settles down. But, no, she will stay here. It's not like punishment. Not really. She wants to stay here because of the boy inside who needs her.

She must have nodded off, because suddenly she is awoken by a clatter across the yard and an almighty shout of pain.

She half suspects a bear, until the swearing starts. A string of curses no bear would be likely to use. Apparently Tank has stumbled across her trap.

She can't resist the urge to sneak to the corner of the lodge to see him, in the light spilling across the yard from above the doorway. He appears, swearing and hobbling, rain streaming off his ball cap. Limping badly.

The Moon opens the door. "What's all the racket?" he asks.

"My foot!" yells Tank. "A fucking nail."

Kitty makes her way back to her safe corner and only makes it just in time, because lights suddenly appear in the woods, like a false and hurried sunrise. It's a car coming. She dives into the bush as the vehicle enters the yard, its headlights raking the back wall of the lodge as it turns around.

It's a black SUV. A man jumps out and runs, covering his head, toward the door. He's lanky. So is this the Snake at last?

He enters the lodge, slamming the door behind him, but almost right away returns to the vehicle, followed by two more figures: the Moon and, under a black umbrella, Jack Niven, a briefcase in his hand.

Kitty waits, fearfully, expecting Tank to appear next with Blink all trussed up and gagged. There will be nothing she can do. Create a diversion? Throw herself in front of the SUV? Or drive the ATV like crazy back to the Jeep and pursue them? But considering the speed at which the Snake pulled into the yard, the SUV will have put many miles between her and them by the time she would be able to follow.

Her horrifying speculations arise and are resolved almost instantaneously. No sooner has the car door shut on Jack Niven than the SUV wheels around in the yard and takes off up the road.

So, as far as Kitty knows, there is just Tank left now—Tank with a wounded foot. Better odds, she thinks.

Chapter 39

You wake up with a start. You must have drifted off. You have no idea what time it is. You turn your head slowly toward the door. You see nothing, not even a light under it. The darkness is complete. And yet you heard something. The wind gusts. The rain pelts down. The window rattles. That's what you heard. Freed from the buildup of paint, the window is rattling. You're kind of rattled yourself.

You switch on your flashlight and scan the room nervously. It's as if you're in the middle of a horror movie. You switch it off again and listen hard; there's nothing but the creaking of this big old building under the battering of the wind, the squall of rain. You throw back the sleeping bag and place your bare feet on the cold floor. You stand and make your way by memory to the window, your hand out in front of you, finally coming to rest on the chilly glass. You've got your flashlight in the other hand and only now do you switch it on. You dig your knife out of your pocket, open it, and lay it carefully on the windowsill. With the flashlight between your teeth, you lift the window slowly, slowly. You test to see if it will stay up, but it won't; the painted-over pulleys in the grooves are no longer connected to anything.

How to keep this thing open? Because there's no way on earth you can undo those fasteners on the shutters and hold this window at the same time. You lower the window. Listen again. That storm is heaven-sent for your benefit, Blink Conboy. If there is a God up there, he's an angry God, but maybe something else has gotten his attention right now. The house seems almost to rock, like a great boat out on the sea. The trees shake and crack under the weight of the deluge, their branches rustling and clicking against the sides of the lodge.

You check under the mattress to see if there are boards there but, no, just springs. You look at the chest of drawers. The two top drawers are each something less than two feet across, maybe six inches high. You slowly pull out one of the drawers. It's empty except for a couple of mothballs. You pull it all the way out, ditch the mothballs, and carry the drawer over to the window, where you turn it on its side. You lift the window again with one hand, then carefully place the drawer in the gap, hard against the sash. You lower the window until the bottom rail rests on the upended drawer.

You step away, breathing hard, holding in the desire to say something proud and foolish. To shout "Yes!" to the night. You smile grimly. Keep that "yes" inside you, Blink. Hold on to it tight.

*　*　*

The longest blade of the Swiss Army knife slips through the crack between the shutters and pushes up the lower fastener with only a few minutes of effort. You push tentatively on the shutter, and a thin whoosh of wind and rain comes in on you. Cold as it is, you have never felt anything so refreshing. Next you slip your arm up into the narrow space between the upper window and the shutter. There is not much room to maneuver in, but you wedge your knife into the widened crack right under the upper fastener. It doesn't give. You press harder. You try to hammer the blade upward, and suddenly the knife springs from your grip and clatters down on the windowsill beside you. You switch off the flashlight.

You freeze. Wait.

Despite the cold, you are sweating like nobody's business. Slowly, carefully, you find the knife in the dark and lift it, cursing your slippery fingers. After an eternity, you try the fastener again; no hammering this time, just even pressure upward. It budges. Good. You lean your back against the right-hand shutter and press the knife upward. Then suddenly there is a snap and a clatter, and the shutter flies open.

The upper S-shaped clasp has broken off and tumbled down the roof. With your flashlight, you can see it resting in the leaf-clogged gutter three feet below you, down the steep pitch of the roof.

The shutters waver in the air and are about to slam against the gable wall when you reach out and grab them. You are hanging half out the window, your feet no longer on the floor, and the shutters are tugging on you like a kite in a gale.

Was there a kite in your life, Blink? Yes, out on the Beaches with Granda. Him getting it up there and then you holding

303

on, two-fisted to the reel, sure you were going to be lifted clear out across the lake all the way to America on the far shore.

Again you catch your breath, wondering how much breath you have left in you. You need your moccasins. The wind is on your side for the moment, pressing the shutters closed, though any minute it might swing them both open.

Go, quick!

You race to your bed, slip the moccasins on, race back, and in one fluid motion fling open the right-hand shutter and crawl out onto the roof.

You didn't count on the rain-slick moss.

Your feet no sooner touch down on the steep slope than they fly out from under you, and you are on your backside sliding down, down, and over the lip of the roof into space.

You cry out.

Crash!

You lie in a heap on a grassy hummock. You are winded, but nothing feels broken. Above you, out of sight from where you lie, the shutter to your cell slams shut, then flies open and slams again, sounding the alarm.

Get up, Blink. Go!

And with a new surge of energy, you roll to your feet in the wet grass and take off, only to run right into a thicker darkness — a darkness you bounce back from, recoil from. Then out of that darkness comes a flashlight beam, blinding you.

"You just made my day," says the Tank-shaped darkness, now revealed as he switches on the row of lights on his ball cap brim. He says it loudly, so as to be heard above the storm, loud so you can hear him good, like a man who's been feeding money all day into a slot machine and just hit the jackpot.

Before you can find your feet again, Tank grabs you by your shirtfront and lifts you up in one fluid motion so your face is inches from his, and the row of brightness on the underside of his cap blinds your eyes. What you can see of his expression is filled with hate and triumph.

"Nobody's gonna blame me for this," he says. He raises his hand, and there's the rifle he wanted you to see earlier. The black metal catches the glow of his lights. He holds it so you can see it. He'd like to hold it there awhile, shaking it in his massive fist, to give you a good long chance to fully appreciate how terrified you are.

"I'm going to let you go in a minute," he says, pulling you closer still, so you can smell the wet rankness of him, the stench of his breath. "And you are going to wish you were never born."

You wish you could tell him that you've thought that before, nearly every day of your life after Stepdaddy moved in. But you had left that behind. And as hard as the street was, you knew you were alive every single day, alive and hungry.

"Are you ready to go now?" he says, almost sweetly, like he's your daddy putting you to bed and about to turn off the lights.

Then all of a sudden, his face contorts with pain, his thick lips grimace, his eyes squint shut. His grip on you loosens enough to pull yourself free and fall backward onto the sandy, wet, leaf-strewn ground, skittering away from him while he howls with pain and rage, the Swiss Army knife protruding almost up to its shaft from his thigh.

You skitter out of his light, try to get up, fall again, and crawl.

Then you hear the click of the rifle.

And the night explodes.

Chapter 40

"**G**ood trigger action on this model," says Kitty. "Very smooth."

She is standing with a rifle of her own aimed down at Tank. His cap has fallen to the ground, and now he is blinded by the light coming from her head: not a guardian angel any longer but an avenging angel. The lights from her hat reveal the Hulk curled up like a giant baby.

"Who the hell are you?" he shouts, as if maybe he thinks she is something supernatural.

Her answer is to work the bolt action on the rifle, sending a shell flying, then to push the bolt forward, reloading it.

"Take it easy!" says Tank.

Beyond him, she sees Blink, his back pressed against the lodge wall, like an execution victim who's wondering if he's just woken up in heaven.

Tank makes a move for his rifle, lying near his feet, and Kitty fires again. The kick is huge. The muzzle leaps a foot above her target. The first shot was in the air. This shot sends up dirt beside Tank's hand, making the man squeal and throw his hands over his head.

Kitty lowers the rifle, quickly works the bolt again, and then, raising it to her shoulder, takes a careful bead on Tank.

"I got my first rifle when I was twelve," she says. "This one here's got a lot longer barrel. It's a .308. Nice walnut stock, knurled bolt handle—the whole Winchester deal. And there are three more bullets left in the magazine. So are you going to try anything?"

Tank doesn't move.

"Nod your head," she says. Reluctantly he nods. "Good. Now use your foot to push that rifle of yours toward me." She wonders if Tank can hear the trembling in her voice that the tough words try to hide.

Tank does what she says, darting his head back and forth to try to see past the wall of light coming from her brow. She edges toward him, the .308 aimed at his chest.

"Now get back," she says. "I mean it."

He does as he's told, making a face at the pain of moving. She sees blood on his thigh and wonders if she shot him without knowing. The thought freezes her. Did the bullet ricochet up from the ground? Something got him.

"Farther," she says.

And maybe something of her own fear lodges itself in that

single trembling word, because suddenly Tank grins through his pain. "Hell, you're just a kid," he says.

"You are so wrong," she says.

With her own rifle trained on him, the butt tucked in at her elbow, she picks up Tank's firearm and lays it carefully on the lake side of her. With her foot, she pushes it deep under a bush. Thunder rumbles in the distance.

Kitty steps carefully aside. "You," she says to Tank. "Get on your feet and walk real slow and careful along the wall past me and head into the building. One sudden move and I'll shoot you."

"No, you won't," he says.

"You have *no* idea how angry I am!" she shouts.

Tank jerks backward, as if her shout had a caliber all its own. He gets painfully to his feet. His arms hang loose at his sides, and he tries to swagger, which is hard with his wounded leg. She sees it's the same leg with the wounded foot. His right leg has taken a beating tonight.

"Country girl, eh?" he says. "Think you could really shoot a man?"

He's aiming for bluster. But his words shake her. He mustn't see it. Must not figure out that were he to saunter across the three or four strides that separate them, he could take the gun from her hands as easy as pie.

She waggles the rifle. "Move it," she says. She thinks of Merlin and hardens her voice, replacing Tank with someone she'd have a better chance of murdering if he were standing there against the wet logs of the lodge.

Lazily he raises his hands in mock surrender. "You are making such a big mistake," he says.

She doesn't answer, only waves the barrel of the rifle in the direction she wants him to go.

"You okay, Blink?" she asks without looking his way.

"Uh-huh," he says.

"Pick up his rifle very, very carefully. Don't even think of touching the trigger. I mean it!" She is yelling at him, like some toddler she's found playing with cat turds in a sandbox. "You hear me?" she says.

The whole lake can hear her. There are people waking up in Toronto right this minute wondering what the noise is. She is on the verge of hysteria.

"It's okay," he says soothingly. "I hear you."

Tank hasn't moved. "Give me that thing before you do an injury to yourself, little girl," he says.

So she fires again and reloads before his scream has died down.

The next part is tricky. Glancing at Blink, she knows he has never held a rifle in his hands before, and she's not about to try to teach him how it works. So it's all on her. She has two bullets left, and Tank must never know she is incapable of shooting him. That even holding the rifle is the hardest thing in the world. So when they get back into the lodge, she is glad for the dimness of the lights, but she warns him not to turn around.

"I don't want to see your ugly face," she says. But what she means is that she doesn't want him to see her ugly face.

And she makes him sit on the couch, his hands on his knees, while she stands behind him. She is shaking all over, and she's afraid the man will smell her fear. This has to happen quickly, she thinks, before she breaks down completely.

"We should tie him up," says Blink. She looks at him, looks into his face, and sips a bit of courage from his wide-eyed stare. Then she shakes her head.

"I don't want you to get anywhere close to him," she says. "And, anyway, we don't have time to find something strong enough, you know?"

Blink nods. He glances at Tank and shudders, as if the impossibility of tying him up has finally dawned on him.

The wind suddenly bangs the palm of its big hand against the house, making the windows tremble in their sockets.

"The gun rack," she says, gesturing toward the south wall. "There's a steel cable strung through all the trigger guards. Take his rifle and put it back, string the cable through, and replace the lock. The key's still in it." Blink does as he's told. "Thanks," she says.

"It's okay," he says.

"No, I was thanking Tank here, for leaving the cable off when he took his gun up to bed with him. Where I come from, that's a big no-no."

Tank is about to turn his head, and she screams at him not to, scaring him — scaring herself.

"You're a whack job," he says.

"Yes," she says. Then she glances at Blink. "When you're finished, throw the key in the fire."

The fire has burned down to hot embers, but it will be enough of a deterrent, she figures. Has to be.

Blink throws the key into the fire and then takes a poker and stirs up the coals to cover it.

Tank's head turns, watching Blink. Kitty can read his mind,

read the muscles in his shoulder, and sees his huge hands grow taut, the veins popping. He is calculating the distance to the boy. Can he get around the coffee table and get to him quick enough to take him hostage?

She does something horrifying. She presses the muzzle of the rifle into the back of Tank's neck. He stiffens and swears again, but there is way more anger in his words than fear, and that frightens her—frightens her terribly.

"Blink," she says. "Here are the keys for the ATV." She throws them; he drops them, picks them up. "Have you ever driven one?" He shakes his head. "Well, it's not so hard. Take one of the caps with headlights and figure it out." He starts to move right away, giving Tank a wide berth. "Bring it to the door facing toward the road. You got that?"

"I got it," he says. Then he's gone, and it's just Kitty and Tank.

"You think you're pretty clever," he says, his voice calm again. She presses the muzzle into the flesh at the back of his neck. He doesn't flinch this time. He rolls his head as if she were giving him a massage. If he could see the look on her face, he would see a nightmare playing out in her eyes.

"You have no idea what you're messing with," he says. "The boys are on their way back. Right now. Should be here any minute, I'm guessing. And, oh, they are not going to be pleased."

"Shut up," she says.

"You give me that gun, darling," he says. "And we'll pretend none of this happened. What do you say?"

She hears the ATV start up, hears Blink revving the motor.

"We can be reasonable," says Tank. "Ask the kid. We can work something out, okay? Because I gotta tell you, you will not get far. That vehicle up there—your get-away car—is traceable. We'll be on to you so fast."

She's just about to tell him to shut up, when she realizes what he's saying. Realizes something she hadn't even thought about.

"Give me your cell phone," she says.

"I don't got no cell phone."

"So how were you planning on letting the others know?" He doesn't speak for a minute, and she almost smiles at how he has blundered. She pokes him hard with the muzzle. "Your cell phone," she says.

"You're not going to shoot me, darling."

He says it so unemotionally that it reminds her of the therapists after Spence's death. They would listen to her and watch her and then tell her things as if they were reading her mind.

"You're right," she says. "But this walnut butt would lay you out cold if you so much as move a muscle. Now give me your goddamned cell phone."

The ATV is outside the door.

She pokes Tank's skull now, twice, three times—hard, feeling the rage growing in her. He grunts with pain and reaches up suddenly with his hand to grab the barrel, and she pulls back just in time. She's losing it. She can feel her control seeping away. She glances around the room for a solution. Because the thing is she's not going to really hit him any more than she's going to shoot him. She would be afraid of hitting him too hard and afraid of not hitting him hard enough.

"You see that lamp?" she says.

"What lamp?"

"The one over the table in the dining room. The one with the blue shade."

312

His head swivels to look. "What about it?"

She steps back two paces from him, turns, aims, and fires. The bullet pings off the metal lamp shade, which snaps back and swings crazily, casting weird shadows around.

"What happened?" It's Blink, standing at the door.

"Nothing," says Kitty. "I'm trying to convince this guy to give me his cell phone, and he won't cooperate!"

Her voice is swinging as crazily as the lamp shade now. Time seems to be closing in like a vice on her head. She can't take this much longer.

Blink runs over. From across the coffee table, he looks Tank over. "I don't think he's got it on him," he says. Then he turns for the stairs and, taking them two steps at a time, runs up to the rooms.

"You are so dead," says Tank, and she can tell by the tone of his voice that Blink has figured out where the phone is.

"I've got it," yells Blink from the end of the upstairs hallway. Then there he is again, clambering down the stairs, waving a cell phone in his hands.

"I am not kidding," says Tank, his voice sounding heavy with implications and violence and angry dreams of payback. "You two are so dead."

But now Blink is running to the door, and Kitty is backing up carefully, her gun still trained on Tank, who stands despite what she told him.

"You are going to die!" he says.

She is at the door. They won't have much of a head start. He'll come after them, and despite his injured leg, she can see the bloodlust in his eyes. She has that one bullet left.

"How do you know I'm not already dead?" she says.

Then she's out the door and climbing on the back of the ATV, clutching on to Blink with her left arm.

"Ready?" he says.

She just clutches him tighter, and they take off.

Chapter 41

At some point you feel her lurch behind you, and she must have ditched the rifle, because the next thing you know her right arm is clutching you as well. Her head is pressed against your back, and she is sobbing, huge choking sobs that threaten to heave you both off the ATV. You hang on for dear life. You are astonished and filled with something bigger than strength.

You shake the stinging rain from your eyes and glance at the dense bush to either side of the cone of light, wondering if you could veer into it if a car was approaching. There would be no room for two vehicles on this rough path. Part of you wonders if you would just crank up the acceleration and hold your path. Die big.

Then you are at the turn, you swing left, and a tense few

minutes later, you are at the Jeep. Kitty seems to almost fall off the ATV, and then she stumbles away from you, away from the car, and you are afraid she is going to take off into the cedars, leave you standing there. But all she needs is to throw up.

The sound that comes from her is like some monster's death throes. You want to go to her, steady her, because she is shaking like a leaf. You're still sitting on the ATV with the headlights on. In your head, Tank is running in Hulk-like strides up the road, maybe sweeping up the abandoned rifle on his way. But you don't say anything. Finally she straightens up, and without looking at you, she finds the keys to the Wrangler in her pocket and hands them to you. You take her elbow and guide her to the passenger seat, like you imagine you would with a girl you were taking to the prom. Some prom.

Only after you've started the Jeep do you get out and stop the ATV. You hurl its ignition key into the bush, climb back into the Jeep, and take off.

The road south is as empty as it was coming north and twice as lonely. Neither of you speak, not in words at least. But you wonder if maybe your blood is talking to her blood. It courses through you like a wild imprisoned thing that hasn't yet realized you have been set free. You glance at her, stooped over in the seat beside you, her hands collected together in her lap. She might be a girl in church sitting in silent prayer. She might only be asleep. Then she sniffs, and you are so glad to hear it.

The cell phone rings, making you both start.

"Don't answer it," she says, which is odd because she's the one holding it now; you gave her the thing when you took the wheel. When it stops, she stares at its face. As a passenger on

316

the way up, you had a chance to look around the cab and so you know where the inside lights are. You turn them on, and she checks the voice mail. It's another one of those cell phones, like Niven's, with a fat antenna that can get reception from anywhere. There's no password on Tank's cell.

"Hey. This thing might take a while. Feed the boy some breakfast, eh? Don't do anything foolish."

"Wallace," you say.

Then she turns off the lights, and you are in the comforting darkness again. She's still shivering, worse than you. You turn up the heat but not too high. Already the effects of adrenaline are wearing off, and you have no idea how long this drive is going to be.

At first you thought she was letting you drive because getting stopped by the cops was not a problem anymore, not as far as you can see. But the truth is she couldn't have driven. What she did back at the lodge sapped every ounce of strength from her, as far as you can tell. She needs you, Blink. How's that feel?

After another little while, you hear her breathing change, and, glancing sideways, you see that she is asleep, her head against the window. Your right hand snakes out and touches her hands, still clasped together in her lap. Wet and cold despite the warm air pouring into the vehicle from the heater.

You're on the beach with Granda. He's carrying the kite in one hand and holding your hand with the other. He's saying something about your dad, something about how he and your mother can't seem to make it work. You gaze at his belly, at the kite folded up under his arm. Mikey the Monkey. You didn't want to stop flying Mikey the Monkey. You wanted it to lift you right up into the crazy

317

wheeling summer sky. But Granda said it was time to go, and maybe you even knew what that meant — that there was something he and Nanny had to talk to you about — the thing you didn't want to hear.

"Whatever happens," he says, "Nan and I will still be your grandparents, lad. Don't forget that, will you, boy? Hold on to that."

"BLINK!"

You jolt awake, and Kitty's hand is on the steering wheel trying to get the Jeep back on the road.

You take control, breathing hard, your eyes opening and closing worse than ever.

"Sorry," you say when at last you're on an even keel.

"Bad dream?"

You wipe the sleep off your face. A dream? No. Something you had forgotten. Granda had told you not to forget it, but you had until just this moment.

You reach Highway 7, look both ways, then turn west.

"Where we going?" she says.

You shrug. "Not to Kingston," you say. It's as good an answer as any. A few minutes later, the Jeep rolls past an Ontario Provincial Police station. There are two cruisers parked in the parking lot. You slow down.

"Don't stop," she says.

"I wasn't. Just don't want to be speeding."

Then Sharbot Lake is left behind, and you're on a long deserted stretch of two-A-empty highway.

"The cops aren't going to be any help," she says.

You don't bother to answer.

* * *

318

You see the motel ahead and start to slow down. It's after three, and your little snooze at the wheel back on 509 only really reminded you how deep this well of tiredness is that you're carrying around inside you. You're fading fast.

You pull off onto the gravel lot, and Kitty jerks awake. She must have drifted off again and figures you're heading into a ditch.

"Where are we?"

"Don't know. Don't care."

She leans forward to peer at the motel. "This looks like a setting for a horror movie," she says.

"Yeah, but there's a vacancy."

"You're not kidding," she says. "There's not one single car here."

"Good," you say as you pull up to the office, hoping that the lights on in there means somebody's on duty. "That way we can pick any room we want."

You turn off the motor and turn to look at her.

"I don't like this," she says. "They can track the car."

"I've been thinking about that. Unless Tank had another cell phone somewhere, nobody knows what happened."

She stares at you, her eyes quizzical. "What happened to you?"

"Back there? Not much."

"I'd say a whole lot. You sound like . . . I don't know. You sound like you're forty or something."

"Is it that bad?" you say.

She doesn't laugh, doesn't even smile, but her eyes look at you as if you've changed. Well, maybe you have. Then suddenly you swear under your breath and smack yourself in the

319

forehead. "The van! I totally forgot the van."

Kitty reaches over and pats your leg. "I didn't," she says.

You stare at her, but all she does is smile. So you shrug and reach for the door handle, but now it's Kitty's turn to cry out in alarm. "Wait a second," she says, grabbing your arm. She turns to stare at the motel. "What are we going to do about money?"

Tired as you are, you can't stop yourself from grinning. You pat her on the leg. "Leave it to me. I'm forty, remember?"

Chapter 42

By unspoken consent, neither of them turns on a light in the room. Light from the parking lot drifts in through a slit in the curtains. Blink doesn't ask, just heads to the bed farthest from the door, where he starts stripping off his jeans and sweatshirt—not what he arrived at the lodge wearing. His brand-new clothes from the Army Surplus are gone.

Too tired to care, she strips herself down to her bra and panties, and climbs into her bed, shivering at the touch of sheets they might have been keeping in a deep freeze. She curls up tight.

"Night," he says, but she wonders if he'll even remember having said it in the morning.

"Night," she says. The cold has woken her up a little, though the clanging baseboard heater is pumping out some kind of second-rate warmth, tinged with the scent of mildew, household cleaner, and stale cigarette smoke.

"Kitty?" he says, his voice only half conscious.

"What?"

"Thanks."

She can't speak. Thick hands seem to have come right out of the mattress under her and wrapped themselves around her neck, choking off her windpipe. The horror movie she had been afraid of.

By the time she has recovered enough to respond, she knows Blink is asleep. She lies there, listening to his breath go in and out. She listens as a car drives by, waiting for it to slow down, turn into the motel, and stop—expecting it to. What was this place even called? She hadn't noticed. Journey's End? They have not gotten away; she has resigned herself to that. She will keep on escaping and keep on being caught. This could go on for millions of years. It will be tiring, she thinks.

Spence is lying on the end of the dock.

"Hey," she says. "No goofing off."

He doesn't move, and as she approaches him, she sees the way his arm lies under his body, the palm up in a way that would be too uncomfortable to bear.

Then she sees his iPod dangling just above the surface of the water, still plugged into his ears. There is a fly on his cheek. A tiny red stain on the back of his collar. A hole at the base of his skull.

Her arms are around you, her face pressed against your back. She is sobbing. You are confused. You are back on that ATV hurtling through the night. But somehow now you are naked, and as she presses her body against you, you realize that she is mostly naked, too. So it's a dream, but if it's a dream, why is she crying like this?

Her hands claw at your chest, as if she can't hold you tight enough. She is holding on for dear life, hurtling through some other darkness, far worse than this cheap and musty room.

You want to turn and face her, hold her, and kiss away her tears. It isn't love she's after—you know that. She's clinging to you the way the survivor of a shipwreck clings to a piece of door, anything that will float. She loves you like a raft, Blink.

Her breasts are pressing hard against your back. And now her legs coil themselves around your legs as if to keep them out of the treachery of the waters. There are sharks down there, circling this queen-size bed. You are her raft—all that separates her from cruel, unforgiving teeth and the freezing darkness of the deepest ocean.

She is struggling, and you are struggling. She's wearing only her underthings. You've never been this close to a girl wearing this little, but even when she loosens her grip on you enough for you to turn and face her, you know that holding her is all that is going to happen for now, despite the crying out in your body.

Her wrenching sobs slacken, and then the tears come, staining your face. You wipe her tears away with your free hand, while the other cradles her head. After a few light-years, she starts to relaxe, and her arms hold you less in desperation now and more as if in passion. A part of you—that restless male part—will not listen to reason. It pokes away at her with a mind all its own, and you pray that it will not drive her away because holding her is enough right now.

She isn't fighting. And you worry that maybe she thinks there might be a price to pay to have climbed onto this raft that is you.

"Shhh," you say into her hair. "It's all right." And what you mean is just that—this is all right. You expect nothing more than this. And you wonder if this is what love might be. And you wonder if you knew it would take so much for it to happen. And you wonder how anything that felt like this could ever die. And then, because you can't help yourself, you wonder again if you *are* dead and this isn't purgatory anymore but a kind of heaven suitable for the likes of street urchins and losers. And you know that it is enough of a heaven as long as it includes her.

There's one good thing about thinking you're dead: the merciless poker down there between your legs has stopped prodding away. There is sadness in that, but it makes things a little easier.

"Shhh," you say again, you're not sure to whom. "It's all good."

She sniffs and hugs you.

"I wouldn't mind," she says. "If you want to."

"It's okay," you say, your voice just a tattered bit of white cloth now, a flag of surrender.

"I would like it," she says.

You press her head into your bony shoulder. "This is good," you say, your voice raw with emotion and weariness and thankfulness.

She sniffs again. "Sometime," she says. You can hear the sleep in her voice taking her over. It is so sweet.

"Sometime," you say.

You wake up and she's gone.

It's light outside, dim inside. You roll over and look at the other bed. She's not there. From where you are lying, you can see the bathroom door, open, dark.

She is gone. What did you expect, Blink? Did you really expect that you deserved anything so good to happen?

You hurt all over. So many bruises. Falling into boats. Falling out of windows. Falling in love. None of it gets you anywhere. You shift your gaze to a chair by the window. The foolish designer jeans Wallace gave you hang over the back, nicely folded. You left them in a heap on the floor. You left the money in the pocket—what was left after you paid for the motel room.

On another morning you might have leaped out of bed to see if it was still there. But you don't bother now. You have come such a long way, young man. Such a great distance. And where will you go from here? How will you get there? She will have taken the Jeep. The keys were there, conveniently, in the pocket with the cash.

You are rested now. You feel as if you slept deeper than you have in years. Maybe that's why you are so calm.

Something happened to you last night. It wasn't a dream. And if she has stolen all that money and the car as well, that was the least of what she got away with. You can't summon up anything like rage. That would require having a heart, and she took that as well.

Then the door to the room opens, letting in a flood of daylight. You shield your eyes, and when the door closes and you can see again, she is standing there.

"Sorry," she says. Then she holds up two handfuls of paper bags. "Turns out we were only a couple of kilometers from civilization. I bought us breakfast."

Chapter 43

Oh, the glory of a good night's sleep and a long, hot shower! It is not nearly as much sleep as you need, and you have woken, prodded by the uncertainty of . . . well, everything. The hot car you are driving, the strange wonders of what happened in the night, the knowledge that the motel wants you out of there by eleven o'clock. But still, the blood in your veins seems renewed. Your mind seems razor sharp. You hit the road with something very like hope beating in your chest.

Kitty drives. She keeps looking in the rearview mirror. You ask if she's looking for cops, and she says yes, she's expecting one any minute, its lights going haywire, forcing the two of you over to the shoulder. She laughs.

"Can you imagine how cool that will be?"

"It'll be great," you say. "I can't wait." Then you suddenly turn on the radio to see if there is any news about the kidnapping of Jack Niven, but all you can find is hip-hop and country and static. You are between places. Signals come and go.

"We'll get thrown in the can," she says, her voice up-tempo and kind of proud. "They'll throw away the keys."

"We'll have a criminal record," you say, getting into the spirit of it. "Hey, Kitty, we're going to Juvie."

She laughs. Then she says, "They'll probably lock us up in a mental hospital."

"Yeah," you say. "In a rubber room."

"And put us on meds?"

"Hope so. But as long as we're real good and not a danger to ourselves or anyone else, they'll let us get together sometimes to play cards or, like, make craft things—maybe potato prints."

"Paper flowers," she says.

"Knitting—except without needles."

You laugh again, but the knitting made you think of Nanny.

Though neither of you knew it last night, this highway is taking you to Toronto. So, a round-trip after all. You are wanted by the law in Toronto, she is wanted by the lawless, but all you can think of right now is that it's a good place to get lost in, a good place to dump the car.

You pull Tank's cell phone from your pocket. "They'll phone," you say. She nods. "What do we say?"

That gets you both going again. The ideas pour out. Soon you're both laughing. And then the laughter dies down, and you just look out at the passing scenery. You're going home, you think. And then you wonder what exactly that means. You're a little bit excited about it.

"Where are you going to go?" you ask without looking.

"I'm not sure," she says. But you get the feeling she is. "What about you?"

"I'm not sure, either," you tell her, but you have a pretty good idea yourself. You glance at her, and she blushes.

"Keep your eyes on the road," you say.

You grew up sometime last night. Even before Kitty came into your bed. You grew up when you were talking to Niven. When you could put together what it was he was talking about, because it mattered to you—because it was a matter of life and death. Because you had read up on it.

She turns south on 115, easing down to 401. About ten minutes later, the cell phone goes off in your hands—tinny rock 'n' roll. It is just before noon.

"You ready?" she says.

You think a bit, nod, push Talk.

"Ontario Provincial Police," you say. "How may I direct your call?"

You wait. There is nothing. And then the phone goes dead. In another couple minutes, it rings again. This time you don't bother with the snappy answer.

"Hey," you say.

"Brent?"

"No, this is Tank, Mr. Niven."

"What is going on?"

You hold the cell phone up, and Kitty beeps the horn. "Did you hear that?" you say into the cell.

"I gather you're on the road," says Jack. He doesn't sound

328

annoyed. He's all business, and that's intimidating. "You do realize you are driving a stolen vehicle and that it is being tracked, don't you? Right this minute."

"Yeah," you say. "We've been expecting the cops all morning. Oh, or maybe you didn't go to them."

"Have you forgotten our little conversation? Do you really expect that anyone would believe your story?"

"Nope. But there's two of us," you say. "They might believe two people telling the same story. Oh, and there's some saved messages on this cell phone that sure sound suspicious. Tank doesn't have a password, so it was really easy to listen to them."

There. You finally slowed him down. But you wait, breathlessly, for the next move. It's like when you played chess with Granda, and you'd do something clever and hope he hadn't noticed that his king was exposed.

"Brent," he says, "I thought we had a deal."

"We did have a deal. And then, after I accepted the deal, you decided to lock me up. That wasn't part of the deal. So, I guess it was a kind of open-ended deal."

"Nobody locked you up. You were a visitor, lost and far from home. We offered you accommodations. You've got a very active imagination."

It sounds as if he isn't really talking to you anymore. It makes you nervous.

"Well, I didn't like my accommodations," you say.

"What is this about, Brent?"

"It's about Tank trying to kill me. It's about getting away, okay?"

"Do you have some new extortion scheme up your sleeve?"

You hold your tongue. You're not sure.

"Is that it?" he says. "Are we entering round two of negotiations?"

Does he really mean he might offer you more? Get a grip, Blink! Have you learned nothing? Can you really trust this man? Please, boyo, get it through your head: something for nothing is a fool's game.

"How about forty-eight million?" you say.

Kitty whoops with laughter.

"I see," says Jack, and the two words send shivers down your spine, as if he really can see—see you and Kitty and this yellow Jeep. As if he were the Wicked Witch watching Dorothy in her glass ball. You grasp at straws.

"You try anything, and we just hand over this phone to the cops," you say, your voice more wobbly than you would like. You sound a lot like a sixteen-year-old talking to the CEO of a big mining operation.

"Good-bye, Brent," he says. "For now." And the line goes dead.

Kitty doesn't ask you what he said. It's as if she can tell. You are nervous again, and it's his fault. You were fine five minutes ago, on top of the world. Now you're angry. You open your window and want to toss the phone out.

"Don't!" she yells. And you roll the window back up. Then you sit there in silence watching the road, the cell lying in your lap. You want only to be somewhere—anywhere. So many things you have thrown away lately.

Without any warning, Kitty tells you her story, the story that led her to Toronto. It's the story you've only heard snatches of that you weren't entirely sure were true. She tells you everything. How she was shooting in the meadow out back of their place up north and how she missed the target Spence had set up and how that stray bullet passed through an acre of bush and across rough ground the length of three football fields and lodged in the base of her brother's skull. She tells you how the bush was dense and there was no way in a million billion years such a thing could have happened but it happened anyway. It was a shot no marksman could have made. A tragic fluke. The most terrible thing that had ever happened in the history of forever.

She tells you about the inquest and the therapists and the breakup of her parents. She tells you about leaving home. No one blamed her. Everyone knew how much she loved her brother. But there was this one person who couldn't stand her anymore: Kitty Pettigrew.

Then she stops talking, and you sit there and sift through it all, like the victim of a fire looking for anything that might have been saved from the blaze. She has told you everything, and when you can speak, you say, "And the worst thing is you were mad at him when it happened, right?"

She is watching the road, watching the speedometer, her hands on the wheel at ten and two, her back straight, like this is a driving test. She shakes her head. "No, the worst thing is that he is dead."

You don't argue. Of course she's right. But you know, somehow, that you were right, too.

There is a huge shopping center in Pickering, just east of metropolitan Toronto, and Kitty pulls off the highway. It's mid-afternoon, and the place is crawling with kids your age. You are just another couple of teens, hanging out at the mall. But you have about three hundred and fifty dollars, and your purpose for being there is anything but casual. You divvy up the money and go to work.

You buy nice clothes—not the kind of clothes you like—*nice* clothes. Well, cheap nice clothes. "You're all kitted out," says the salesman, who looks relieved that you want to trash the clothes you came in wearing. "Were you, like, at a costume party?" he asks.

"Something like that," you say. He looks pleased, as if he just helped to do something good, as if selling you these clothes was an act of charity. You've made his day.

At the cash register, you buy sunglasses, too. Yellow for her, blue for you.

Then you go to get your hair cut. You come out stylish and blond. This is real camouflage gear, Blink. Time to blend in.

Kitty does the same. When she arrives at the food court, you're already digging into a large French fries and a gallon of Coke.

"What do you think?" she says, just like a girlfriend might.

Her hair is almost gone, buzzed down to a fine nubble. She's wearing a Fair Isle sweater dress in a cool rainbow of colored stripes, an icy-blue faux-leather jacket, icy-blue tights, and argyle low-tops.

"I think you look hot," you say. And she blushes. Then you hand her the yellow sunglasses. "A present."

She gets some Japanese noodles and joins you, sitting on your side of the table. "Let's move here," she says.

You look around. "That's cool with me," you say. "We could live here forever." And then suddenly she's crying again, softly, leaning on your shoulder. The game of the day has just about drained completely away.

It's five by the time you head outside again, but you are in no hurry to go to the Jeep and possibly walk into a trap in your nice new clothes.

So many clothes you've gone through lately. Like snakes growing so fast, you have to shed every few hours or so.

You watch the Wrangler for a long time, trying to figure out if it's under surveillance. You parked in a far corner of the lot, which thins out more quickly as closing time approaches. You both look for someone sitting in a car reading a newspaper. Someone hanging around.

"We could just leave it," you say after a while. "I think the GO train comes all the way out here."

She shakes her head. "I need it," she says. You don't ask why. You have shared so much, become so intimate, and yet your separation from one another is this secret—an unspoken pact. The time is fast approaching when you will have to say good-bye—at least for now. There is nowhere you can go together, though you keep thinking about it.

Your next stop is the Yorkdale Shopping Centre in the north end of the city. It's a place from which you can catch the subway south.

"Are you going to be all right?" she says, taking your face in her hands.

You nod. "You?"

She nods.

"I'll miss you," you say. She rolls her eyes, and you both laugh nervously. Then she leans her forehead against yours.

A passerby might have mistaken the kiss that follows for two suburban teens at the end of a first date. The kiss is so tentative, nervous, as if the matinee is over and the movie wasn't all that

333

good and neither of you are sure there's going to be another date. It's not nerves; it's fear: fear that if you kiss her like you want to kiss her, then the next bit—the hard bit—would be impossible. You'd both just have to climb back into that bright yellow time bomb and take off to who knows where and keep traveling until the money runs out. Which would be in one more tank of gas.

She pulls away and rests her hand gently on your arm. She looks at you and grins. "Now I owe you way more than sixty bucks," she says.

You nod. "And I want it back, okay?"

She nods. Then she writes Wayne-Ray's phone number on your arm. You watch her do it so carefully and think how odd it is that just that morning in the motel you had scrubbed off what was left of Alyson's number from pretty much the same spot. She finishes and then kisses your arm, and you have to wipe the wet ink off her lips.

"Is that where you're going?" you ask.

She shakes her head. "But he'll know where I am. What about you?"

You write a number on her arm, amazed that you still remember it.

The next kiss isn't a good idea, but it is inevitable. You hold her head in your hands. As much as you love the flesh of her, you love the bones of her, too, this tough skull. Your lips are chapped but so are hers, and it doesn't matter even though it stings a bit. Your hands slip down the length of her to her waist. You feel her arms around your shoulders, and you are glad for that because you feel as if you might fall right over were she not holding you up.

"You saved my life," you say. "Did I tell you that?"

334

"You saved mine," she says.

For a moment it looks as if there will be a third kiss, but you both come to your senses.

"Phone as soon as you can," she says. "As soon as you . . . you know . . ."

You more or less know what this thing is that cannot be named because it is so uncertain: home. Phone when you find a home.

It's after nine when Kitty pulls wearily into the sprawl of the mostly empty parking lot of the Northgate Shopping Centre in North Bay. It's been a day of shopping centers, but none of these stores is open. She is completely exposed. She parks the Wrangler, leaving the keys under the floor mat and locking the doors manually. She walks away, then runs. All day she has expected to be caught and has been philosophical about it, to a point. When Brent was with her, it hardly mattered if they got arrested. They lent each other strength neither of them had on their own. But now that she is on her own, she must face the fact that she wants her freedom desperately. She starts crying as she runs. She crosses the highway—the Trans-Canada— darting through traffic, putting herself as far as she can from the Jeep and everything it stands for.

In a McDonald's, she makes the call. It's Saturday night and either Mom will be at Auntie Lanie's, or Aunt Lanie will be at Mom's. Wahnapitae is over an hour away.

"Sit tight, honey," says Lanie. She has to take over the conversation, because Mom can't talk, she's sobbing so much. "You hear me?"

"Yes," says Kitty. "I won't budge. Promise."

Chapter 44

The cottage in the Beaches looks just as you remember it. Smaller perhaps. It feels like half a lifetime ago you were last here. Then you notice in the light from the porch something that isn't the same. The postage-stamp front garden is overgrown with weeds. Granda used to keep it neat as a pin. You used to help him sometimes: watering things, raking, planting stuff with his big hands guiding yours so that the bulb went into the hole just so.

You imagine the worst. And you almost leave—almost give up, just like that—as if nothing has really changed inside you, even though you know that everything has. You stop yourself from running. You walk up the cracked path to the front door that is the same blue you remember but not so brilliant any longer. There are bits of white showing through. You ring the doorbell, knowing a stranger might answer and being prepared for that, even though you have no idea—no idea in the whole wide world—what you will do if that happens.

"Coming," says a voice inside. And you dare to think it is Nanny's voice. She cracks the door just a wee bit and looks out at you.

"What is it?" she says. She's older, of course. And like the house itself, she seems even smaller, her eyes no longer as brilliant. But it is her all the same.

"It's Brent," you say.

She looks confused. "He doesn't live here," she says. "I told the policeman that." And then she tries to shut the door. You stop it with your foot.

"No, Nanny," you say. "It's me. I'm Brent."

She opens the door another inch, no more, and stares at you good and hard, curious who this boy could be with the blond hair. You stand still under her gaze, waiting for her to see herself in your eyes, waiting and hoping you haven't left it too long.

"By the saints," she says. "Brent?"

"Nanny Dee," you say. And only then do her eyes light up. Because if she's not entirely sure she knows you, she knows her own name, for goodness sakes. And there is only one person in the world who ever called her that.

"Brent," she says. And there—now it's official.

"Yes, you can stay. As long as you want, as long as you need. We always said that. Can you have forgotten?

"And, yes, I'm lonely without Trick. But, oh, no, Brent, Granda's not dead. Just gaga, my son, that's all. In a home

337

now—in the locked ward, so he can't wander off and get himself lost. They cook onions every evening at five so that the residents don't wander away," Nanny tells you. "Sundowner's syndrome they call it. The poor old ladies and gents just want to go home for their tea. We'll visit him, but don't be alarmed if he doesn't know you, Brent. He scarcely knows me. Well, he does of course. He's just not sure who I am."

The next day is Sunday and you go. You and Nan. There is a code to get in, and you must clean your hands with special soap so that you don't infect the fragile souls inside with the infections of the great wide world.

Granda is not in his room.

"Not likely," says Nanny. "He'll be down in the lounge entertaining the troops. Granda the storyteller. Even now, when he can't remember his own wife, he can remember his stories."

But when you get to the lounge, the crowd is watching cartoons, and Trick is over by a window looking east at where there is a garden, though there are no flowers in it so late in the fall. You wonder if he is dreaming about flowers, about gardening. He seems so frail, sitting in his wheelchair. He who hoisted baggage onto trains for all those years. He who got your kite in the air for you, running along the beach.

"Trick," says Nanny. "Look who the cat dragged in, will you."

He turns his wheelchair to face you both. His eyes go directly to the voice. He doesn't see you right off. He smiles at Nanny as if this is a face he likes.

"Oh?" he says.

"Look who's come back," she says, her hand pushing your elbow to make you step forward.

You do—a little reluctant, a little scared. And now he sees you. His eyes are cruelly blind. Not entirely blind, Nanny had explained, preparing you for the sight of him. Macular degeneration, it's called. She'd said, "Put your fist up to the bridge of your nose and try to see around it. That's what he's got left of his sight."

But he is seeing you. Some of the smile he had for Nanny is still there.

"Is this that boy?" he says.

"It's Brent, darling. Ginger's son."

"Hello, Granda," you say.

He nods. "Brent," he says speculatively, as if he's tasting something new to see if he likes it, to see if he wants a second helping.

"I told him how much we've missed him all these years," says Nanny. "How Linda wouldn't allow him to see us, she was that mad at Ginger. But he's come on his own. And he's going to stay with me, aren't you, Brent, and help out around the place—with the shopping and whatnot. He'll go to school, of course . . ."

And on she goes chatting away while the old man just stares at you, nodding, nodding.

"Brent," he says again. As if he's taken another mouthful. Then, "Brent!" As if—no, it can't be—and yet . . . "Brent. Yes."

Nanny stops her chatter and looks at you happily. As if she's saying, *There, what did I tell you?*

He reaches out a shaky hand to you. You take it, all dry bones wrapped in paper.

"Brent, my boyo," he says. "I've been thinking about you for days now."

"Yeah?" you say.

"Oh my, yes," he says. Then his other hand comes up to join the first, and now he is holding your hand with both of his. "I have such a wonderful story to tell you," he says.

Later . . .

Despite what you said to Niven on Tank's cell phone, there is nothing all that incriminating in his voice-mail. Niven would never have been so foolish as to say anything important to Tank. After all, he had been planning to leave his very own BlackBerry behind in that hotel room, assuming it would be found by the cops, and you doubt there was anything but business calls on it; business calls and calls from his wife and the daughter who was his password.

When you are settled in at Nanny's place, you try to write down everything you know; what Niven told you; what Alyson told you; what the newspapers have told you; and how it all weaves together. You made a deal with Niven that you wouldn't go to the press, but you want to have it all written down, clear as you can make it, in case the police come calling again. They were here, Nanny said, when they were looking for that Black-Berry. Your mom must have told them you might be there. Anyway, if they do come back, you don't want to stutter and stammer and lose your cool. Those days are over.

More than the papers or the police, you wish you could contact Alyson and tell her that you didn't steal her car and abandon it, that you carried out the mission she had set for you. You remember her cell phone number. It has long since been erased from your arm, but it is etched in your memory. You'd like to set the record straight. But something in you holds back. Something in you says enough is enough. No use tempting Providence, as Nanny would say. There might be something in that.

Then, barely a week after your escape, Niven is in the news again. He's been picked up on a road near Owen Sound. You look it up on a map: Owen Sound is nowhere near the hunting lodge. You're not surprised. When he's picked up, Niven says he has no idea where he is or where he was kept captive. SPOIL has driven him there blindfolded and let him go, he tells the police—just like that. Simultaneously, SPOIL sends out a news release stating that they feel they have made their point, and they want to show their goodwill by letting Niven free. But the speculation in the media is that things were getting too hot, that they let him go out of fear. The police are extending their search for the phantom terrorist organization. Meanwhile, there are those who believe the whole thing was phony.

Ah, the story you could tell, Brent.

You talk it over with Kitty. You e-mail back and forth to her. She reminds you of how close you came to getting your fool head blown off—except she doesn't say it that way. She says she'll back you, whatever you decide to do, but maybe it would be best to lie low. You wonder. But as you are wondering, you are learning how to read the business section of the newspaper; how to read the stocks. Queon is not doing well. You're taking a course in business at high school. The teacher explains it to you.

The protest up at Millsap Lake just won't go away. The tide of public pressure has built and built. The government is willing to talk to QVD again about buying the land off them, but they aren't offering nearly as much as they did before.

And then in late January, you see on the front page of "Report on Business" in the *Globe and Mail* that QVD has been bought out by the Japanese company ANS. Niven has been relieved of his post as president and CEO but has been kept on as a consultant, whatever that means. In a sidebar, there is an interview with him. He needs a rest, he says. He needs time to be with his family. He needs to reconsider his options.

And somehow, that is enough. You feel pretty much the same way, don't you, Brent?

In the spring, Kitty, her mother, and aunt drive down to Toronto with a baked ham for Wayne-Ray. He's so busy now, balancing school and his job at the music store, that they bring Easter to him. He has been able to go back to school early. Kitty helped him decide.

She is to drive because she knows the city better than her mom or Lanie. This is a truth she would rather not admit. They do not talk about the time she was gone, only that she is back.

As they cross the top of North Bay, they pass the shopping

343

center where she left the Jeep six months earlier. She half expects to see it there, but of course it is gone.

The car veers onto Highway 11, heading south to "the Big Smoke," as her mother calls Toronto. Her mom is sitting in the backseat. She leans forward.

"Only was ever in the Big Smoke three times," she says. "Once, when I was a kid for the Royal Fair, once with Byron for a little getaway weekend, and that one time we brought Spencer down to set him up in his new apartment."

Auntie Lanie is sitting in the front passenger seat, and she nods. And Kitty just holds tight to the wheel and thinks how strange it is that Spencer's name can now be mentioned like this, as a passing fact in a conversation rather than the whole sad subject. She feels a hand on the side of her head and leans into it without taking her eyes off the road.

"Look at you," says Aunt Lanie, and chuckles.

Kitty's hair has grown back—well, three inches of it—the reddish color grown out. It's in jaggy layers with lots of product. She had looked at her face in the mirror that morning, chubbier now, living at home. She is plumper all over. She warned Blink in her last e-mail. She hopes he will still find her pretty.

She is finishing high school by correspondence. There was no way she could return to school, where everyone knew her and what she'd done. There were kids her age who had known Spence, kids he'd coached in soccer. No, that was not something she could do. But she had noticed sometimes when she was in town that people would say hello to her. Just hello. And she was learning how to say hello back.

There had been talk of her going to school up the road in Sudbury, living with her dad. But while she spent weekends with him now and then, she wanted to be at the house. She wanted the daily reminder of her brother. She wanted him nearby to talk to, out on the frosty meadow or down by the frozen lake. She didn't want to trouble him anymore with her heartbreak and wretched guilt. So she tried to tell him things he would be interested in.

"I finished *Anna Karenina*," she told him one day. "I'm glad things work out between Kitty and Levin. Too bad about Anna. I didn't ever really like Count Vronsky. Did you?"

There were other books on his shelf she was tackling. If she could read a novel with over eight hundred pages, then she could read anything.

One day, she sat at the end of the dock, where she had found him. She was tying on her skates. She told Spence about Brent. How when he jumped off the end of the dock into the boat, it had been, for her, this totally unexpected, wrenching experience. She had no idea why at first. She had screamed, she told Spencer. Luckily no one heard her.

"Eventually, I figured it out," she told him. "It was as if it were you, Spence. As if Blink were you. You, finally escaping the end of the dock, jumping into this silver boat . . . well, aluminum. It was like I was letting you go. I don't know. Something like that."

She knows, of course, that she will never let him go.

Her favorite things to tell Spence are about what Serina is up to. She e-mails regularly with Tamika, who sends pictures all the time. As soon as Wayne-Ray learned that Kitty had returned home, he insisted she get in touch with Tamika, because there was something important Tamika needed to tell her. Kitty figured it would be about the money again. All that money shoved through the mail slot in the dead of night with that pathetic little note.

But that was not the most important thing Tamika needed to say to her, although the money had been a huge surprise. It was being held in a trust by a lawyer. One day, Kitty was going to have to claim it because Tamika wanted nothing to do with it. Kitty didn't want anything to do with it, either. So Tamika suggested she might give it to some charity. That was something to think about. No, this was not the most important thing.

Merlin would never see the money. He was in jail. Brent found out. He'd become a compulsive newspaper reader. Merlin had been nabbed for possession and resisting arrest. The police ransacked Merlin's apartment and found enough drugs to keep him off the streets for a long time. But this wasn't the most important thing, either.

The most important information—what Tamika had not had the opportunity to say to Kitty on that terrible October night, with Merlin tracking her down—was that Serina was not Spence's child.

"What do you mean?"

"Not his birth child is what I mean, Kitty."

"But—"

"You listen to me, sister," Tamika said to her, firmly but with such love. And she listened and learned.

Spence was the closest thing to a father Serina had. The real father had been an accident. He had no knowledge of the child he had sired. Spence had become friends with Tamika after she conceived and had been there through it all, right up to her labor. He was with her when the baby was born. He had been as close to the child as any father could be. The love that drew

Spence and Tamika together grew more slowly, without Spence even knowing it at first. So Serina was his first love, and then he fell in love with the baby's mother.

Kitty had so wanted Serina to be her niece—her *real* niece—that at first this news almost rebroke her heart. If Serina were her real niece, it would mean that there was a part of Spence still left in the world.

"I know," Tamika had said in an e-mail. "It would be so convenient, wouldn't it?"

It had seemed to Kitty a cold thing to say, maybe even spiteful. But it wasn't meant that way.

"Oh, heavens, Kitty. Think, will you? *You* are the part of Spence still left in the world." Kitty had never thought of that before. And she came to understand that Tamika wanted her for a sister and wanted her for an aunt for little Serina, as much as Kitty wanted those things.

"I want the baby to know you and to know him through you. You get that? Is that clear?"

And Kitty got it. It was clear.

So on this road trip, they would visit Wayne-Ray and Tamika and Blink. Kitty's mother wanted to meet the young man who had saved her daughter's life.

"Don't blow it," she told Blink on the phone. "Act like a hero."

He had laughed so hard.

They are having a lady's kind of high tea at Tamika's when the doorbell rings. Everyone grins at Kitty.

"That'll be your gentleman caller," says Auntie Lanie. Then she laughs and slaps her knee.

347

Kitty makes her way down the narrow hallway with Serina toddling after her. There is no way to send her back to the others. The two-year-old holds out her arms to be picked up. Holding her close, Kitty decides that it is nice to have a beautiful shield with her.

He has grown taller, thicker through the chest and shoulders. She isn't sure if he looks younger or older. His hair is brown again; he has let his camouflage fade. He was so emaciated when she met him that he looked kind of bony and older. But he also looked like a frightened rabbit half the time, which didn't help.

"Hey," she says, stepping out onto the porch and pulling the door closed behind her. She will invite him in, of course, but she wants this time alone with him — well, almost alone. She can't really speak, she's so tongue-tied.

"Hey," he says.

And then they are kissing, which isn't easy with a giggling child in your arms, squished between you.

"This is Serina, right?"

Serina beams and shows off her Easter-egg–yellow dress, which Blink tells her looks very nice. That is all the child needs, and the next thing Kitty knows the toddler is leaning out to Blink, her arms up.

He takes her without hesitation. Figures out how to hold her, lets her feel his cheeks with her chubby hands.

"Hey," says Kitty again, chuckling, as if she had forgotten entirely how to talk. Her hand touches his hand, now full of shining, golden Serina. Her hand rubs his arm, and he finds a way around the toddler to kiss her again. He's as tongue-tied as she is, but she can see words in his tea-colored eyes and almost hear

348

them assembling on his lips. Deep inside her, words are forming, too, possibly the same words he is slowly putting together. Yes, she thinks that's likely from the look in his eyes. His eyes. She touches his cheek and looks into his eyes, and he looks back at her, unblinking.

AFTERWORD

When I was sixteen, a friend of mine was shot and killed by his younger brother in pretty much the same way that Spencer Pettigrew was shot and killed. It was a freakish accident—a statistical improbability that was right off the scale. That death has always haunted me. And the fate of the person at the other end of the rifle has haunted me equally. Whatever anyone might try to tell you about how it's people who kill people, not guns, they're wrong.

ACKNOWLEDGMENTS

I'd like to thank Kristina Watt, Xan Wynne-Jones, Geoff Mason, Martine Leavitt, Jim King, and Amanda Lewis—always Amanda—for various bits of help and encouragement they have provided. Oh, and Nicole Feret for the tonsorial advice.

The stately hotel at the corner of Bloor and Avenue Road has gone under more than one name in the time I have known it and I have taken the great liberty of giving it another, fictitious name for the sake of this novel. (If Blink hadn't been quite so hungry, he could have gotten himself a free and delicious lunch across Avenue Road at The Church of the Redeemer. They've been feeding street people really good food for a very long time.) I've also added an extra lake to the wild and beautiful countryside of Eastern Ontario. There is no Millsap Lake, but if there were, you'd have to be crazy to want to spoil it by putting a uranium mine anywhere nearby.